Published by: GladEye Press
Interior Design: J.V. Bolkan
Cover Illustration: Kate Poirier
Cover Design: Sharleen Nelson
Marketing and Publicity: Kaylee Crum
ISBN-13: 978-1-951289-20-1
Library of Congress Control Number: 2025930094

This is a work of fiction. All names, characters, places, and events are
either a product of the author's imagination or are used fictitiously. Any
resemblance to real persons, businesses, organizations, or events are totally
unintentional and entirely coincidental.

10 9 8 7 6 5 4 3 2 1

The body text is presented in Adobe Jenson Pro, 11 point for easy
readability.

Quilts of a Feather

Arlene Sachitano

GladEye
Press

Springfield, OR

CHAPTER ONE

Harriet looked around the banquet room of the Cafe on Smugglers Cove, her husband James's restaurant in Foggy Point, Washington, a peninsula that sticks out into the Strait of Juan de Fuca, and from above, resembles the head and front claws of a Tyrannosaurus Rex. The banquet room's windows looked out at the sailboats moored at the dock below. Harriet thought the view might be the only enjoyable part of this meeting.

Harriet and Lauren sat down at a back table. James entered and set two glasses of iced water on the table. He smiled, kissed Harriet on the cheek, and left the room.

Lauren shrugged out of her jacket and dropped her messenger bag to the floor beside her chair.

"These people invited us to their meeting to ask us to do something, right?" Lauren said.

"I will be shocked if that is not the case," Harriet said. "Why else would the bird-watching club invite a group of quilters to their meeting? Especially when they're planning some sort of gathering."

"Have we missed anything?" Harriet's Aunt Beth called as she came in with fellow quilters Mavis Willis and Connie Escorcia.

"Unfortunately, no, the meeting hasn't started yet," Lauren replied. "I hope they don't make us wait too long before they ask us for whatever they want. I'm working on a project for one of my clients, and I can already tell it will take some time."

Harriet shook her head. "You know they're going to ask. I've got a shelf full of quilts to stitch, so I hope it's nothing too big."

Beth had given her long arm quilting business to Harriet several years before, when the wear and tear on her shoulder became too much for her to continue. Harriet had believed she was coming to Foggy Point to babysit her aunt's business while her aunt went on a cruise. Beth was going on a cruise, but she was giving her niece the business as well as her old Victorian home which housed the quilting studio. Harriet didn't think her aunt should be making those sorts of decisions for her, but in the end her aunt had been right, and Harriet loved living in Foggy Point and running the quilting business.

Connie smiled. "I'm happy to have a new project. My kids and grandkids have more quilts than they can use, and I'm tired of making simple charity quilts. Maybe they'll ask for something challenging."

Lauren sighed. "Great."

Harriet's phone buzzed in her jeans pocket. She pulled it out and glanced at the screen. "At Arinda's - 911."

Harriet grabbed her purse. "Come on," she said to Lauren. "We have to go; Luke's got a problem at Arinda's."

"Do you need us?" Aunt Beth asked.

"I don't know, I'll let you know when I get there."

She hit Luke's name on her phone's friend list as she hurried down the stairs, followed by Lauren.

Luke answered immediately and started talking before she could say anything. "I think Arinda OD'd," he shouted.

"Hang up and dial 911."

"I already did. And Ta'sean had some of that naloxone stuff, so we squirted that up her nose, but I don't think it's working. He's doing CPR while we talk."

"Do you have another dose of naloxone? If you do, give her a second dose."

Harriet and her friends had attended, Beyond the Band-Aid, a first aid class at their church and had learned about naloxone, a medication to rapidly reverse opioid overdose. She knew the naloxone being distributed locally was boxed two to a package. They'd all been given a package at the end of the class.

Lauren jumped into the driver's seat of Harriet's car and started driving while Harriet climbed into the passenger seat and talked to her foster son. Harriet and her husband were in the process of adopting Luke. He had been living with them since his junior year of high school. Before that, he'd spent years in the state foster care system. Luke believed Arinda was his stepmother, but the state had found no documentation to prove she'd been married to Luke's father. Luke stayed in touch with Arinda because she was the mother of his half-brother Ta'sean. Harriet knew that Arinda lived in a low-cost housing development only a few miles from the restaurant.

They pulled into the parking lot of the Spring Meadows apartments. The paramedics and fire department truck had already arrived. Lauren parked, and they walked to the apartment entrance area as the paramedics wheeled Arinda out on a gurney. They raised her head up slightly, and she struggled against the straps holding her onto the bed.

"My baby," she shouted. "I can't leave my baby."

Lauren nudged Harriet. "So, she can't leave her baby, but she can OD on drugs in front of her."

Harriet shook her head and closed the distance to the ambulance. "Arinda," Harriet said in a loud voice. "We'll take care of the baby."

"Harriet?" she said in a bleary voice.

"Yes, it's Harriet. Luke and I will make sure the baby is taken care of."

Arinda flopped back against the gurney. "Thanks," she said and turned away from Harriet and the paramedics.

"Are you a relative or friend?" A paramedic she'd never met asked her. He was a short man with startling ice-blue eyes. It was hard not to stare. He cleared his throat.

"We're not exactly either," Lauren answered for her. "Harriet's foster son is the half-brother of Arinda's son Ta'sean. She's sort of Luke's ex-stepmother, but I'm not sure they ever got married, so she's probably not related."

"Thanks," the paramedic interrupted her. "We have the police and a social worker coming to deal with the kids."

"Are you related to Dr. Jalbert?" Lauren asked him.

"Why do you ask?"

"Your eyes," Harriet said, finally regaining the ability to speak. "I've never seen anyone besides Aiden with ice-blue eyes like his." Harriet had dated Aiden when she'd first moved to Foggy Point, but it hadn't lasted.

The paramedic smiled. He lifted the edge of his jacket, exposing the name patch on his shirt. "Jalbert," it said.

"We're cousins." He reached his hand out. "I'm Philippe Jalbert. When the families emigrated from France, my father chose to settle in Canada. He's still there. I was close with Aiden's older brother, Marcel. He convinced me to come out here after his mother died. I'm an RN. I need to get my license in Washington to work at the hospital. In the meantime, this pays the bills."

"It's nice to meet you."

The second paramedic signaled to Philippe from the back of the ambulance.

"Gotta go," he said and jogged to the ambulance, jumped in, and closed the door.

When the ambulance pulled away, Luke exited Arinda's apartment carrying the baby. Harriet put her arm around his shoulders and hugged him awkwardly.

"Are you okay?"

Luke sighed. "Not my first overdose, although I've never used naloxone before."

"What happened when you didn't have naloxone?" Lauren asked him.

"Some died, some didn't. Depends on how fast the ambulance got there."

"I'm sorry, sweetheart," Harriet said.

The baby reached up and grabbed at Luke's cheek. He bounced her up and down. "What will we do with you?" he asked her.

"We'll talk to the social workers when they arrive, but I'm guessing they'll send her to an emergency foster care family. Our church has a registry of people available at a moment's notice," Harriet explained.

Could Ta'sean come to stay with us for a few days? I know we can't keep him forever, but it would help him to stay with people he knows while he gets over the shock of seeing his mother like that. I know he'll try to act tough and say it doesn't bother him, but you can't unsee things like that."

"Let me call James," Harriet said. She stepped away from Luke and the baby and pulled her phone from her pocket.

CHAPTER TWO

Harriet returned to Luke, Lauren, and the baby just as the social worker arrived. She spoke to the police, who had arrived and were themselves talking to the firemen.

"James says it's fine with him as long as it doesn't cause problems for Luke," she told Lauren.

"He'll be fine," Luke said. "He's a good kid. Look how he's been pretty much raising Baby. He never complains. Staying with us will be a vacation for him."

"So, tell me this," Lauren said to Luke. "I've noticed you all call this child 'Baby.' Does she have a proper name? Or is 'Baby' her given name?"

"Her proper name is Nevaeh."

"Nev-a-eh?" Lauren stumbled over the three-syllable name.

"It's heaven spelled backward," Luke explained. "Baby is a lot easier."

A young woman joined the trio. "Hi, I'm Jennifer Green with children's services." She reached out for Baby, who clung to Luke's shirt. Jennifer dropped her arms and turned to Harriet.

"The fireman said there were two minor children."

"Ta'sean is in the apartment," Luke said.

"Jennifer, we would like to take Ta'sean home with us," Harriet said. "We could keep him until a longer-term arrangement is made. He's Luke's half-brother, and my husband and I are licensed emergency foster care providers."

Jennifer smiled. "We can make that work. I'm sure you know how critically short we are of foster families. And if children can stay with family, it's usually a better situation all the way around."

"What will happen to Baby?" Luke asked.

"We have families who are set up to take babies and toddlers in on an emergency basis."

"Can Ta'sean and I visit her?" Luke asked her.

Jennifer sighed. "That will depend on the family taking care of her."

"Ta'sean's her brother. Or at least her half-brother, I'm not sure." Luke told her.

"In that case, visitation can be arranged," Jennifer said.

Luke handed Baby to Harriet and headed for the apartment to fetch Ta'sean.

Ta'sean came out of the apartment before Luke reached the door. He had a bulging backpack slung over one shoulder.

"I packed Baby's things," he told Luke. "Do you know where they're taking us?"

Luke put his hand on Ta'sean's narrow shoulder. "They aren't sending you together this time. Baby is going to an emergency foster care that does babies and toddlers. You're going to come home with me to Harriet's house."

A look of concern crossed Ta'sean's face. "Won't she be afraid without us?" he asked Luke.

"They have families who know how to care for little ones," Harriet told Ta'sean.

She looked at the baby. She won't look back once Baby has had a few nutritious meals, a warm bath, and clean clothes, Harriet guessed, but didn't share the thought with Luke and Ta'sean.

"That kid will think she's hit the jackpot," Lauren said under her breath to Harriet.

"Will we be able to visit her?" Ta'sean asked.

"You will, but they probably won't want you to visit until she has a chance to settle in," Harriet told him.

"I'll bring some papers by your place this afternoon," Jennifer said to Harriet as she took Baby from her.

The baby started crying, and Ta'sean reached for her, but Luke took his hands and held them.

Jennifer reached into the bag over her shoulder and pulled out a colorful stuffed unicorn with large plastic eyes. Baby stopped crying and grabbed the stuffed animal. Jennifer picked up the backpack Ta'sean had dropped and headed for the car seat in the back.

Harriet put her arm around Ta'sean's shoulders. "Let's get you guys back to my house so you can get settled in. Do you need to pack your stuff?"

Ta'sean hung his head. "I don't have anything."

"What happened to your stuff?" Luke asked incredulously.

"It was my fault," Ta'sean said. "I mouthed off at Scott, and he made Mom gather all my stuff and put it in the dumpster. By the time they let me out of the apartment, the dumpster had been emptied."

"You don't have any clothes or anything?" Luke asked, his voice rising.

Ta'sean shrugged. "I wash my undies every few days in the bathroom sink."

"T, when stuff like that happens, you need to call me," Luke said. "I can help. I get an allowance, and Grandpa pays me to do chores for him."

"Let's lock the apartment, and then we need to take Lauren back to the restaurant. And then," she drew out the word, "then"... we can stop at the store on our way home and buy a few things for Ta'sean."

Luke jogged to the apartment, disappeared for a few minutes, locked the door, and returned. "It's a good thing I checked," Luke noted. "Arinda had left her curling iron plugged in."

"She fixes her hair?" Lauren chuckled.

Luke smiled. "I know, right?"

Lauren tossed the keys to Harriet, and they all got into the car. As soon as Harriet started the car, her phone rang.

"Hi, Aunt Beth," Harriet said. "You're on the car speaker."

"I'm just checking to see how it's going."

"Arinda went to the hospital from an overdose, the baby went with a social worker, and Luke's brother Ta'sean is going to come stay with us for a little while. We'll stop at the store to pick up a few supplies before we go home."

"Mavis and Connie are here with me at your house. We figured it would be easier to find out what's going on and to tell you about the meeting if we were all together."

"Sounds good," Harriet replied.

"While we wait for you, we can set up the little nursery room for Ta'sean."

Ta'sean looked sharply at Luke. "Hey, I'm not a baby."

"Don't worry," Beth laughed. "It hasn't been a nursery for a hundred years. The nurse used to stay in my room in the old days, and the baby stayed in a room that connected to it."

"It has a regular bed," Connie said in the background.

Ta'sean looked skeptical. "If you say so," he mumbled.

"See you all in a little while," Harriet said, ending the call.

Harriet pulled into her garage two and a half hours later with two grumpy boys and bags full of clothes, school supplies, and assorted grooming items. Beth, Mavis, and Connie were seated at the kitchen table, with a plate full of chocolate chip cookies in the center and a steaming mug of tea in front of each of them.

9

"Perfect timing," Mavis announced when they came in. "We just finished fixing the room and thought we'd have a break. Help yourself to the cookies," she said to the boys. She didn't have to ask twice.

When they heard the new arrivals, Harriet and James's dogs, Scooter and Cyrano, came barreling into the kitchen. Ta'sean collapsed on the floor, and Scooter climbed over him, licking and wagging for all he was worth. Luke picked up Cyrano, who was pacing back and forth between the two boys.

"Well, show us what you got," Aunt Beth said when Scooter calmed down.

Ta'sean looked up at Luke. "You didn't tell me you had dogs."

Luke laughed. "We're a regular zoo," he said, looking around the kitchen. "There's a cat around here somewhere, and we also have a horse."

Ta'sean's eyes got big. "You have a horse?" he said.

"Show Aunt Beth your clothes. Then we can put your stuff away, and maybe later Harriet will take us to the stable, where you can meet Major."

"Cool," he said and stood up.

Ta'sean brought the bags over to the table and started pulling clothes out.

Aunt Beth, Mavis, and Connie oohed and ahhed over the selections as if the jeans, T-shirts, and sweatshirts were fit for meeting the king. Luke pulled a jacket out of a bag from the Outdoor Store. It was a smaller version of Luke's own jacket. The three women suppressed smiles.

Luke had a bag of his own, containing a pair of hiking pants that zipped off at the knees, and a sun-protective shirt.

"Looks like you two did pretty well for yourselves," Mavis said. "Why don't we go upstairs and show you your room."

Luke led the way upstairs. Harriet stayed downstairs with Connie and Aunt Beth. She reheated the kettle and made herself a cup of tea. Glancing at the stairs, she sat down at the table.

"While they're out of earshot, I have an ask. A big one. Ta'sean has been staying home with his mother and the baby, caring for them both. I'm guessing he's behind on his schoolwork."

"Say no more," Connie said. "I'd be happy to evaluate and tutor Ta'sean. I'll go by the school and talk to his teacher tomorrow."

Harriet let out the breath she didn't realize she'd been holding. Connie had been a teacher in Foggy Point until her retirement, but Harriet didn't want to take advantage of her expertise. She said as much and Connie assured her again that she loved working with kids even though she was retired.

"Thanks."

"Are you sure you're ready to take on another boy?" Aunt Beth asked.

"I couldn't leave him to the system. Arinda's boyfriend was abusive. He made Arinda throw out everything Ta'sean owned. If they send him back to Arinda after a few days, who knows what the boyfriend might do to him."

"Surely, after her overdose, they wouldn't return him to her," Aunt Beth said.

"They've returned Baby and him before," Harriet told them. "She promises to stop using, goes to rehab, and they are short enough of foster families that they are willing to believe her."

"We'll be fine for the few weeks that he'll be here. Tell me, while Lauren and I were gone, what did you learn from the bird people?"

Aunt Beth sipped her tea and then set her cup down. "They have quite the event planned. Classes, bird counting ..."

"... bird-themed items for sale for a fundraiser, lectures, hikes ..." Connie continued Beth's description.

Harriet sipped her tea, then took a cookie. "I assume they want us to make quilted something?"

Connie laughed. "That's not all. The organizer wants us to lead hikes since they think we know the trails through the hills around here."

"And don't forget the classes," Beth reminded Connie. "Not just Connie, but all of us."

"I need to take classes about birds myself," Harriet chuckled.

"Not to worry," Connie said smiling at her. "They figure those of us who aren't bird experts can teach the kids activities."

"If we can teach them, I'm guessing it's more like babysitting," Harriet said.

Beth laughed. "You got it in one."

Harriet sighed and picked up her tea. "Great."

CHAPTER THREE

Tuesday's Loose Threads quilt group meeting was about birds. Beth, Mavis, and Connie explained the event to Robin, DeAnn, Jenny, Carla, and Sarah, the other quilters in the group.

Lauren came in as Beth finished describing the quilting part of the project. "Sorry, I'm late. I had a client call. And if no one has claimed pillows yet, that's what I want to make."

Mavis pulled a tablet and pencil from her bag and began drawing.

"Here's what I'm thinking." She turned the tablet toward the group. She'd drawn a circle with bird images around the outer perimeter. "This is going to be a table topper. The birds will be appliquéd, and the background will be pieced."

"Is the edge actually scalloped, or did your pencil wiggle," Lauren asked.

"It's scalloped," Mavis replied.

"Wow, that's ambitious," Lauren commented.

"Oh, thank heaven I've found you," a woman screeched as she entered the classroom where the group was meeting. Her gray hair was sticking out from under a worn canvas bucket hat at all angles. There's a witch in the forest; I've seen her."

Aunt Beth got up and went to the woman, guiding her to a chair at the table while Connie brought her a glass of water from the kitchen.

"Maylene," Mavis said. "Sit down and tell us what happened."

Maylene spluttered and sipped and made whimpering noises before she finally spoke.

"Betty asked me to walk all the trails we've marked on our maps and ensure they are passable and match what we've drawn."

"Who's Betty," Lauren whispered to Harriet.

"Betty Ruiz is organizing this whole event," Harriet said quietly. "You'd know if you've ever encountered her. She has a really, and I mean really, strong personality."

"Great," Lauren said with a sigh.

"I started with the main trail that goes up Miller Hill. The Equestrian Center is letting the bird people hike on their property, so I started at the back of their arena. Once you get about a quarter of a mile up the trail, you see game trails and hiking paths cutting across it.

"I took the third branch to the left side of the main trail. It's a deer trail. I had just started up the path when I heard chanting. It was getting louder as I kept going. I came around a bend, and there was this witch. She was in a little clearing and had things that looked like dream catchers hanging from the trees. When she saw me, she started screaming and waving what looked like a giant cigar and ran at me. I've never been so scared in my life."

"Is that deer trail on the map?" Mavis asked her.

Maylene took out her map and studied it. She ran her finger up the main trail but struggled to find her deer trail.

"I guess it's not on the map, but if I found it, our visitors will, too."

"The first thing we need to do is talk to the Equestrian Center and see who else has their permission to be on their property. Whoever your 'witch' is, she may have permission to be here," Harriet said.

"No offense," said Lauren, "But I'm pretty sure your encounter wasn't with a witch."

Maylene shook her head. "You didn't see her," she said darkly.

"What's your plan now?" Harriet asked her.

"I have to go back and check out the trails, but I'm bringing my dog. I'd bring another person, but everyone I know is doing other projects for this event."

"Unfortunately, we've all been signed up for tasks, too," Beth told her.

"I'll take Puff with me, and we'll be okay. Once my nerves settle, that is."

Harriet looked at Lauren. "Puff," she mouthed. Lauren smiled and shook her head.

Maylene stayed another half hour and then left. She'd decided she was done for the day and was going home.

"What do you think of her witch story?" Robin asked.

Sarah set her mug down on the table. "We all know a witch isn't in the Miller Hill woods. As you all know, I live on the other side of the hill. If there was a witch, I think I'd have seen or heard something."

"There are other people who live on your side of the mountain, aren't there?" Lauren asked.

"The short answer is yes. But the mountain isn't just a smooth mound. There are many little valleys and gullies and a few cabins tucked here and there all over."

"Any hippie types?" Mavis asked.

"I'm the anomaly. Most of the people are the homesteader wannabe type. Maylene could have seen any of them and concluded they were witches."

"Not our problem, though, right?" DeAnn said.

"True," Harriet agreed. "We need to get cracking on our quilt project ideas and divide the teaching responsibilities."

"Okay, let's see what we've got," Connie said, picking up the stack of class information. She then separated each project into its own pile.

Harriet looked over Connie's shoulder. "What's your selection criteria?"

Connie straightened as she set the last papers down. "Age. Teenagers will do bird journals or sketchbooks. The older grade schoolers will make juice carton feeders. Any age group, especially the younger ones, can plant flowers in pots that attract hummingbirds. We can also do a separate project decorating the pots before we plant in them. The younger teens and grade-schoolers can make window guards to put on their windows at home to deter birds from flying into the windows. The older kids can walk in the woods and look for owl pellets. Lastly, the organizers would like the kids to make posters about rare or endangered species that can be displayed in the local businesses for the next month."

"That should keep the kids busy," Mavis said. "How many kids are signed up so far?

"We do not know," Beth said.

Robin pulled a yellow legal tablet from her bag and made a note: Find out how many kids are coming.

"Do we have any other questions to put on our list?" Robin asked.

Connie flipped through the pages of the first project and set it back down on the stack.

"I don't see anything that says how much time we have for each class."

Robin noted: How much time per class, and are all times equal?'

"What else?" she asked.

"Do we have to gather our own supplies?" Carla asked.

"Good one," Lauren said, causing Carla's face to flush.

Robin noted that question.

"Do we have helpers with our classes?" Connie asked. "If someone needs to go to the bathroom, we need someone to take them or watch the class while we take them."

"I hadn't even thought about that," Harriet said to Lauren as Robin added it to the list.

A few more questions were added to the list. Several had to do with first aid-related issues.

"Who wants to take our list to Betty?" Robin asked.

"I vote you do," Lauren said before anyone could suggest her. "If Betty has a strong personality, as Harriet says, we need our courtroom advocate to face off with her."

Robin sighed, ripped the list off her pad, folded it, and stuffed it into her bag. "Should we meet for coffee, say, Thursday? I should have answers by then, and we can divide the teaching duties."

"Sounds like a plan," DeAnn said as she gathered up used mugs and carried them to the kitchen.

"See you all then," Harriet said as she and the rest of the group picked up their bags and left.

CHAPTER FOUR

The Loose Threads met two days later at the Steaming Cup. Although there were several coffee shops in Foggy Point, the Threads most often ended up at the 'Cup'. It was centrally located and had upholstered chairs that were much more comfortable than the hardwood ones the other shops in town provided.

Mavis put her cup of tea beside the plate that held her chocolate croissant. "Before we talk about bird business, can we get a report on how your new house guest is doing?" Mavis asked, directing her question at Harriet.

Harriet twirled her spoon in her teacup. "We're still in the honeymoon phase. Ta'sean walks like he's on eggshells; he never raises his voice, and asks permission before doing anything. It's not natural."

"He'll crack," Mavis predicted. "A young boy can't keep that up forever."

"He hero-worships Luke, and all boys love James," Harriet countered.

Beth grinned. "I'm with Mavis. He can't keep it up forever."

"Now that we've settled that," Lauren said as she joined the group at the table, "How did it go with our exalted bird leader?"

Robin laughed. "Harriet wasn't joking when she said Betty has a strong personality. I used every trick in the book to keep her from taking over our conversation and telling me what we wanted or needed. Eventually, I got her to be quiet and listen to our questions and requests. She gave me the names of a couple of people to get some answers. I wrote them down and can email them to everyone. The most notable item is that we have to get our own volunteers."

Everyone started to protest at once. Robin put her hands up.

"Calm down, everyone. It's better than it sounds. We don't teach all day, every day. When one of us teaches an activity, some can be volunteers. Then we can switch off. I'll go through all the schedules, and if there are any times when all of us are teaching simultaneously, I'll call the Small Stitches Quilt Group. They owe us one; as far as I've heard, they're all healthy."

"If we're lucky, maybe we won't need them," DeAnn said.

Robin was about to respond but was cut off by Maylene rushing into the coffee shop. She slid to a stop at their table, but not before banging into it and spilling about half the drinks.

A barista rushed over with two white bar towels, mopping the liquid from the tabletop before it could spill on the floor.

"Maylene, honey," Mavis said. Beth brought a chair over and slid it behind Maylene's pudgy legs. Robin went to the bar and got a glass of water for Maylene.

"Now, calm down and tell us what has you upset," Connie said.

It took Maylene a minute to gather her wits and speak. She took a deep breath. "I was walking up through Fogg Park on the main trail. I took a trail off to the north, and a group of aliens were wandering through the brush." Tears filled her eyes, and she sagged back into her chair. The Threads looked at each other.

"Aliens?" Lauren mouthed from her position behind Maylene.

Beth put her hand on Maylene's shoulder. "Are you sure they were aliens?"

"Positive," Maylene said firmly.

Harriet crouched down in front of Maylene. "Can you describe what they looked like?"

"Their skin was white, except for their hands and feet. Their hands were orange, and their feet were green. Oh, and they had long black noses."

Harriet stood up. "James took the boys to the restaurant this morning to work with the baker. They were experimenting with rolls, so James said he'd have many extras to share with the homeless camp. He bought a couple of bricks of cheese to go with them. I'm going to be taking it up this afternoon. They should be able to tell us more about what's going on in Fogg Park. If there's been an alien landing, they'll know."

"Robin and I need to go pick up our kids," DeAnn said. "Can we give you a ride home, Maylene?"

"My car is here," Maylene said with a frown. Her face was still flushed.

"DeAnn and I rode here together. I could drive your car, and you can ride with DeAnn," Robin suggested.

"Oh, thank you," Maylene said.

Robin and DeAnn gathered their purses and bags, walked Maylene out, one on each side of her, and settled her in DeAnn's car. Robin shut the car door and turned to Harriet and Lauren, who had followed them out.

"I'll be home this evening. Text me and let me know who was really in the park," she said with a smile. Lauren gave her a mock salute.

"If you don't mind coming by my house on your way to the camp, I'd like to go with you," Beth said when Harriet returned to the coffee shop.

"Fine with me," Harriet answered. "Are you coming, too?" she asked Mavis. Connie had already told the group she was going by the church to drop off some clothes she'd collected for the closet, where they collected items for people without resources.

Mavis set her cup down. "Count me in," she said.

Sarah stood up. "I've got to go back to work," she said. "I'm only working part-time, but today is my afternoon."

Harriet followed Beth home to drop off her car. "Come in for a few minutes," Beth invited her. "I've got to find a sweatshirt. It's going to be cold in the woods. Do you need to borrow something?"

Harriet smiled at her aunt. "Thank you, but I have a jacket in the car." She wandered over to her aunt's favorite chair to see what was in her sewing basket. She picked up a block Beth was working on. It was an appliquéd bird sitting on a tree branch, with a background of pale blue batik. "Your bird block is nice," she called to her aunt.

"It needs leaves and some smaller branches," Beth called back from her bedroom.

"I think it looks good now," Harriet muttered to herself.

"Okay," Beth said. She came out wearing a lavender sweatshirt with a screen print hummingbird image on the front. "Let me grab a few cookies for the ride." She went into her kitchen and filled a quart-sized zipper bag with chocolate chip cookies.

"With all these cookies and goodies, how do you and Mavis not weigh a thousand pounds?"

Beth laughed. "Mavis and I have been walking. We're up to five miles daily and do t'ai chi classes twice a week. Connie joins us part of the time, too."

"Good for you," Harriet said and headed for the car.

CHAPTER FIVE

Luke and Ta'sean were in the kitchen when Harriet, Beth, and Mavis arrived at the restaurant. They'd entered through the back since multiple cars parked in front meant James would be busy. The boys each picked up a large square insulated box.

"Is James busy out front?" Harriet asked them.

Ta'sean looked up at Luke. "The mayor came by and wanted to talk to him. One of the waiters said the mayor wants to have James cater a dinner for special guests during the bird thing," Luke told them.

Harriet smiled. "That's good." It was on the tip of her tongue to comment about the work helping keep the boys in shoes, but Luke was very sensitive about being a burden to Harriet and James. She'd tried to assure him that he was not a burden and, in fact, was very helpful to have around the house. He wasn't convinced.

"Looks like you boys are ready," Beth said. "Did you wear coats today?"

"Mine's on the rack at the back door," Luke said. "Ta'sean didn't wear one."

"It's cold up in the woods," Mavis commented.

"James has a spare jacket in the back of the car. It'll be big, but he won't mind if Ta'sean borrows it," Harriet said.

Ta'sean gave her a small smile and followed Luke to the back door.

"We can put the boxes of food in the back, and you can get the jacket," Harriet told Ta'sean.

"Who do you think Maylene saw near the homeless camp?" Mavis asked Harriet.

"I'm pretty sure it wasn't aliens," Harriet said with a grin.

"There's aliens in the woods?" Ta'sean said from the back of the car. He looked at Luke. "You said we were going to see some homeless people. You didn't say anything about aliens."

"Calm down," Beth said from the middle row of seats. "There aren't aliens in the woods or anywhere else. Maylene has a very active imagination."

"You're sure?" Ta'sean asked.

"We're positive," Mavis and Beth said in unison.

"By the way," Beth said to Harriet. "Did you check with the Equestrian Center about Maylene's other sighting?"

"What other sighting?" Luke asked. "Is someone bothering the horses?"

"No, nothing like that," Harriet assured him. "I think some bird watchers are trying to get a jump on the rest of the attendees. The Center said a few birdwatchers have been hiking the trails, looking for nests. For the most part, they've asked for permission. The Center doesn't turn out any horses on that property. They only use it for trail riding, so they don't care."

"Are these homeless people dangerous?" Asked Ta'sean in a small voice.

"No, sweetie," Mavis assured him. "What gave you that idea?"

"A group living in tents on Fourth Street down by the river. My friends and I were downtown, and some guys pulled us into the alley and stole our stuff."

"What stuff?" Luke asked.

Ta'sean smiled ruefully. "They didn't get anything from me because I didn't have anything, but they took the other guys' backpacks and phones."

"The people we're going to see aren't like that," Beth said.

When Harriet led the boys into the homeless camp area, Joyce Elias was tending the fire.

"Good afternoon," she said with a smile. "You boys can set the boxes on the big table."

"James had the boys come to the restaurant this morning and work with the baker, learning how to make rolls," Harriet told her. "He sent you a couple of bricks of cheese and some butter to have with them."

Joyce watched as Luke and Ta'sean opened the two boxes and removed packages of rolls. "You seem to have acquired another young man," she observed.

"We've been remiss," Harriet said. "This is Ta'sean. He's Luke's little brother. Ta'sean's mother is dealing with some stuff, so he's come to live with us for a while."

"You're a lucky lad," Joyce told him, her English accent apparent.

Ta'sean looked at her. "You talk funny," he said.

Luke poked him on the shoulder and shook his head. "You don't say stuff like that."

"It's okay," Joyce said with a laugh. She looked Ta'sean in the eye. "I do sound funny. That's because I'm from England. Where I'm from, everyone sounds like I do."

"Don't you want to sound like everyone else?" Ta'sean asked her.

"I never really thought about it. In any case, I'm unsure I know how to talk any other way."

"What have you brought us?" came a booming voice from across the clearing. A large, shaggy-looking man approached them from a trail opposite where they were standing.

"Hi, Max. My brother and I learned how to bake rolls." Luke smiled and greeted the man.

Ta'sean tried hiding himself behind Luke, but Max wasn't having it.

"Come on out. You don't need to hide from old Max. I won't bite." Ta'sean stepped out to stand beside Luke but stayed close to his big brother.

"Why don't you two boys show Max and Joyce what you've made," Beth suggested. "If you've got a knife handy, I can slice some of the cheese."

Joyce opened a drawer in a large wooden camping box at the edge of the clearing and pulled out a knife. Beth took it and the plate Joyce had handed her and returned to the table.

"Did you brush these tops with egg wash or butter?" Max asked Ta'sean.

"We mixed an egg with some water," Ta'sean answered him seriously.

"Max is good with kids," Harriet observed quietly.

"He's been volunteering at the church preschool," Joyce told her.

Harriet sat down on one of the log benches near the fire. "We have a question for you while we're here."

Joyce smiled. "Hopefully, I have an answer."

"One of the bird people was tasked to walk all the trails on the map that all the attendees will be given. When she was up here, she came out very shaken. She said she'd encountered aliens."

"She said they were dressed head-to-toe in white," Beth added.

Joyce thought for a minute and then started laughing.

"The Chamber of Commerce paid for a team of gardeners to come through the forest and remove all the poison hemlock and giant hogweed. They were also going to trim back the poison oak. They were dressed in white coveralls and orange gloves. I think they had on face masks, too."

Beth and Mavis looked at each other and shook their heads. "That solves that mystery," Mavis said.

Two more women and a man came into the clearing from the trail.

"You boys can leave the boxes here. We'll get them when we come next time," Harriet told Luke and Ta'sean.

"Come see us again," Max said with a wave as he went to the big table and found a seat.

"He's kind of a cool old guy," Ta'sean said when they were out of earshot.

"Not what you expected?" Beth asked him. Ta'sean grinned.

"Anyone want to stop by Rime for an ice cream?" Harriet asked her passengers.

"Silly question," Harriet said when everyone said yes.

CHAPTER SIX

"Is Beth here?" Mavis asked as she came into Harriet's kitchen. Harriet dunked her tea bag up and down and then swung it into the kitchen wastebasket.

"I just got in from my run, but I've not seen or heard from her. I'm going to drink my tea and then shower before we start stitching."

"Beth told me we were going to start early. Maybe I misunderstood."

The door from Harriet's studio to the kitchen opened. "You didn't misunderstand; Betty Ruiz asked me to swing by and pick up the class schedules she printed up." Beth waved a stack of papers she held in her hand. "Besides our classes, this tells us when the other activities are scheduled." She flipped the first page over. "Did you guys know we had a wildlife rescue center on Miller Hill?"

"Where?" Harriet asked.

Beth flipped another couple of pages.

"This doesn't say. It just says—Miller Hill Wildlife Rescue Center.

"We can look it up on the internet," Mavis said.

Harriet stood up. "You guys can check that out and make tea for the rest of the group while I shower."

Thirty minutes later, Harriet joined the stitchers in her studio. Beth handed Harriet a cup of tea, and Mavis set a blueberry muffin on a napkin at Harriet's customary spot around the big worktable.

Robin and DeAnn brought their Featherweight sewing machines to stitch pieced squares for the quilt they were making together. Today, Robin was making birds in the air blocks, and DeAnn was making flying geese, which she would later assemble into blocks the same size as Robin's.

Harriet was cutting strips of fabric for her lap robe when she heard a soft tap on the studio door. She opened it and found Sarah struggling to drag her Featherweight sewing machine up the steps. Sarah had injured her arm more than a year ago and had never regained her strength. Harriet stepped onto the porch and took her machine.

"Is this okay?" she asked as she set Sarah's machine in an empty spot to Robin's right.

"Thank you," Sarah said. "This is great. I'll be back in a minute— my fabric is in the car."

"Do you need help?" Robin asked her.

Sarah smiled. "No, thanks. I can handle it."

Mavis watched the studio door. When it was closed, she leaned toward Beth.

"I can't get used to this new 'Sarah,'" she said. "I'm glad, but she's so much nicer; it's weird."

"She's been going to counseling for over a year," Robin said. "It was bound to have an effect."

The door opened again, and everyone busied themselves with their sewing.

"Sarah," Mavis said. "Do you know about a wildlife rescue operation on Miller Hill?"

Sarah stuck the pin she was holding into her first place mat.

"I'm not sure what Avelot Solace does rises to the level of a wildlife rescue operation, but I know she and her son take in injured squirrels and crows and whatever.

"My neighbor said Avelot's son came to live with her sometime last year. The neighbor said he's doing online college classes of some sort. I ran into him and Avelot at the grocery store a few months ago, and I have to say, he doesn't look like the college type."

"What makes you say that?" Harriet asked her.

"Not to be judgmental, but his tattoos have a white supremacist look to them. I'm not an ink expert, but that's what they made me think of when I saw them. And there are many of them, including on his mostly bald head."

"That's interesting," Harriet mused. "Just when I think I know everything that goes on around here, I find out there's more."

"I had no idea we had a wildlife rescue operation, and I've lived here forever," Mavis commented, picking up a leaf to appliqué to a tree branch at the center of her round table topper.

"Avelot hasn't lived in that cabin for a long time," Sarah told them without looking up from the place mat she was stitching. "There was an old falling-down cabin on the site, and I think it belonged to older relatives. Then someone moved a house trailer onto the back part of the property, and I think Avelot's mother lived there; then someone rebuilt the cabin, and according to my neighbor, that's when Avelot showed up. Avelot's mother died, and she must have inherited the property. I'm unsure when her son arrived, and I don't know if she has more than one child. I also don't know if anyone lives in the house trailer."

"Wow, you know a lot," Harriet said to her.

Sarah smiled. "In our little section of the hill, our mailboxes moved up the paved road together. Most of us walk up to get our mail around five since we all know that's when it's delivered. We learn a lot around the mailboxes."

Harriet chuckled. "I guess I'm missing out, having my mailbox at the end of my driveway."

Everyone had just returned to stitching on their project when the studio door opened again, admitting Connie and Lauren to the group.

"What did I miss?" Connie asked as she settled in a chair beside Harriet.

"Did you know there was a wildlife rescue center in Foggy Point?" Harriet asked her.

"I did not," Connie replied with a laugh.

"Sarah was just telling us how much she learns at her mailbox, which is in a group with her other neighbors," Harriet told her.

"Our mail gets delivered into a slot beside our front door. The mail person walks the neighborhood with our mail in a bag that he carries over his shoulder."

"On a different subject," Connie said as she got her quilt block out and started appliquéing feathers on a bird. "I just finished my tutoring session with Ta'sean. He's a very bright boy, I have to say. But, when we were working, a cell phone rang. It was in his pocket. Did you know he had a cell phone?" she asked Harriet.

"No, I didn't, but continue."

"He glanced at it and tried to stuff it back in his pocket. I held my hand for it, and luckily, he handed it to me. I don't know what I would have done if he hadn't. Anyway, it was a cheap phone, like the one you buy at the checkout counter at Walmart. While I was holding it, a text message came in. His mother has been sending him texts, telling him he has to find out where Baby is. The social workers won't tell her. They told her she had to get clean before they would tell her anything about Baby. It sounds like she's trying to get her boyfriend to take Baby from wherever she is."

"Okay," Harriet said. "Let me go call the social worker."

"James?" Harriet said after she dialed his cell phone. She'd gone upstairs to ensure privacy. She wasn't trying to keep Ta'sean's trouble secret exactly, but the earlier Loose Threads discussion underscored how gossip traveled around their community.

"What's up?" James asked her, and she repeated what she'd learned from Connie.

James was quiet for a moment.

"Do you think the social workers would let me take Ta'sean out of state?" he asked. "Before all this, I'd planned on taking Luke to some spring training baseball games. Since he's a senior in high school this year, we're running out of opportunities. If they let me, I could take Ta'sean, too, and get him away from his mother's clutches. That would give the state time to devise a plan for the baby and take the pressure off Ta'sean."

"You are the best," Harriet told him. "I haven't told the social worker about the phone yet. I'd better call her, and I can feel her out about the baseball trip."

"Let me know what they say. I might ask my dad, too."

"That would make for a fun trip. Are you sure you can handle all of them?"

James laughed. "It'll be fine. I hope the social worker will go along with it."

"You're the best," Harriet said.

"Love you, too," James replied.

Harriet called Jennifer Green and explained what had happened. It turned out Jennifer was out visiting a foster home not far from Harriet's. She asked if Harriet was up for a face-to-face chat.

"Sure," Harriet told her. "I have a house full of quilters in my studio working on things the bird people will sell to raise money for their projects."

Jennifer laughed. "Our office got roped into providing snacks for the kids taking bird classes."

"In addition to making quilted items, we've been asked to teach those classes," Harriet told her.

"You have to give it to Betty Ruiz. She's got everyone in this community working for her."

Harriet chuckled. "Who doesn't like a bird?"

"Okay, I'll see you in a few minutes. I'm at the bottom of your hill."

Harriet led Jennifer into the formal dining room, where Connie joined them. "I thought Connie could give her input since she's been tutoring Ta'sean and was the one that found the secret cellphone," Harriet told Jennifer.

"I talked to my supervisor while driving up your hill," Jennifer began. "Believe me, we've been dealing with Arinda for years. Ta'sean and Baby are not the first children we've had to take away from her."

"What?" Harriet said. "Do Luke and Ta'sean know that?"

Beth brought three cups of tea and set them down in front of Connie, Jennifer, and Harriet.

"Holler if you need anything else," Beth said, returning to the kitchen.

Jennifer picked up her cup and sipped. "Luke and Ta'sean share their father. Ta'sean and Baby belong to Arinda. Arinda has given birth to at least four other children. One is a full sibling to Baby, but the others were from different fathers. The other four children were born before Ta'sean was old enough to remember them. The oldest two are twins.

"At any rate, we took the others because of neglect, her drug use, the various fathers abusing Arinda, and sometimes the children. She's been in a program since Baby was born, and she has been doing better. Not great, but just well enough to get Ta'sean back and keep Baby. She has a social worker who believes the birth family should stay intact. If anyone had been checking up on Ta'sean's school attendance, he'd have been taken from her."

Connie picked up her spoon and stirred her tea. "We all know Arinda is a mess, but did you get an answer from your supervisor?"

Jennifer smiled. "It turns out Arinda had some complications from her overdose. I think she fell and hit her head. They're running tests related to concussion protocols. Because of that, Arinda is not in a position to try to take her kids. She can complain to her social worker, but Arinda has no relatives to help her. She's burned all those bridges long ago. Anyway, she can't do anything while she's in the hospital. The boss and I decided it would do the boy good to get away from here. She says she can stall Arinda's social worker long enough for Ta'sean to have a nice vacation."

Harriet leaned back in her chair. "James and Luke will be pleased."

Connie chuckled, "Ta'sean will be ecstatic. He's very impressed James played college baseball."

Jennifer finished her tea. "If you don't have any questions, I'd better move on to my next home visit. Thanks for the tea."

"Thank you for your help," Harriet said.

Jennifer smiled. "It's why I get the big bucks," she said, picking up her purse before heading for the door.

CHAPTER SEVEN

Harriet's landline phone rang when she entered her kitchen after her run the following day. "Good morning," Connie greeted her when she answered. "Are you going up to the homeless camp today?"

Harriet affirmed she was. "Oh, good. I was hoping you were. On my way home, I went by Bird Headquarters yesterday and saw Betty's updated class schedule. I noticed that both Max and Joyce were teaching classes. Max is doing art, and Joyce is teaching journal-making. We should ask them if they need us to pick up supplies. I'd ask them myself, but I've got to take my granddaughter to a speech therapy evaluation in Port Townsend. I'm not sure what Joyce and Max's financial situations are but I know they don't have transportation to go shopping."

"No problem. I've got to take the boys shopping after school. Ta'sean needs shorts and T-shirts to wear to Arizona. I'm sure James will get the boys' team shirts, but it will be hot, so they'll need shorts and sandals. James gave us a bag of cut up vegetables to take to them. He's teaching one of his sous chefs to do fancy cuts with carrots, radishes, and jicama. They're making flowers and stuff like that. Needless to say, there are a lot of errors. He sent along a jar of ranch dressing for them. All that is to say, the homeless camp is on our route."

"Let me know what you find out about supplies. I could go by the art store tomorrow."

"Will do," Harriet said and ended the call. After her shower, Harriet spent the rest of the morning working on a complicated long-arm quilting project for one of her clients. She walked the dogs but still wasn't ready to switch to her bird quilt.

She pulled her cell phone from her pocket and dialed Lauren's number. "Hey, are you interested in getting drive-by coffee and then taking a ride to the homeless camp? I have some food to deliver."

"As it happens, I just finished the project I was working on."

"I long-armed all morning, and my back is stiff, so I'm not ready to work on my bird quilt yet."

"I'll meet you at your house in thirty minutes if that suits you."

"It's a plan," Harriet said and signed off.

"These are wonderful," Joyce said when Harriet handed her the large bag of vegetables.

"James is training his assistant on how to make flowers and other interesting shapes from carrots, jicama, and radishes."

"We're happy to eat the rejects," Joyce said with a smile.

"Connie was at Bird Headquarters and noticed that you and Max are teaching classes next week. We were wondering if you need us to pick up any supplies for you."

Joyce smiled. "That would be wonderful. Paper Chase donated materials for my journal-making class, and, I think, also for Max's drawing classes. We haven't had a way to pick them up yet, so we haven't seen what they donated yet."

"Did I hear my name?" Max asked as he came into the clearing from the trail that led to his camp area. He held a sketchbook under his arm.

"We just offered to pick up your art supplies for you," Lauren told him. "Are any drawings you will teach the kids in your sketchbook?"

Max held the book out to Lauren. "Maybe you two can give an opinion on which birds the kids would like."

Lauren laughed. "I'm the wrong person to ask." She handed the book to Harriet.

Harriet took the book and started turning the pages. "These are wonderful," she told him. Lauren came to stand beside her so she could look.

"Max, you're amazing," Lauren added.

"I'm sure the kids would be happy to do any of these birds," Harriet told him. Harriet kept turning the book's pages, stopping at the image of a woman. She had shoulder-length gray hair with feathers braided into it. She also had a colorful woven band that went around her head.

"Who is this?" Harriet asked Max.

"That's a woman who wanders the woods all over the hill. She picks up injured and abandoned creatures as she goes."

"Do you know her name?" Lauren asked.

"I do not," Max replied. "I've never spoken to her. I've just crossed paths with her as I've hiked the trails."

Harriet chuckled. "I think we've found the 'witch' our friend was scared by."

Max smiled. "I can see how someone might think that."

"Was that the same friend who saw the aliens?" Joyce asked.

Lauren laughed. "Why yes, it is. I think Maylene has a very active imagination."

"I think Maylene will be relieved to know she's met the wildlife rescue person," Harriet said. She reached into her coat pocket and pulled out a bottle of ranch dressing.

"I almost forgot to give you this." She handed the bottle to Joyce. "It's James's secret recipe, ranch dressing for the vegetables."

"This sounds wonderful," Joyce said.

"We'll leave you to it," Harriet said, and she and Lauren headed back down the trail to the Fogg Park car park.

Harriet checked the time on her phone when they got into the car. "If you're interested, we can swing by the art store before I need to pick up the boys for their shopping trip."

"Sure," Lauren replied. "I think I will be working with the little kids painting flowerpots. I thought I'd look for those brushes that are pieces of foam on a stick. After they use them, I can put them in the recycling bin."

"Are you going to be helping them plant the flowers, too?"

Lauren laughed. "If you mean, will I be handing out seeds for them to poke in the dirt? Yes, I'll be doing that. I don't have great hope for the flowers hummingbirds like, but we're giving them each a nasturtium seed since they're as close to guaranteed success as plants get."

"Hummingbirds like nasturtiums. Aunt Beth always has us plant them in the backyard."

"Good to know."

Harriet looked around Paper Chase as she and Lauren walked in. "I've never been in here before," she said.

"I think they've changed hands since the last time I've been here."

"Let's look around a little before we ask about the materials they're donating."

Harriet picked up a Faber-Castell set of one-hundred-twenty colored pencils in a metal box.

"Okay, I must have this. I like to use colored pencils to draw quilt patterns."

Lauren picked up a box of sixty pencils. "What do you need that many colors for? I find sixty is more than I need."

"I don't *need* one-hundred and twenty colors. And I don't even need sixty, but I *like them*."

"That's a relief. I would be worried if you couldn't draw a quilt on a piece of paper unless you had a whole box full of colored pencils."

They walked down another row. "Look, are those your sponge paint brushes?"

Lauren picked up a brush from an open bin. "These are the ones."

CHAPTER EIGHT

"**C**an I help you ladies?" said a deep voice from the end of the aisle. Harriet looked up. A tall man with a bald head and arms covered in tattoos walked toward them. He wore a tie-dyed shirt with Paper Chase printed across the chest.

"Our main mission is to pick up some supplies your store is donating for the bird classes some of the homeless people from Fogg Park are teaching during the upcoming bird count and conference," Harriet told him.

"We also want to do some additional shopping for our classes," Lauren added.

"Have any of you thought about how much damage you people are doing to the forest and the birds?" the man said. "How many birds will be injured, and nests disrupted by everyone stomping through the woods?"

Lauren put her hand on her hip. "Tell us how you feel. Don't you think educating the local people will help keep them from wrecking the habitat?"

"Maybe," he muttered. "Talk to my mother. She's caring for the injured and abandoned birds and animals. They all can't be gone soon enough."

"We will bear that in mind," Harriet said. "In the meantime, if you go gather our supplies, we'll find the brushes Lauren needs and my colored pencils."

He turned around and headed to the checkout desk without saying a word. Lauren laughed. "He's a delight."

"Let's get out of here," Harriet said. "I've got to get the boys and then deliver this stuff to the camp."

"I can do the camp delivery, so you won't have to rush the boys."

"Thanks, that would help. After shopping, we'll meet my aunt and James at Tico's Tacos for dinner. Would you like to join us?"

"Sure, if I'm not intruding."

Harriet laughed. "Never, besides, I think Connie and her husband and Mavis are coming, too."

Jorge Perez owned and cooked at Tico's Tacos and was Aunt Beth's "special friend." Harriet wasn't sure exactly the nature of their relationship, and she wasn't about to ask. All she knew was that Jorge had become part of the family.

"What time are you thinking?" Lauren asked.

"How about six o'clock?"

"Works for me. And if you need to be later, just text. I've got some reading for my next project, and I can do it at Tico's just as well as at home."

With their plan in place, they checked out and headed back to Harriet's house.

Jorge had set dinner up in the back room. "I was going to try a new Birria taco recipe tonight, but I know the boys both like burritos and it's their going away party, so we're having burritos."

"I like your burritos," Lauren said.

Jorge laughed. "Blondie, you like anything I make as long as you get your guacamole."

Lauren smiled. "This is true, but I do like your burritos."

Harriet walked into the back room with bags over both arms, followed by the boys, each holding a bag. "Did you buy the stores out?" James asked, coming into the room from Jorge's kitchen carrying a large bowl of fruit salad. He set it on the big table and came over to relieve Harriet of her bags.

"I brought this stuff in so you could see if I got the boys what they need," Harriet said. She unloaded cargo shorts, UV-protecting shirts, sports sandals, and lightweight jackets. She also bought James two long-sleeved UV-protecting shirts and a new pair of shorts.

James leaned over to Harriet and kissed her on the cheek. "You did good, babe." He turned to the boys. "Gather this stuff up and put it back in the car."

Connie and her husband Rod followed Luke and Ta'sean back in from the parking lot a few minutes later.

"Hola, everyone," Connie said as they came in. She held a canvas bag over her arm. "Before we get to the fun part of dinner, I brought some lessons to take with you on the trip. It isn't going to spoil your trip. You need to do a little each night. Ta'sean, you have worksheets—some math and some grammar. Luke, you have to read. The books are classics that will help you with your entrance exams for college."

Ta'sean rolled his eyes. "Hey," Luke said, "don't complain. I'll help you. You don't want to be the dummy in the class. You're smart; you need to do the work."

"Okay," James said when people finished eating their burritos, and Jorge's waitress was serving flan for dessert. "The boys and I are leaving tomorrow and will be gone for ten days. I hope your bird adventure goes well and you will keep an eye on Harriet and our little beasts. Jorge, I'd appreciate it if you would swing by my restaurant to ensure my assistant has everything under control."

Jorge nodded. "Don't worry. It will be fine, but I will check more than once."

"Speaking of little beasts," Lauren said, looking out the window into the back parking lot. "Isn't that Maylene's little dog, Puff?"

Harriet stood up and went to the window. "That is Puff, but where is Maylene?"

"And how did Puff get so dirty?" Lauren added.

"Let's go look," Harriet said.

James stood up. "What is it?"

"Lauren and I are going to go outside for a minute. We think that's our friend Maylene's dog in the parking lot. She shouldn't be out there by herself."

"Do you need help?" He asked.

"I don't think so. We'll be back in a minute," Harriet replied. She and Lauren went into the kitchen and out the back door.

"Puff," Harriet called. The little dog ran over to Harriet. She was a muddy mess. She ran in circles and then took off for the driveway.

"Come back," Lauren called to her. The dog returned and then ran to the end of the driveway again. "Is she trying to do the Lassie thing, telling us that Maylene fell in a well?"

"She certainly seems distressed. I don't think we should let her run loose, though. Let me get her a leash from my car, then see if she still wants to show us where Maylene is."

Lauren put her hand out. "Give me your keys. I'll get the leash from your car, and you can tell James and your aunt what we're doing. I assume it's in the back?"

Harriet handed Lauren her car keys. "Yes, in the back, on the left."

Lauren picked up Puff and headed for Harriet's car. Harriet went in to tell James and the rest of the group what they were doing.

Harriet returned and took the leash with its attached slip collar over Puff's head. When she was done, Lauren set the little dog down.

Puff looked back at Harriet and Lauren and trotted to the end of the driveway and out onto the sidewalk.

CHAPTER NINE

Puff was on a mission. The dog trotted along the sidewalk, eventually slowing to a walk as she became tired. Puff led them away from the direction of the park and into downtown, where she turned left on Second Street toward the Muckleshoot River.

Harriet looked at Lauren. "This is not the direction I expected her to take us."

"And not where she got covered in mud," Lauren commented as she glanced around the tidy sidewalks.

They walked past Steen's insurance, past the alley next to Annie's coffee shop, where Puff paused briefly for a drink of water from a bowl left by Annie for passing dogs, then on toward the river.

In another block, a driveway into a series of high-rise condo buildings crossed Second Street. Puff stopped again, this time sniffing the pavement. She started moving again, winding her way between buildings. Most of them had shops or restaurants on the ground floor. A man exited a dry cleaner's shop and held out a small dog bone. Puff sat down and delicately took the treat.

"Where's Maylene?" The man asked. "And what happened to Puffy here? She looks like she took a mud bath."

Harriet stepped closer to the man and held out her hand. He clasped it and shook hands with her.

"I'm Harriet Truman, and this is Lauren Sawyer. Puff here showed up at Tico's Tacos, where we were having a group dinner. Maylene was not with her, and as you noticed, Puff is a mess. We're working with Maylene on the bird festival, which will start in a few days."

"We decided to see if Puff could lead us to Maylene," Lauren added.

43

"I'm Bill Park. I own this dry cleaning shop. Maylene and Puff come by nearly every morning on their walk down to the river. As you can see, Puff collects her treat whenever she passes."

"Can I assume Maylene lives near here?" Harriet asked.

Bill pointed to a building farther down the path. "These buildings are all named after birds. Maylene lives in Raven One. It's the second one down from here. I don't think she's home, though. She and Puff left around eight this morning. Puff had her dog treat and hasn't returned until now. If Maylene had come home, they'd have stopped by for her afternoon biscuit, but I haven't seen them." He reached down and picked Puff up. "Until now. You can ring her door buzzer just in case they snuck past me. I can't imagine Maylene would come home without Puff, though."

Harriet took Puff from Bill. "Let me know what you find," He called after them as they headed for Maylene's condo.

According to the buzzer panel, Maylene lived on the fifth floor. Lauren pressed the buzzer, but there was no response. She looked at Harriet. "What do you think?"

Harriet put her hand over her mouth and thought for a minute. "I'm not sure we have enough information to get the manager to go inside her condo. The same goes for having the police do a wellness check. At this point, we only know that Puff got away from Maylene and came home."

Lauren scratched Puff's head. "Is your mama out in the woods looking for you?" she asked the little dog.

"Anything?" Bill Park asked when they'd returned to his shop.

"No answer when we pressed the door buzzer," Harriet told him.

"Do you want me to keep Puff?" He asked.

Harriet let out a breath of air. "I think we'll hang on to her. Our next step will be to see if we can figure out where Maylene was hiking today. She's been checking the trails on the maps we're

44

giving out to our visitors to be sure they're accurate. She may be hurt out on the trail."

"If we get her close, Puff may be able to help us locate her," Lauren added.

Bill stepped back into his shop and picked a couple of cards from his counter, returning to the sidewalk in front of his store. He handed the cards to Harriet and Lauren.

"Here's my number. Call me if you find her or need me to take Puff or anything."

Harriet put Bill's card in her pocket. "We'll let you know what we find out," she said, and she and Lauren turned and walked back down the sidewalk.

"The dog led you to Maylene's condo?" Aunt Beth asked when Harriet and Lauren had returned.

"She did," Harriet replied. "And we met the man who runs the dry cleaners in their complex. He gives Puff a treat every time they come by. He assured us Maylene left this morning and hasn't been back. We rang her door buzzer just in case, but no one answered."

"Do we know who Maylene was working with?" Mavis asked. "Checking the trails, I mean. Someone must have given her that task."

Connie sat forward in her chair. "Good point. One of the organizers probably has a list of the trails she's checked already and the ones she had left. We all know she wouldn't have organized the task by herself."

Beth took her phone from her pocket. "I'll sacrifice myself and call Betty. She can tell us who oversaw verifying the forest locations." She pulled her phone from her pocket and stood up, walking to the back of the room where it was quieter. She returned a few minutes later.

She came back, shaking her head. "Betty hasn't gotten any sweeter," she laughed. "I had to listen to an earful of how we are all behind schedule on our tasks, how the park ranger assigned to the festival, Gregory Lewis, is making himself scarce, and finally, how Maylene has only walked half of the trails the festival is using."

"Did she tell you who was working with her?" Mavis asked her.

Beth nodded. "It took three tries, but she finally told me Mason Sanders, the location and facilities manager for the event, has been managing Maylene, if anyone can be said to manage Maylene."

"Betty said the contacts list was at the festival headquarters, which, as you know, is at the Chamber of Commerce building. She was unwilling or unable to meet us tonight but said she'd be there at eight sharp tomorrow morning."

"Does anyone know Mason Sanders?" Harriet said, looking around the table.

"I'm on a fundraising committee with him at the high school," Connie's husband Rod said. "I don't know where he lives or how to contact him, though."

"I don't think there's much point in wandering the woods in the dark looking for her," Harriet said. "I'm pretty sure the police won't take a missing person report based on what we know, and that Maylene's only been missing for several hours."

Lauren scooped up a chip full of guacamole and sat down. "We're assuming that Puff running around alone means Maylene is missing. The fact of the matter is we don't know if she's missing. All we know is that we don't know where she is, and her dog doesn't seem too either."

"She's missing," Ta'sean said to Luke.

Luke smiled at him. "I'm with you. People don't leave cute little dogs like Puff running the streets unless they are in trouble."

The boys high-fived each other.

"I'm sure the boys wouldn't mind wearing their new clothes without being washed. We can do laundry at the hotel after that."

Harriet leaned back and gave James a look. "My children will not wear scratchy, wrinkled clothes on vacation."

"Your children?" he laughed. "They're my children, too, and I'm trying to teach them how to dress like guys."

Harriet swatted at him with the shirt she was holding. "I'm not having 'our' boys taking their first trip together looking like hooligans.

"I was just thinking you might want to go to bed; besides, wrinkled or not, they aren't going to look like hooligans wearing …" James searched the shirt he was holding for a label. " …whatever high-end label this is."

Harriet set a folded shirt on Luke's pile of clothes. "I'm not sure I could sleep if I went to bed now anyway."

James reached over and took Harriet's hand. "If Maylene hasn't shown up by tomorrow, you can report her missing and let the police take over."

She squeezed his hand. "I wish it were that simple, but I've got a bad feeling about this. Maylene would never leave her dog, and Puff would never leave Maylene if he could. Something is keeping them apart."

"Well, worrying about it isn't going to help. There's nothing we can do tonight."

"I've got one last load in the dryer. When it's finished, I'll go to bed. You don't have to wait."

James leaned toward Harriet and kissed her. She put her arms around his neck and kissed him back. He picked up a shirt from her laundry basket and started folding.

"Your laundry is my laundry," he said with a smile, putting the folded shirt into the pile of folded clothes.

"Call me when you guys get to Arizona. And text if your plane is delayed leaving Seattle."

James laughed. "Sweetie, we're going to be fine. Ta'sean has never flown before so it will be an adventure."

"Make sure he doesn't run off."

"I'm pretty sure he will stay glued to Luke's side. Luke will stay with my dad, and I'll watch all three. You can relax and enjoy your bird counting or whatever you're doing."

"Your mom told me your dad bought the boys baseball gloves to catch foul balls. He's not giving them to the boys until you get there."

James chuckled. "Dad's loving this. He bought me a glove the first time we went to spring training. Of course, I was a lot younger. He had my baseball career planned from before my birth."

"Don't forget to take pictures."

"Yes, ma'am."

Harriet picked up another T-shirt and folded it, sighing. She was pretty sure the baseball trip would be much more relaxing than the bird festival.

CHAPTER TEN

Harriet ran early the following day. Lauren was coming over, and they wanted to be at the festival headquarters when it opened. "You guys behave while I'm gone," she instructed the dogs and cat when she came downstairs from her shower.

Lauren came into the kitchen from the studio. Most of the Loose Threads had keys to Harriet's studio door. The connecting door to the kitchen had a different lock if she and James wanted privacy, but they rarely used it.

"James and the boys just left, didn't they? And already you're talking to yourself. This doesn't bode well for your senior years."

"Oh, stop," Harriet laughed. "Don't tell me you never talk to Carter. I was instructing these hooligans to behave themselves while we're gone."

Harriet grabbed a light jacket from the closet. "Let's get over to headquarters so we can start searching."

"I'm ready," Lauren grumbled as she returned from the kitchen to the studio.

A dark-haired woman stood behind a table stacked with printouts. She appeared to be collating schedules. "Can I help you?" she asked. She wore a plastic name badge that identified her as "Kath."

"Yes, you can, Kath," Harriet said. "We'd like to speak to Mason Sanders."

"Is he expecting you?" Kath asked them.

"No," Lauren said firmly. "But he'll want to talk to us," she added.

"I need to tell him what this is about. He's swamped getting ready for the festival."

Lauren pressed her lips tightly together. "We're wasting time," she said.

"You're right," Harriet said as she turned back toward the door. "We'll be back with the police," she told Kath.

Kath came around her table and blocked Harriet's path to the door.

"I'm sure that won't be necessary. Let me see if Mason's in his office. Now, what was your name?"

"Harriet. Harriet Truman, and this is Lauren Sawyer."

"Wait here," she said and went down a hall that divided the back half of the room.

Lauren and Harriet looked at each other, shrugged, and followed Kath down the hallway.

"Mason, two pushy women here insist on seeing you. I tried to put them off ..." Harriet pushed past Kath and into the office.

"We'll only keep you a minute," Harriet said before he could react. "Maylene Harris went missing last night. Her dog came home without her. We need to know which trails she's already verified so we can narrow our search perimeter."

"Kath, can you get Maylene's maps for me? She's been turning in a new map daily with the completed trails."

Kath rolled her eyes and picked up a stack of papers from his desk. She quickly paged through them, pulling two of Marlene's maps as she came to them. "Here," she said and pushed the papers toward Harriet's hands.

Mason intercepted the papers. "This isn't enough. Maylene's been doing the trails for over a week. We've been having a little trouble with the organizers over the spaces they've reserved, and I'm afraid that's taken all my attention. Maylene came by the office at the end of the day every day. I assumed she was dropping off her maps. We said hello, but I didn't look at what she was turning in."

He handed the two pages to Harriet. "These look like they're from last week."

"At least it's something," Lauren said.

By the time they reached the Miller Hill area, Harriet had studied the pages and made her best guess where Maylene would have gone next and how much she had done in the past few days.

"I think we should park on the road that leads to Sarah's cabin and then work our way through the woods to this trail." Harriet pointed to a thicker black line on the map she was holding. "This line looks like it was drawn in with a marker—like it wasn't part of the original map copy. I wonder if Betty is adding areas not given initially to Maylene."

"If this isn't part of the original plan, it's probably a good place to start," Lauren agreed. She drove them to the agreed upon spot and parked. "I packed a couple of bottles of water and some protein bars," she said as she exited the car, taking a small backpack from the rear seat.

"Hopefully, we're going to find Maylene or some sign of her before we need provisions," Harriet said, starting down the trail.

They walked for most of an hour without any sign of Maylene. The trail had a series of switchbacks, which caused them to walk at least a mile with very little downward progress. The surface was loose dirt. It was surprising Betty wanted any of her guests to walk on this.

Lauren handed Harriet a bottle of water and opened one for herself.

Harriet took a few sips of her water, and when she went to put the cap back on her bottle, it flipped out of her fingers and into the brush at her feet. She bent down and carefully separated the berry vines and other branches. Harriet reached in and picked up the cap, but as she pulled her hand out, she noticed a flash of pale blue a little farther into the bush. She reached back in and tugged at the scrap of cloth.

"Did you find something?" Lauren asked.

Harriet showed her the scrap of fabric. "Doesn't this look like the scarf Maylene had on the last time we saw her?"

"It's hard to tell. That scarf had big blue butterflies on it. That scrap could be part of a butterfly." She took it from Harriet and rubbed it through her fingers. "I think you're right. She wrapped it across her face when she was in the woods to keep those little bugs from getting into her mouth when she was huffing and puffing."

"You don't happen to have a plastic bag in your pack, do you?"

Lauren rummaged in her pack. "No bags, but I've got a fresh napkin." She wrapped the scrap in the napkin and handed it to Harriet.

"I'm not sure if this is useful to the police, but we can give it to Detective Morse just in case. Let's keep going."

"It's hard to imagine how a piece of Maylene's scarf got into brush that dense," Lauren commented as she started down the trail.

They'd gone about five hundred yards when Lauren stopped and reached into the brush beside the trail. She pulled another piece of cloth out.

"This looks like more of the scarf."

"And that brownish spot looks like blood," Lauren observed.

Harriet looked closer. "I think you're right. Maybe Maylene scratched herself on the berry vines. At least we know we're going in the right direction."

They continued hiking and stopped again when they reached a steep section of the trail.

"I wish we'd brought hiking sticks," Harriet commented. "I guess I thought the bird people would use the easier trails around the hill."

"I wonder if this is one of the 'spaces' Mason was discussing with the bird people."

"Who knows," Harriet said. "Well, here goes nothing," she said, starting down the steep grade.

Harriet had gone about twenty feet when the trail dropped away suddenly, and her feet slid out from under her. She could see trees rushing at her and grabbed at vines to try to stop her slide, but only managed to rip open her palm.

"Help," she yelled as she twisted around, forcing her body sideways across the trail, hoping she could wedge herself against the rocks and brush. Her slide slowed, but Lauren crashed into her from behind before she stopped, her speed controlled by the thick branch she held in her left hand.

Harriet tried to pull herself upright, but her feet were tangled in something soft. Lauren stood up, still holding on to her branch, and stepped carefully to Harriet, grabbing her arm and pulling her toward herself.

"Are you okay?" Lauren asked.

Harriet reached down to free her foot from whatever was still wrapped around her ankle. "Oh my gosh," she said, slumping back.

"What?"

"We just found Maylene, and she saved me from going over this escarpment."

"Let's get you away from the edge before you both go over," Lauren said.

Harriet crawled up the trail, grabbing the fallen tree Lauren's branch was attached to. She pulled her phone from her pocket as soon as she was in a stable position.

"I don't have a signal, do you?"

Lauren looked at her phone. "Nothing here either."

Harriet turned back to the trail. "Let's see if we can get back up to the car and get some help."

"Lead the way," Lauren said.

CHAPTER ELEVEN

Climbing back up the slope was easier said than done. Lauren used the branch of her fallen tree, climbing hand over hand. She stopped to see if she had reception yet. She didn't have reception, and when she tried to restart her climb, the root ball of her tree became dislodged, and she slid backward, crashing into Harriet.

Harriet rolled to the side, into the blackberry brambles, before reaching Maylene's body again. "Alright, what's plan B?"

Lauren wiped her sweaty forehead with the back of her hand, smearing mud across her face. "Can we go sideways around the slope?"

Harriet scooted herself to the side, and the dirt and rock slipped away as she did. "Not in this direction," she said. "How about your side?"

Lauren was looking around her feet when she heard a voice. "Grab the rope," it said.

"What rope?" she said quietly to Harriet.

Harriet pointed up the slope. "Here it comes," she said. The rope stopped dropping, and the person at the other end must have shaken it because the end of the rope landed at their feet all at once.

"Tie the rope around your midsection," the disembodied voice instructed. "And only lightly use your toes to keep you from going to either side. We don't want to cause any more dirt to fall away."

"Rock paper scissors to decide who goes first?" Lauren suggested.

Harriet sighed. "That's big of you, but you're closer to the rope, and we might both go farther down if we try to change positions."

"I'm not bleeding, though."

Harriet looked at the palm of her hand that had been gashed by the thick vine. "Better to lose a little blood than go over the cliff."

"Good point," Lauren said as she wrapped the rope around her waist and secured it. "Ready when you are," she called up the hill.

"See you at the top," Harriet said, watching Lauren slowly make her way up the cliff face.

Harriet was face down when Lauren and a woman she didn't recognize took her arms and pulled her up and over the cliff edge. They rolled her over.

"I'm okay," she gasped. The older woman had waist-length gray hair with feathers woven into it. Her face was tanned and deeply wrinkled. She took Harriet's injured hand and gently examined it.

"Bring her to my cabin," she instructed and didn't wait to see if Lauren complied.

"I can walk myself," Harriet mumbled to Lauren.

The woman led them down a narrow path that branched into the woods. At the base of a sizeable old-growth fir tree sat what looked like it might be a log cabin. It was hard to tell.

"If she calls us Hansel or Gretel, run," whispered Lauren.

They reached a door made from wide pine boards with a curved top and an iron latch. The woman opened it and led the pair into a large room lined with cages and enclosures of various sizes, outfitted with perches, nests, beds, and burrows. A fire burned in a small woodstove in the corner. Clearly, this was the wildlife rescue operation Harriet had heard about.

"Come through here," the woman said, leading them to a smaller room at the back of the structure. It was a combination kitchen, sitting room, and bedroom. To one side of the kitchen area was a wooden worktable. A row of dried herbs hung from a cord above the table, and a shelf at the back held bottles of various tinctures and several mortar and pestle sets.

"You can sit there." The woman pointed to a worn, overstuffed chair that sat to one side of a second woodstove. Harriet sat, and the woman turned and went to the sink in the kitchen, filling a large, thick ceramic bowl with water and returning to the woodstove, setting the bowl on its surface.

"My name is Avelot Solace," the woman said when she turned back to them. "This," she gestured to the cabin around them, "is the Wildlife Sanctuary. If you don't mind my asking, who are you two?"

"I'm Harriet Truman, and this is Lauren Sawyer."

Avelot took the warm water bowl from the stovetop and carried it to her bench. "The dead woman is Maylene Harris," Lauren added.

Avelot stopped working. "Dead woman?" she asked.

"It's what we were doing in the woods," Harriet explained. "Maylene was checking out the trails the bird festival people will use—making sure they were safe, which clearly this one wasn't. Maylene didn't come home, so Lauren and I went looking for her."

"This section of the woods was to have been taken off all their maps," Avelot said as she kept working. She poured a cup of water from the bowl and added a teaspoon of dried slippery elm bark before setting it on the woodstove. She took the remainder of the water, added a few drops from a bottle labeled chamomile, and then added a few more drops from a bottle marked tea tree oil. When she'd stirred it thoroughly, she took it to Harriet, set it in her lap, and then submerged her wounded hand in the bowl. She glanced at the face of a heavy pocket watch she'd pulled from her pocket.

"When we had all that rain in October, several trails slid, making them too dangerous. I told Betty she couldn't bring people up here."

"I don't think she scheduled any group activities here, but it is on the maps for people trying to add birds to their life lists."

"Well, it shouldn't be. Would you like a cup of tea?" she asked Harriet, and when she nodded, Avelot glanced at Lauren. And you?"

"Yes, I would. Something to settle the nerves, please," Lauren answered.

Avelot went to her workbench. She muttered the names of the teas as she put them in a pot. "Rooibos, valerian root, a little peppermint, I think—and lavender." She wrote the names on a slip of paper and handed it to Lauren. If it works for you, you can blend your own. At bedtime, add a little chamomile. If you put the chamomile in now, you'll be asleep before you leave my door."

"For you," Avelot looked at Harriet, "Green tea, peppermint, and lemongrass. There are many more antimicrobial herbs, but these will do for a start."

Lauren pulled her phone from her pocket and checked for a signal, but there was still nothing.

"What do you do in case of emergencies?" Harriet asked.

"Gregory Lewis, the park ranger, comes by once a day, and my son Bob Solace comes by to help with all the sick and injured birds and animals. He also has a couple of falcons he flies in the evenings. He has a car, so he can go for help."

She checked the cut on Harriet's palm. "You need to soak a little longer, and your tea needs to steep longer." She brought their teapots to the table between their chairs. "My son should be coming by to help feed a hawk we have. When we're done, he can take you to town."

"I'm worried that the forest creatures are going to snack on Maylene before we get help for her," Harriet said.

Lauren shivered. "That's a terrible thought."

"While we're waiting for Bob, I'd like to clean some of the thorns and little pieces of gravel from your hand if you'll let me," Avelot said to Harriet.

Lauren chuckled. "That sounds like fun."

Harriet sighed. "It has to happen, and it's probably better sooner than later."

Avelot took a clean cloth from a cubby on her workbench. She came over, pulled a stool close to Harriet's chair, and then set Harriet's hand onto the cloth in her lap. She unwrapped a bundle of tools she'd taken from her apron pocket.

"I'm sorry, but this is going to hurt."

Harriet took a sip of her tea. "Let's get on with it."

Avelot worked for about fifteen minutes. Beads of sweat gathered on Harriet's brow. Avelot set her tweezers down. "We'll take a break. Please put your hand back in the bowl of water."

Harriet had three sessions of Avelot picking and then soaking her hand again before Avelot declared that she'd done as much as possible.

"You should go by the emergency room when you return to town. In the meantime, keep the bandage on it until a doctor sees it." Avelot squeezed an ointment onto the cut; Manuka Honey, Harriet read on the side of the tube. She finished by placing a gauze square on Harriet's hand and wrapping it in more gauze from a roll.

"That's as much as I can do for you," Avelot said. "Would you like some more tea?"

Harriet lifted the lid on her teapot. "I've still got plenty."

Harriet was on her third cup of tea when a familiar, large, heavily tattooed man entered the cottage. He stopped at one of the cages in the front room to check on one of the patients.

"Bobbie," Avelot called out, "come on back. We have guests, and they have a bit of an emergency."

Bobbie entered the living quarters and stood with his hands on his hips.

"Well, well, well, what have we here? As you can imagine, we don't really get visitors up here. So why are you two here?"

"That's enough, Bobbie," Avelot said in a firm voice. "These two were looking for their friend who didn't come home last night, and they went over the bluff. I had to throw them the rope, and before I did, Harriet tried to use a thick blackberry vine and got a nasty vine burn in the process."

"That wasn't very smart," Bobbie said.

"We were a little short on options and didn't realize we were this close to your cabin," Harriet said.

"If you're done critiquing our dilemma," Lauren said. "Could you take us into town or at least into cell reception range?"

"We found our friend at the bottom of the slide, dead," Harriet said.

Bobbie turned to Harriet. "You should have led with that," he said gruffly.

"Correct me if I'm wrong, but you didn't give Lauren or me a chance to get a word in edgewise."

Bobbie looked down. "I'm sorry. And I'm sorry about your friend. I just spent my morning going three rounds with Betty Ruiz. She can't grasp the concept that we have several fragile nesting areas and we can't have a bunch of tourists tromping through them. If you're ready, I can take you and your friend into Foggy Point now."

Harriet stood up. "Thank you for tending to my hand," she said to Avelot and followed Bobbie through the kitchen, the animal area, and out the door.

Avelot put her hand on Bobbie's arm and whispered something before patting him on the back and sending them on their way.

CHAPTER TWELVE

"Could you just drop us at the police station?" Harriet asked Bob.

"Are you sure you don't want to go to the ER first?" he asked.

"Your mother cleaned it up well enough for now."

"She told me to take you by the hospital first. My mother is an excellent herbalist, but if she says you need to go to the hospital, you need to listen. To emphasize his point, he turned his car toward the hospital when they reached the bottom of the hill.

"I'll trust you can find your way home," Bob said. "I'm off to the police station with a map of the hill to tell them where you found your friend."

"I didn't see that coming," Harriet said to Lauren when they were through triage and waiting in a cubicle.

"You didn't think they would want to look at your hand?"

"Not that; I knew I would be here a few hours. I didn't expect Bob to volunteer to report Maylene's death. He didn't see her, and frankly, he didn't seem exactly choked up when he heard she was dead."

"He did seem more preoccupied by his argument with Betty Ruiz."

"Maybe Maylene's death wasn't a surprise."

"What? Do you think he could have killed Maylene? We don't even know if someone killed her. The ground may have given way like it did for us."

"We knew we were going on a trail that didn't look like the others on the map. Maylene may not have realized she was going on a sketchy trail."

"Surely, after walking the other trails, she could recognize the difference," Lauren said.

"Bob didn't want people walking by the wildlife center. Maybe he dug up the trail to discourage people from hiking it. He must have known they were sending someone to check the trails."

Lauren shook her head. "I think your hand pain is affecting your thinking. We need to find out whether Maylene was killed by anyone, much less Bob."

"You have to admit he looks like the type who could kill a little old lady."

An older man in a white coat with matching white hair entered the cubicle. Lauren stood up. "I'll call your aunt while the doctor cleans you up."

The man traded places with Lauren and slid his hands into a fresh pair of gloves before gently picking up Harriet's hand. He swung a magnifying lamp on a stand into place to better examine Harriet's palm. "From the looks of your hand, you were hanging on for dear life," the doctor said. The patch on his coat read Wilson.

"As a matter of fact, I was. I felt like Tarzan, except my vine was a very stickery blackberry vine."

"It must have been pretty thick," Wilson said as he turned her palm this way and that.

"It was, and I was very thankful. It was painful, though it was helpful."

"Unfortunately, the vine may have saved your life, but it did a little damage to your hand. You've damaged one of the tendons that operates your middle finger. Fortunately, it didn't rip through, but I'm afraid you'll need some repair. I'll call one of my colleagues in

Seattle, and we'll get you bundled up and sent there this afternoon. If things go well, they'll send you home tonight."

"Can I drive myself to Seattle?" Harriet asked him.

He smiled. "That would save you some money, but I'm afraid you'll be going in our medical transport due to liability issues."

"Great," Harriet said with a sigh.

"I'd like to soak your hand for a few minutes in antiseptic soap while we make your arrangements, and then an intern will bandage up your hand. A nurse will bring you some pain medication. You've not said anything, but your hand must hurt like a son of a gun."

"The herbal tea Avelot gave me seems to have helped," Harriet said.

"She's a skilled herbalist, and we at the hospital are glad she understands where her job ends and ours begins. Her herbs can be useful, though."

"Can you have someone send my friend Lauren back in?"

Dr. Wilson stood up. "Sure," he said. "And no more swinging in the jungle for you."

Harriet smiled. "Don't worry," she said.

"Okay," Lauren said as she sat in the guest chair in Harriet's cubicle. "First, your aunt is on her way, probably with one or more of the Loose Threads. They should get here before they get done soaking your hand and making your arrangements.

"Second, I called Detective Morse to ask about Maylene. They have a mountain recovery team trying to bring her body out. She mentioned our friend Bob is making things difficult, preventing them from accessing certain areas that are fragile wildlife environments."

"They are sending me to Seattle for hand repair."

"So, I heard. They told me on my way in that they will transport you there, but you will be released from the Seattle hospital, so we'll have to bring you home."

"That's dumb, but whatever."

"How far along is your quilt project for the bird benefit sale?"

"I've got the quilt basically finished. It just needs the binding put on."

"Oh, great, my favorite part," Lauren said.

Harriet smiled. "Hey, it could have been worse. I got the appliqué done last week and found a few minutes to throw it on the long arm a few days ago."

"Ya, ya, yeah … I'm so lucky."

"Stop complaining," Aunt Beth said as she followed a nurse into the cubicle. "We all know your pillows have been done for a few days. Now, tell me what's going on here."

Harriet and Lauren explained how they'd chosen the trail that led to falling down the slide and finding Maylene. Harriet assured her aunt that her hand would be fine after a minor surgery in Seattle this afternoon.

"Mavis will come to Seattle, and Connie is already on her way to your house to care for your animals. Are you going to tell James now or later?"

Harriet looked at her hand. "I won't spoil their trip over something this minor."

Aunt Beth pressed her lips together. "Something you need to go to the hospital for is not minor."

"You know what I mean," Harriet said. "I'll apologize for not telling them when they get back."

"What if you suffer a complication?"

"I won't. If I do, I'll deal with it, and depending on what happens, I can tell James then. Now, on to more important things. Can you ask Robin to keep on Detective Morse and find out what happened to Maylene? Depending on what the detective finds out, it may not be safe for the bird festival to send people out into the woods."

"Don't you think Detective Morse will figure that out?"

"Probably, but we don't want to leave it up to chance. And, before I forget, do Connie and Rod still have Puff?" Harriet asked.

"Yes, unless anyone else shows up to claim him, Connie and Rod may have a new pet."

A nurse came into the cubicle and chased everyone out so she could give Harriet her pain medication and set up for the intern to bandage her hand.

"There you go," the nurse said when Harriet's hand was dry and ready to be dressed. "You're lucky that vine didn't cut any deeper."

"I suppose," Harriet mused. "I don't feel fortunate right now."

"You'll feel better when your medication takes hold."

Harriet yawned.

CHAPTER THIRTEEN

Aunt Beth buckled Harriet into the passenger seat of her car in the hospital's loading area. Lauren had driven Harriet's car because it was roomier than her own, and after much discussion in Foggy Point, Beth, Mavis, and Connie all came to Seattle with Lauren to wait for Harriet.

It was late afternoon when Harriet was released. The surgery had gone well with no complications, but it was clear she wasn't going to be doing any handwork in the near future. Being right-handed, she'd grabbed the vine with that hand, and of course, that was the hand she used to hand stitch.

"We got your prescriptions filled at the hospital pharmacy," Mavis told Harriet.

"The doctor wanted you to start the antibiotics immediately," Connie explained.

"Can we go to Molly Moon's Ice Cream on the way home?" Harriet asked.

Beth laughed. "Did I spoil you by taking you to get ice cream every time you visited the doctor when you were a girl visiting me?"

Harriet sighed. "I love their Earl Grey ice cream."

"Since you've been a good patient," Mavis said, "I think we can detour."

"So, what do we know about Maylene?" Harriet asked as she licked her ice cream cone.

"She is, in fact, dead." Lauren offered.

Harriet frowned. "I got that part when I slid into her, and she didn't move."

"We've all been so worried about you that we haven't followed up with Detective Morse yet," Mavis said.

"She did call looking for you," Aunt Beth said. "I told her you wouldn't be available for the rest of the day."

"She left a message on my phone, too," Lauren said. "I figured I'd call her back when we get home."

"I couldn't do a full exam from my spot on the trail, clinging to the vine that was killing my hand, but it was curious; I didn't see any blood or injuries."

"That seems curious," Connie said. "How could she fall hard enough to kill herself and not have any scrapes."

"Hopefully, Morse will have some answers for us," Beth said. "Now, when do you get your stitches out?"

They reviewed what Harriet's doctors had told her, as well as going over the accident multiple times for the rest of the drive.

When they were thirty minutes from home, Mavis called Morse and arranged for Morse to meet them at Harriet's.

"I made a unilateral decision, as you heard," she said. "I figured we needed to find out what happened to Maylene as soon as possible. And Morse is anxious to talk to Harriet and Lauren."

They drove the rest of the way in silence. It was dark when they pulled into Harriet's driveway. Detective Morse's car was already parked by her studio door. Lauren pulled into the garage, and Aunt Beth got out and walked to the studio to let Morse in.

"Let's go upstairs to the TV room so Harriet can sit in a comfortable chair with her feet up," Aunt Beth suggested.

"I'll make some tea," Mavis said.

Lauren helped Harriet up the stairs and brought her a pillow from her bedroom. "Do you need anything else, Madam?"

"This is good. And if I haven't said it, thank you," Harriet said.

Lauren smiled. "Now, don't go getting all mushy on me."

Morse joined them and sat down on the sofa. "If you two are done with your mutual admiration society, can I ask you a few questions?"

"I don't know about the patient, who is under the influence of drugs, by the way, but I'm ready," Lauren said.

Morse took her notebook from her pocket and opened it to a blank page. "Let's start at the beginning. What were you two doing hiking around on those unstable trails?"

"We were ..." Lauren began.

"Maylene's dog ..." Harriet said at the same time.

"One at a time," Morse said. "Lauren, you start."

"Maylene was missing, and we knew she'd been walking all the trails the birders would be going on. They could only find two of her maps, so we had to guess which trails she'd been on. The trail we took had been marked with a felt-tip pen."

"Why was that do you think?" Morse asked.

"We weren't sure," Harriet took over. "It quickly became obvious that it wasn't a trail anyone should be hiking on, much less the birdwatchers coming to town. Obviously, we should have turned around and gone for help, but we were anxious to find Maylene in case she'd injured herself and was unconscious on the trail somewhere."

"It seemed like a good plan to jeopardize your lives just in case?" Morse said in a matter-of-fact voice.

"Of course not," Lauren said. "We didn't expect there was going to be a slide unexpectedly in the middle of our trail."

"You're both lucky you weren't hurt worse," Morse said. "How did you happen to be looking for Maylene?"

"Her little dog showed up at Jorge's without her," Harriet said.

"The dog was pretty dirty and looked a mess," Lauren added.

"And Maylene was nowhere to be found," Mavis said as she entered the room with a teapot, followed by Aunt Beth with a tray of mugs, sugar, and milk.

"What did Maylene die from," Harriet asked.

"I'm afraid I can't share information from an ongoing investigation," Morse said.

"We didn't see blood in the dirt around her," Harriet said. "And I didn't see any open wounds on her."

"Did you contaminate our crime scene?" Morse demanded.

Lauren laughed. "Not on purpose, we didn't. If Harriet hadn't slid into Maylene's body, she would have gone over a cliff. Maylene was stuck on the escarpment, but luckily, when Harriet crashed into her, she didn't come loose."

"As you can imagine, I scooted around to both get in a more secure position and to separate myself from Maylene," Harriet explained. "It did give me a fair look at her body, so I know a few things that didn't cause her death."

"Since you've already 'examined' the body, as it were, I can tell you that you're correct that she didn't have any obvious injuries other than scrapes and bruises from sliding down the trail. And you're right about there not being any blood to speak of," Morse confessed.

Aunt Beth poured a cup of tea and handed it to Morse. "Does that mean Maylene was dead before she got scraped?" Beth asked, even though she already knew the answer.

"That's generally what it means," Morse sighed.

"Hmmm," said Lauren. "So maybe she was strangled?"

"No," said Harriet. "I had a close-up and personal look at her neck, and she didn't have any marks that could have been strangulation."

Morse stared at her. "You're an expert now?"

Harriet laughed. "Don't pretend that everyone in this room hasn't seen more than their fair share of dead bodies in this community."

"And don't make me remind you that Foggy Point didn't used to have all these murders until you came back to town," Morse said.

Beth stood up and glared at Morse. "Stop right there. You know as well as we all do that Harriet and Lauren, for that matter, have not had anything to do with the increase in crime in this community. Don't try to lay a guilt trip on these two."

"And let's not forget that Harriet and the Loose Threads collectively have helped you solve any number of deaths since Harriet moved back," Mavis added in a firm voice.

Morse held up her hands. "Okay, okay, you're right. I'm just frustrated. We have no idea yet how Maylene died, and we have a large group of strangers coming to town in a couple of days. The bird festival committee is not happy. I don't have to tell you what Betty Ruiz is like."

"No, you don't," Beth said.

"Now, do you two have anything else you can add to your description of finding Maylene?"

Harriet sipped from the cup of Earl Grey tea Aunt Beth had prepared for her. "No one has asked us, but we were rescued by Avelot Solace and brought back to town by her son Bob," Harriet told Morse.

"Who are they?" Morse asked.

Lauren stirred sugar into her tea. "She or they rescue injured wildlife—birds, raccoons, squirrels, that sort of thing," she told the group.

"And she's an herbalist," Harriet added. "And her son Bob ..." She looked at Lauren.

"He works at Paper Chase," Lauren finished for her. "And it's a little hard to tell his deal."

"What do you mean?" Morse asked.

"He's big and bald," Lauren said.

"And covered in an interesting assortment of tattoos," Harriet said.

"That doesn't mean anything," Mavis said. "Most of my boys have tattoos."

"Bob is definitely not a fan of the bird festival," Harriet said. "He says they'll be taking people into fragile environments. He tried to talk to Betty about it, and you can imagine how that went."

"He's the one who drove us back to town," Lauren said.

Morse made notes. "I'll pay them a visit tomorrow."

"Don't drive your own car," Harriet cautioned her. "It's pretty rough up there."

"I will make a note of that," Morse said and stood up. "Now, I'm sure you ladies are ready to relax and talk things over yourselves, so I'll get out of your hair."

"I'll walk you out," Beth said.

CHAPTER FOURTEEN

Beth and Connie were sitting at Harriet's kitchen table when Lauren arrived. Harriet came down the stairs, having just showered.

"I guess I didn't need to come to pick Harriet up," Lauren commented as she poured a cup of coffee for herself and then sat down at the table. "Who made the orange sticky buns?" she asked and put one on a plate. "I'm pretty sure Harriet didn't do any baking."

"I confess," Connie said. "Rod wanted me to make some for him, so I did a double batch and brought the second one."

"What are you teaching today?" Harriet asked.

"Your aunt and I are making juice carton feeders with the older grade school kids. What are you doing?"

"Lauren and I asked Betty if we could double up since our classes don't take the full amount of time. A kindergarten teacher is taking the little kids on a nature hike after we finish planting flowers to attract hummingbirds in Fogg Park. Then we're taking the older kids in the woods to search for owl pellets."

"We got some pamphlets about owl pellets for the older kids to study up on while we're working with the little kids," Lauren said. "We'll take both groups of kids to Fogg Park. The teens can read there."

"Since you two are going to Fogg Park and Beth and I are making our feeders at the community center, you can go ahead and take her with you," Connie told Lauren.

"Sounds like a plan," said Beth. "Now, I'm going to take your dogs out before we go."

Lauren drove by the Fogg Park maintenance shed, where the park ranger, Greg Lewis, met them with a box of hand shovels, seed packets, and a big bag of potting soil.

"I can carry the soil," Harriet said.

Lauren shook her head and took the bag.

"I hurt my hand, not my whole body."

"Fine."

Harriet and Lauren had just laid out three planting areas within the tilled-up beds the gardeners had prepared. They'd divided the seed packets and shovels between the beds when a bus pulled up and off-loaded nine children and one adult.

"Over here," Lauren called, and the group headed for the flower beds.

Harriet looked back toward the bus while she waited for the kids to cross the grassy area. She heard a raised male voice and could see Bob Solace, who appeared to be arguing with Gregory Lewis.

"I wonder what he's doing here," Harriet told Lauren.

"He, who?" Lauren asked.

Harriet pointed to Bob. Gregory had walked away.

"What would Bob be doing here?"

"Oh, I don't know. Something to do with bird rescue, I'm guessing."

"I suppose. He didn't strike me as the type to volunteer for something like this."

"Hi, kids," Lauren said as their group arrived. "We will be planting flowers that will grow up and become food for hummingbirds."

A red-headed girl who looked to be about six-years-old raised her hand. "Yes," Harriet called on her.

"Can't they just hang a bottle of that red juice out here?"

"They could do that, but someone would have to clean and refill the bottle every few days. Besides, it's better for them to eat natural food instead of sugar water."

"Okay," Lauren said and divided them into three groups. "Let's get started."

"Done already?" Aunt Beth asked Harriet and Lauren when they met again at the community center.

"We're going back into the woods with the older kids to look for owl pellets."

A woman with a bushy gray ponytail approached the trio and pushed her way into the middle of them. "Ouch," said Harriet when the woman bashed her injured hand with her notebook.

"Where do I go to see the Northern Flickers? I need to put it in my book."

"Excuse me?" Lauren said.

"I need to know where the Northern Flicker habitat is. I've only got half an hour until the shorebird tour, and I need to find a Flicker."

"Not my problem," Lauren said.

Beth put her hands on the woman's shoulders, turned her around, and pointed over her shoulder. "See that group of women over there by the snack table? The ones wearing the badges that say 'Ask Me.' I suggest you walk across the room and go ask them."

"Well done, Auntie," Harriet said with a smile.

"Some people don't have the brains they were born with," Beth said, shaking her head. "I better go help Connie. I'm supposed to be getting paint from the supply room."

"Are we meeting at the Steaming Cup when we all get done?" Harriet asked her.

"We are now," Beth said. I'll spread the word."

"I'll go get our owl pellet maps," Harriet said and headed toward the office.

"Okay, where are our teenagers?" Lauren asked.

"According to Mason's secretary, who I had the distinct displeasure of encountering in the office, it was decided that the teens couldn't be trusted to read the information they were given about owls by themselves, so Gregory Lewis will read it to them. We'll find them by the restrooms in Fogg Park, where the trail goes into the woods by the homeless camp."

Harriet went to the front of the group beside Gregory and said, "Are you finished orienting our group?"

Greg sighed. "They're all yours. I think you've got about three kids who are interested in owls. The rest are here because their parents wanted to be here and had nothing else to do with the kids."

"Geez," Lauren said under her breath. "They aren't five-year-olds."

"Does anyone need to use the restroom before we enter the woods?" Harriet asked them.

All six girls did, so they waited while they did their thing. While waiting, Max came out of the woods and joined Harriet.

"I've located several nesting owls along the trails. If your students are willing to be quiet enough, we could see some of our beautiful owls."

"Okay," Harriet said to the group. "I don't know if you heard Max, but he has located several owls along our trails. You must be very quiet as we walk along. Lauren and I will point out areas where we can look for owl pellets, and Max will signal us when we approach the nest areas."

"I've got plastic bags available if any of you want to collect an owl pellet," Lauren told them.

"That is so gross, one of the girls said under her breath, and the two girls beside her snickered.

"Please spread out along the trail," Max told the group. "We don't want to sound like a herd of elephants tromping through the woods."

"Okay, let's go," Max said in a firm voice.

"He's good," Harriet said quietly to Lauren. I wonder what he did when he was younger."

"Hard to tell," Lauren said. "I hope he used that rich voice of his."

They walked for about fifteen minutes before Max raised his hand, halting the group. "Look up and to your left when we come around the bend ahead. You will likely see a barred owl sitting on a branch outside its nest. It looks very similar to the tree bark, so look carefully. Look, and then keep walking. If you stop and gawk, it's likely to take off."

Max was at the front of the students' line, while Harriet and Lauren were at the back of the group. The back half of the line ground to a halt while the front part slowed to maximize their viewing.

Harriet unzipped her waist pack to take out a small bottle of water when a panicked girl pushed her way up from the very back of the line.

"Harriet, come help. Something's wrong with Carrie."

Lauren and Harriet hurried to the back of the group and found a girl slumped on the ground.

"What happened," Harriet asked.

"I don't know," the girl who had gotten Harriet said.

"What's your name?" Harriet asked.

"Cyd," the girl said.

"Does anyone know if Carrie has a medical condition?" Lauren asked.

Cyd and two other girls looked at each other. "Has she taken something?" Lauren demanded.

"She could die if you don't tell us," Harriet added.

"She took a pill, okay?"

Harriet fumbled left-handed in her open waist pack. "Help me," she asked Lauren. "I've got a box of Narcan in here. There are two doses. Get one out and give it to her."

Lauren ripped the box open and popped the cap off one of the doses, sliding the nozzle into Carrie's nose and squirting the medication.

"I'm going back down the trail to find a signal and calling 911. You stay with Carrie and the kids. One of you kids, go up to the front of the line and tell Max we're stopping."

Harriet ran back to the parking area and called for help. Moments later, she heard sirens.

"Gather around everyone," Harriet said to the students. "We probably aren't going to see any owls in this area after all the activity we've just had, but we can look for owl pellets."

"As I'm sure you read and were told," Lauren took over, "owl pellets are not owl poop. They are rodent parts and small bird parts, and on occasion, you will find one of the rings that were put on a small bird to identify where it's traveled. If you find one, turn it into Fish and Wildlife or the local Audubon Society."

"Lastly," Harriet said. "If you want to take your pellets apart to look for skulls or bird rings or whatever, you should sanitize them either by putting them in the freezer or baking them in the oven to kill any pests they may have picked up."

"Everyone ready?" Max called from a few feet further up the trail."

The group was subdued and followed Max without comment.

CHAPTER FIFTEEN

Harriet's palm was throbbing when she and Lauren reached the Steaming Cup. Beth, Mavis, and Connie were already sitting at the large table.

"Robin, DeAnn, and Jenny were still finishing their projects and will be along in a minute," Beth told Harriet. "What can I get you?"

"You can dig in my waist pack and get me out a pain pill. After that, hot chocolate would be nice. I can get that, though."

"Just sit down," Mavis told her. "I'll get your cocoa, and Beth can take care of your pain pill and some water."

Harriet leaned back in her chair, stretched her legs out in front of her, and turned to Lauren. "I don't know about you, but I'm a little stiff after our plunge over the slide."

Lauren stretched her legs out before her and massaged her thigh muscles. "I've got a bruise or two myself."

Mavis came back from the coffee bar carrying two drinks. She put Harriet's chocolate in front of her and then put a vanilla latte before Lauren.

"I didn't ask, but it seems like you've been drinking a lot of lattes lately," Mavis said.

Lauren took a sip of her drink and closed her eyes. "This is perfect, thank you."

"We heard you had a little excitement in Fogg Park this afternoon," Connie said.

"Wait, wait," Robin called from the door. "Don't start without us."

"Well, hurry up," Connie told her.

Robin, DeAnn, and Jenny hustled over to the coffee bar, ordered their drinks, and then came to the table and sat down.

"Okay," Robin said.

"What happened in Fogg Park?" Aunt Beth asked, looking at Harriet and Lauren.

"One of our kids overdosed," Lauren said. "We haven't heard how she is, but she was lucky Harriet had a pack of Narcan in her bag."

"She was breathing when we last saw her," Harriet said. And I have to say, since our episode with Ta'sean's mother, I don't leave home without Narcan."

"Where do you get it?" Robin asked.

"You can buy it at the pharmacy, but you can also get it free from the paramedics at the fire station," Harriet said. "Given the fentanyl crisis in our community, I think all of you would be wise to carry it in your purse."

Lauren sipped her latte again. "You can't go wrong with the stuff, either. If the person isn't OD'ing on an opioid, it doesn't do anything to the person," she told them.

"Speaking of overdosing, I heard a group of our kids talking about Maylene. One of the girls has a mom who works at the morgue, and she was telling her friends that she heard her mom on a phone call telling someone that Maylene died of an overdose of fentanyl."

"What," Beth said, her voice rising as she said it. I can't believe she was a drug user."

"She did have that back surgery a year ago," Mavis reminded the group.

"She's been doing physical therapy for that," Connie said. "My daughter-in-law used to see her in the hospital when she was there for her appointments. And when I talked to her about it, she said the therapy was really helping."

"You never know what a person does behind closed doors," Lauren said.

Harriet sipped her cocoa. "I just have a hard time picturing Maylene taking street drugs," she said. And I don't see why anyone takes fentanyl. People are dying left and right from that stuff, and apparently, it only takes a little bit to kill you."

Lauren sipped her latte. "What I don't get is why the dealers are putting it into all their other drugs. I get that the users are going for a higher high and don't have the best judgment, but won't killing off the users eventually put the dealers out of business?"

"I agree, it makes no sense," Mavis said.

"Has anyone heard anything of interest while mingling with the birders?" Jenny asked.

"I saw Bob Solace and Greg Lewis arguing in the staging area when Lauren and I were gathering our little kids this morning," Harriet volunteered.

"Could you tell what it was about?" Jenny asked.

"No, I was too far away, but Bob looked really angry," Harriet added.

Lauren chuckled. "Seems like angry is Bob's everyday look," she said. "Then you add all those tattoos, and he looks pretty scary."

"Apparently the injured animals he takes care of don't mind the tattoos," Mavis said.

"I suppose not," Harriet mused.

"Have any of you looked at the other items people have made to sell?" Beth asked. "I haven't looked yet and wondered how our stuff stacked up against the others."

Harriet laughed. "That's my fear; my lap robe will be the only thing that doesn't sell."

"Like that would happen," Lauren said and shook her head.

"When we finish our drinks, why don't we go look and see how sales are going," Connie suggested.

"I have to go pick up kids after this," DeAnn said, "but if my quilt is the one that is being rejected, don't tell me."

"You all are being silly," Mavis said. "The big crowd won't be here until next weekend, so I don't think we can draw any conclusions yet."

It took another half hour for them to finish their drinks and conversation. They walked into the parking lot, but before Harriet could get in Lauren's car, Ta'sean's mom, Arinda, staggered up and grabbed Harriet by the right arm.

"Where's my baby?" she demanded.

Lauren grabbed Arinda's claw-like hand and pulled it free. "Are you okay?" she asked Harriet, noting that she was cradling her injured right hand with her left hand.

"I'm fine; the jostling is just a little uncomfortable. No real harm done," Harriet replied and then turned to Arinda.

"I don't have your baby and don't know where she is. You know as well as I do that you must deal with your children's social worker. In any case, I have no idea where your baby is."

"You know where Ta'sean is," she slurred.

"Ta'sean is on vacation, so at the moment, I don't know where he is either."

"I want my children," Arinda yelled.

Lauren took her by the arm and guided her away from Harriet. "Here's a word to the wise. If you want to get your children back, don't show up drunk and high."

While Lauren was distracting Arinda, Harriet got in Lauren's car. She called Arinda's social worker, Jennifer, and explained what was happening.

"I'll send someone over to deal with her," Jennifer told Harriet before signing off.

Harriet looked out the window. Arinda pushed Lauren, causing Robin and DeAnn to stand between the two women.

Arinda was shouting expletives when an older sedan pulled up, and a young man in a gray sweater and blue jeans got out.

"Hi, I'm Russ," he said. "Jennifer sent me." He turned to Arinda. "Come on, sweetheart, let's see what's happening at the Muckleshoot Center."

"I don't want to go to detox," she cried. "I want to go home."

"Come on, we'll give you something to help you come down," Russ said in a soothing voice, guiding her toward his car.

Arinda went along with him. He helped her into the backseat of his car, which appeared to have a partition preventing the passenger from climbing into the front seat.

Harriet got out of Lauren's car and joined the group. "Not his first rodeo," Mavis said.

"Clearly," Harriet agreed.

"I assume they'll keep her on a seventy-two-hour hold," Robin said.

Harriet sighed. "We'll have a few days of peace, then."

"Let's go check out our quilt items," Mavis said.

They got in their cars and headed over to the community center.

CHAPTER SIXTEEN

"**D**oes anyone know where the sales area is?" Beth asked. Mavis volunteered to ask and came back a couple of minutes later.

"Okay," here's the deal," she told them. "They've selected some of the things that were donated—not just quilts, but other items, too—to be put in a silent auction on the night of their banquet. The rest of the stuff, including things they bought to resell, are in the Willow room. They're for sale all the time."

Mavis led them to the Willow room. "I see Sarah's place mats and Carla's napkins," Harriet said and pointed to a table of smaller quilted items.

"I only see one of Jenny's tote bags," Lauren said.

"One of them sold the first day," Glynnis Wilson said as she entered the room. Glynnis was a member of another quilt group in Foggy Point, the Small Stitches.

"If you turn the tag over on the one still here, it's already sold, too. The buyer will pick it up at the show's end," Glynnis told them. "Everyone loves Jenny's appliqué."

Lauren fluffed up her pillows. "Don't worry," Glynnis told her. "We have a couple of holds on your pillows, too.

"If you made quilts, table toppers, or other larger items, they are being saved for the silent auction."

"Are they making much money so far?" Harriet asked.

"They're doing alright," Glynnis answered. "Someone was clever enough to order binoculars, small backpacks, water bottles with bird images on them, notebooks, that sort of stuff."

"Thanks, Glynnis," Harriet said. She turned to Mavis and Beth. "Let's go by the office and see if Mason has any word on the girl who OD'd in my class today."

"The good news is, Carrie survived, "Mason said. "The bad is she won't tell anyone where she got the fentanyl. Carrie did say she thought it was oxycodone. She had a bad headache, and someone gave it to her. Neither she nor her friend, who is nameless at this point, expected the fentanyl."

"I'm glad she's okay," Harriet said.

"She was lucky you were carrying Narcan," Mason said.

"We're fostering a young man whose mother has a habit. It's sad, but I put a box of Narcan in his backpack when he visits her; my husband and I carry it wherever we go now, too."

"That is sad," Mason said. "Speaking of sad, I'm sorry you got hurt searching for Maylene." He pointed at Harriet's hand. "Looks like you need to go by the doctor," he added.

Harriet held her hand up and saw that the wound on her palm was soaking through its bandage. She sighed.

"I guess I better go home and rewrap this."

Beth gently took Harriet's hand in hers and examined it.

"We'll take you by the urgent care clinic. You shouldn't be bleeding this much."

Harriet shook her head. She knew her aunt wasn't going to take no for an answer. "Fine," she said.

Beth looked at the rest of the group. "We probably don't need the whole team for this trip."

"I need to go home and make dinner, anyway," Connie said.

"I'll make sure we have the art supplies ready for tomorrow. We're all supposed to work on making posters about rare or endangered birds," Mavis told them.

"What are the adults doing while we're doing all this kid babysitting?" Lauren asked.

"They're walking through the woods on the trails Maylene checked out," Beth said. "They have classes on bird identification, both what they look like and how they sound. There are classes on bird habitat, too."

"We can chat once we get Harriet checked in at the clinic. Sometimes the wait there is long, so if you need more supplies, let me know, and I can pick them up while I wait for Harriet," Lauren said, pulling the car keys from her pocket.

When Lauren tried to pull in, barriers were across the entrance and exit to the urgent care clinic. A woman came out of the clinic, carrying a sign, dressed in a white coverall with gloves and a mask. She hung the sign on the center sawhorse blocking the drive.

"The clinic is closed for the foreseeable future," Harriet read from the sign. "There has been an outbreak of norovirus, and the clinic needs to be disinfected. We will be closed for three days," she finished. Included was a list of phone numbers of other clinics in the area.

Lauren put the car in reverse. "I'm guessing we're on to the ER," she said.

"Don't you think they'll be even busier than usual?" Harriet countered. "Let's get a cup of tea at Annie's Coffee Shop. Peppermint was one of the teas Avelot said was helpful, and Annie has that."

Lauren was able to park in front of Annie's. She, Beth, and Harriet had just settled at a table with their tea and cinnamon twists when Avelot and Bob came into the shop carrying baskets of dried herbs. Aunt Beth explained to Harriet that after their tea, she still had to go to the ER and get her wound cleaned.

"Can I help with something?" Avelot asked Harriet.

"I'm Harriet's Aunt Beth." Beth introduced herself before Harriet could. "Harriet's wound is bleeding and needs to be cleaned and redressed, but there's been an outbreak of norovirus at the urgent care clinic."

"And I'm not anxious to go to the ER because I'm assuming some of the norovirus people have gone there and are spreading their germs," Harriet countered.

"Shall I get your kit?" Bob asked his mother.

Avelot looked at Harriet and then Beth. "If you're willing, I could clean and redress your hand. If Annie doesn't mind us using her private room, that is."

Beth stood up. "I'll go ask her."

Bob went outside and returned a few minutes later, carrying a covered basket. Beth returned to the table and then led them to Annie's private dining room. Avelot took a sterile drape from the top of her basket and spread it out on one end of the table.

She looked at Bob. "Please ask Annie to boil a kettle of water for me."

Bob did as asked without saying a word. A few minutes later, she returned with the hot water. She opened several clean jars from the basket and added a few pinches of crushed herbs from jars that were also in her basket. Bob poured hot water into each jar, and Avelot stirred them. Avelot gently removed Harriet's bandage and pressed a clean white cloth dampened with water onto the stitches.

"We'll soak your stitches to remove the dried blood, then I will soak them with several herbs. When everything looks clean again, I can rewrap your hand," Avelot told Harriet. "It's important to keep your cut clean. Right now, it's looking pretty red and irritated. I want you to drink these teas three times per day. You can drink one cup after another or put all three teas in one big cup thrice daily. When the ER or clinic are open again, you must see a Western doctor to get some antibiotics. My herbs can help you, but the Western medicines are stronger, and you need strong right now."

"Yes, ma'am," Harriet said.

Bob went to the kettle and brewed Harriet a cup of herb tea with a generous dollop of honey stirred in. He handed it to Harriet. "Drink this," he said.

"Can we go home?" Harriet asked after her hand was clean and wrapped and she had consumed two cups of tea.

Avelot repacked her basket. "I've done all I can," Avelot told her. "If you were a squirrel or a baby bird, I'd be much more confident of my work."

Beth put her hand on Avelot's arm. "Thank you so much for everything you've done. None of us wanted to go anywhere near the norovirus locations. That would be all we'd need during this bird festival."

"Like I said," Avelot laughed, "I'd feel more confident if you were a bird."

"Thank you," Harriet said. "I'll think bird thoughts if you think that would help."

Bob walked out to his car while his mother did her herb tea business with Annie. Harriet was almost to her car when she turned and walked over to Bob.

"I know this is random, but do you know where a person would obtain OxyContin or fentanyl in Foggy Point?" she asked Bob.

He stared at her. "Because I have tattoos, I have to be a drug dealer?" he said. Her face turned red.

"No, I just thought you'd lived here long enough, you might know. I've only been here two years. Maylene died from a fentanyl overdose, and someone gave it to her."

"It may surprise you to know that a lot of older people become addicted to painkillers when they hurt themselves and run out of the prescriptions their doctors give them. They turn to street drugs. Maylene may have been a user and got a bad batch."

Lauren honked the car horn. "Let me know if you think of anything to help us figure it out."

Bob looked at her darkly. "Don't hold your breath," he said as she walked away.

CHAPTER SEVENTEEN

Jorge was waiting at Harriet's when Lauren pulled into the garage. He exited his van with a large, insulated bag in each hand.

"Dinner has arrived," he said with a smile. "Beth wants to go to the raptor flying demonstration at dusk, so we figured you'd all want to eat early."

"I made you a burrito," he told Harriet. I figured you could eat it with your left hand."

"Are you getting more customers with the bird watchers in town?" Harriet asked him.

Jorge laughed. "I couldn't ask for better. We've had a thirty-minute wait for people to get in at dinnertime, and the back room is reserved every night."

Beth smiled at Jorge. "What time is the raptor show?" Harriet asked her aunt.

"I think it is about six-thirty, but are you sure you should be going out?"

"I promise I won't do anything else," Harriet said.

Jorge looked at his watch. "You all better eat up to make it in time. I'm heading back to the restaurant."

The falconry demonstration was held in Fogg Park's grassy lawn area. Connie, her husband Rod, Carla, and her daughter Wendy arrived early and set up nylon folding chairs for the Loose Threads. They positioned the group in front of the plywood stage that had been set up for the demonstration. A curtain had been hung at the back of the stage to create a protected area for the birds when they weren't performing.

Aunt Beth carried a pillow and put it on Harriet's lap when everyone was seated. Harriet laughed. "I thought that was for your back," she said.

Beth looked at her sternly. "I want you to rest your hand on the pillow. You need to take better care of your hand if you want it to heal."

"Yes, ma'am," Harriet promised. Lauren snickered.

A man dressed in a satin shirt made from an American flag print with rhinestones outlining the stars and stripes appeared. He wore a pirate head scarf in a matching print and a headset microphone to amplify his voice.

"Welcome to the falconry show," he announced.

"That's Bob," Harriet said louder than she intended. Bob looked down at her from the stage and smiled without stopping his introduction. He gave the audience a short lecture on the history of falconry in America before bringing out his first bird. Bob had explained that the birds he would be flying had all been raised at the wildlife rescue center and that it wasn't possible to release them to the wild after being rehabilitated. He'd begun working with them to keep them from being bored and to allow them to hunt, which was an instinct for them.

The first hunter he brought out was a peregrine falcon. He took her hood off and sent her into the sky. She disappeared, returning a few minutes later with a mouse clutched in her claws. She'd landed on a platform set up for the show and ate her prey. When she'd finished, she hopped onto Bob's arm, and he put her hood back on and took her behind the curtain. He returned with a large red-tailed hawk. He warned the audience that Red sometimes came back with larger prey, rabbits or doves, and that it could be upsetting for younger audience members.

Carla took Wendy across the lawn to a food cart to buy cotton candy before the hawk was about to fly.

Bob removed the hood and sent 'Red' into the air. He continued talking about his three birds and how they had come to the wildlife center.

"Seems like Red is taking her time hunting," Harriet said.

Lauren turned in her chair and scanned the horizon. "I don't see her anywhere," she said.

Bob excused himself and went behind the curtain, returning a moment later with a tablet computer. He pressed a few buttons and then stared at the screen.

"Ahh, she's coming," he said.

He held up the tablet to show the audience. "Each falconer's birds have a chip attached just above their tail. This allows us to locate our birds if they stay out longer than expected, like in this case. "Excuse me just a minute," he said, disappearing behind the curtain. Harriet could hear him talking to someone. A few minutes later, he returned with a great horned owl on his gloved arm.

"This is something you will rarely see. Helen is a great horned owl. She has learned to hunt like a falcon."

Bob talked about Helen, giving the audience her history and explaining how hawks, falcons, and owls hunt. Finally, low over the horizon, Red returned. As she approached the stage, Avelot came from behind the curtain with a falconer's leather glove on her arm. It was clear Red had been injured. Avelot helped Red land and quickly took her behind the curtain while Bob sent Helen into the air.

"I wonder what happened to Red?" Aunt Beth commented.

"I wonder what was in the baggie Red was clutching in her claw," Harriet said.

"Looked like pills to me," Lauren commented.

Helen returned on schedule, clutching a rat in one claw and a mouse in the other as if she'd been trained for the grand finale. Bob raised Helen on his arm when she set her prey on the food platform and returned to him. Helen fluffed her feathers and scanned the audience. She was a natural show bird.

The Loose Threads pulled their chairs into a circle as the crowd dissipated. "What do we think happened to the hawk?" Robin asked the group.

"I don't know," Harriet said, "but she brought a bag of pills back with her."

"That's interesting," Robin commented. "I wonder where she got them."

"She seemed like she'd tangled with something," Mavis said. "Avelot whisked her off stage pretty quickly, but she looked like she'd been injured."

One park worker pulled the curtain off the stage and began removing the framework. This revealed Avelot settling Red into a wooden box lined with nesting material. Bob was locking the smaller carrying boxes the other birds had arrived in.

"What happened?" Harriet asked and walked over to Avelot.

"I'm not sure, but she may have tangled with a drone. Unfortunately, people are flying drones over the woods, and the birds perceive them as a threat."

"Is she going to be okay?" Harriet asked her.

"She has a few scratches, but with a little rest, she'll be fine."

"I could share some great tea with her," Harriet said with a chuckle.

Avelot smiled. "Don't worry, she'll have some herbs in her water."

"I'm glad she's going to be okay," Harriet said, returning to the group.

CHAPTER EIGHTEEN

J ames called early the following day. "How is the bird event going?" He asked.

"All things considered, it's going as well as can be expected," she said.

"Well, that sounds ominous," James said with a chuckle.

"You know Foggy Point. Nothing ever goes completely smooth. One of the teenagers overdosed but survived. She'd gotten what she thought was oxycodone and turned out to be fentanyl. Unfortunately, it's not that unusual these days. Ta'sean's mother paid us a visit at the coffee shop and had to be taken off to the detox center. Again, nothing that unusual. How is the baseball going?"

"The boys are having a great time, and my dad is in his element. We'll have to buy another suitcase to take home all their treasures. Dad is indulging their every desire. Luke, of course, is restrained, but Dad buys anything he shows an interest in."

"Sounds like a good time is being had by all."

"Before I go, could you go by the restaurant and pick up a food box for the homeless camp? Apparently, my assistant made more chicken piccata than they needed."

"No problem; I'd like to see how the group is doing with the bird watchers tromping through the woods in any case."

"Miss you," James said.

"Miss you, too," Harriet said and meant it.

When she'd ended her call to James, Harriet called her aunt to see if she wanted to go to the homeless camp. She did and was free, as was Mavis. They decided to meet at Harriet's in an hour. Harriet was behind on her herb prescription, so she put on the tea kettle and sat down to drink Avelot's tea and wait for her companions.

"I'm going to drive," Aunt Beth said, "and I want no arguments."

Harriet smiled. "You weren't going to get any from me. I would like to take my car, though. Before we go, we need to go by the restaurant and pick up some food for the camp. The three of us and a box of food would be a little crowded in your car."

"How is your hand?" Mavis asked.

"It hurts, but I think it's getting better."

"You need to go to a real doctor," Beth grumbled.

"And when I'm sure the doctor's office won't make me sick, I will," Harriet said.

The group discussed the endangered bird's posters the kids were making for the rest of the ride.

Beth pulled into the parking area closest to the trail into the forest. Harriet walked into the woods, turning off the main trail and onto the entrance path to the homeless camp. "Anyone home?" she called. Max and Joyce came into the clearing from the camping area.

"We're here," Joyce answered.

"Can one of you help carry boxes from my car?" She held her bandaged hand up.

"Sure," Max replied and headed for the parking lot.

"James said his assistant chef cooked more chicken piccata than he needed. And the baker is still teaching his assistants, so there are several boxes."

"That sounds delicious," Joyce said.

Max and Mavis carried the boxes to the big table in the camp's common area. Joyce started putting things away. "Wait here." Max said, and then he went back toward his camping area. He returned a minute or two later.

"I was just showing this to Joyce," he said and set what looked like the remains of a drone on the big table. "This fell out of the sky last night. Just before dark."

Harriet stepped closer to the table. "I think I know what this is," she said, explaining what had happened with the hawk the night before.

"We do hear these things buzzing over us every few days," Max told them.

Harriet examined the most significant piece when the park ranger, Gregory Lewis, joined them in the clearing. He reached out and took the piece Harriet was holding.

"I'll take that," he said. "I've been looking for the pieces of this drone. Kids fly drones around the forest, disturbing our birds and endangered mammals. I've warned them, and now I'm taking the evidence to the police for enforcement."

"Do you know who the kids are?" Max asked Greg.

"We've encountered several groups of kids flying drones with cameras on them, but I need to know which group is flying the ones that are crossing the forest. He held up the drone piece. This will help us figure it out. If you see any of the kids flying these, you let me know," Greg said sternly.

"Yes, sir," Max said.

Greg turned and left. Harriet waited until she heard Greg's car drive out of the parking lot. "Is it just me, or was that weird?"

"It was weird," Mavis said.

"I've not seen any groups of teenagers hanging around the park flying drones," Beth said.

"I'm unsure how Greg will identify the kids through the drone. Wait here," Max said. He went back to his camp in the woods, returning a few minutes later and set a handful of small plastic pieces, along with a memory stick and a cluster of wires, on the table.

"Greg was being so rude," Max said, "and he didn't ask if that was all we found, so I decided he didn't need to know about the rest of what fell out of the sky."

Harriet leaned toward the table for a closer look. "We need Lauren to come take a look at this."

"I agree," Mavis said.

Harriet pulled her phone from her pocket and called Lauren. She explained the situation, and Lauren told her not to touch anything and that she'd be there in a few minutes.

"How is your hand?" Joyce asked Harriet while they were waiting.

Harriet held her hand up. "It's doing well. Avelot Solace has been caring for it, and it's healing."

Joyce raised her eyebrows. "She comes here to check on our health needs, but I'm surprised she's treating your injury."

"She gave me emergency treatment and then sent me to the doctor, but there was a problem at urgent care and the hospital, so I didn't have much choice."

"What do you all think of her and her son?" Beth asked Joyce.

Joyce thought for a moment. "I think Avelot is a credible healer. She seems to know her limitations. She has sent several of our residents to the clinic for bad infections or stitches. I can't say about her son. Max knows him better."

"I've encountered Bob when he was out flying his hunting birds," Max said. "I think he's one of those people who has been battered by society."

"What do you mean?" Mavis asked.

"He's done jail time," Max said. "If what he's telling me is true, his father, who had been missing since Bob was little, returned to Foggy Point and forced himself into Avelot's life, stealing from her and then assaulting her. Bob came to check on Avelot one night and walked in on his dad, beating the life out of Avelot. Bob hit him with a thunderous punch to the side of the head. He hit the sweet spot on the side of his skull, and his dad dropped to the ground and died. He didn't mean to kill his dad. Avelot was badly injured, and Bob was arrested for defending her. He appealed, was defended by an innocence project, and was eventually released from jail. He did seven years before that happened."

"Wow, that's rough," Harriet said.

"It was," Max said, "But after a few rough years, he says he got some counseling and then got in the falconry program and got his life together."

"As you can see," Joyce said, "we've observed Avelot and can tell you she's a good person, but for Bob, we only have his own word."

"Hello?" Lauren said as she came into the clearing. The small group made a place for her around the table.

"Here is part of what fell out of the sky," Harriet said and pointed.

"Only part of?" Lauren asked.

"Not all of it fell into our camp," Max explained. "And the biggest piece was collected rather unceremoniously by our local park ranger, Gregory Lewis."

"That's too bad. This isn't much to work with," Lauren said. She pulled a pen from her messenger bag and poked the pile of electronics, separating the various pieces. The group stood silently, watching Lauren examine the parts until she looked up.

"Could you all go take a walk or something so I can study this stuff without being stared at."

"Follow me," said Max, "I'll show you where I found the drone pieces."

Joyce stayed with Lauren in the clearing, putting the food that Harriet and the group had brought into cold storage boxes. Over

97

time, their camp had various improvements added by local community groups, the most recent being a solar-powered refrigerator.

"Once we get up the first half mile, the trail will level out," Max explained and started walking.

"Can we rest a minute," Beth asked when they'd been walking for fifteen minutes.

"Sure," Max said. I've been hearing someone up ahead of us in any case. We should let them find their birds and move on."

Max had just started their group moving forward again when a group of three people appeared behind them from a side trail. They were dressed in hiking pants with zip-off legs, sun protection shirts, and wide-brimmed nylon hats. One man was carrying a spotting scope on a tripod.

"Excuse me," one of the two women asked. "Can you direct me to a chipping sparrow?"

Harriet looked at her aunt, who looked at Mavis. No one said anything.

"They are fairly common around here," Max told them. "We're looking for something else, so I'm sorry we are unable to assist you."

"Aren't you local people?" The man asked them, looking them up and down.

"We are," Harriet said. "If I were you, I would continue on this side trail for about a mile and then take a branch that goes uphill."

The trio took her advice and headed out, leaving Harriet, Max, Beth, and Mavis to continue up their trail.

"Where did you send them?" Mavis asked Harriet when they'd gone far enough to be out of earshot.

Harriet laughed. "I have no idea."

"By chance, you've sent them on an actual trail. Depending on how far uphill they go, they'll end up at the wildlife care center."

"That's pretty rugged," Harriet said. "That's where this," she held up her injured hand, "happened."

"Hopefully, the trail on this side of the hill is better," Max commented. "Not our problem." He added.

They walked on for another ten minutes, and then Max stopped again. "Be careful but look closely in the underbrush. The biggest piece was sticking out onto the trail. Most of it was in the bush. Mind the little plants while you look. I've been trying to restore our trails to native growth."

Harriet squatted down and gently moved branches back and forth. She didn't see anything, so she moved up the trail a couple of feet and tried again. Mavis and Beth were looking at the tops of bushes. Harriet was pretty sure neither of them had the flexibility to squat down, despite their chair yoga.

On her third try, she was brushing her hand over the dirt when something sharp poked her finger. She carefully dug the piece that poked her from the ground and pulled it out.

"Have you found something?" Max asked, and came over to where she was working. Harriet yanked the plastic piece and pulled out a tangle of wires.

"Stop right there," Beth said, digging in her waist pack. She pulled out a nitrile glove and held it out to Harriet.

"I think you should put the glove on and take this from me," Harriet told her, wiggling her bandaged hand. "I can't put the glove on with this."

Beth did as Harriet suggested and took the piece from her. "Too bad we don't have an evidence bag," Mavis said with a chuckle.

Harriet shook her head. "That's because we're not detectives."

Beth turned the glove inside out over the wire bundle, put it in her waist pack, and then returned to searching. They searched for another thirty minutes but didn't find anything else.

Harriet rubbed her back and stretched.

"Lauren is probably ready to tell us something by now. I say we head back down."

CHAPTER NINETEEN

When the search team returned to the clearing, Lauren's laptop was open on the table. Beth pulled the glove-wrapped bundle from her pack and dropped it on the table.

"Any joy?" Harriet asked her.

"I think this was attached to the drone. If we had the part Gregory took, I could say for sure. My guess is that this drone had a sophisticated transmission system, and this is part of it. Someone was keeping very close track of their bird."

"Do you think they were spying on someone?" Beth asked.

"I think they were transporting drugs," Lauren said. "We need to ask Avelot, but it looked like the bird that tangled with the drone returned with a bag of drugs in her claw."

"It's fine to talk to Avelot, but I think we need to give all this stuff to Detective Morse and encourage Avelot to give the drugs to Morse, too, if she hasn't already," Harriet said. "Hopefully, she'll already have the bigger pieces from Greg, so this won't be a surprise."

Lauren gathered the drone pieces and put them into a bag she pulled from her messenger bag. "I hope we're going to get coffee after all this," she said.

"I need to see Avelot in any case," Harriet said. "Fred knocked one of my bags off the kitchen bar and into his water dish."

"Did he drink the water after?" Lauren asked.

Harriet laughed. "He did."

Lauren left her car at the park and rode up to the wildlife center in Harriet's all-wheel drive car. Avelot was sitting in a worn rocker on her front porch, a fluffy cat on her lap. She started to get up, but Beth told her to stay put.

"Are you okay?" Avelot asked Harriet. "I see you haven't been to the clinic yet."

Harriet's face turned red. "I'm still waiting to be sure the hospital doesn't have norovirus." She held her hand out. "My hand is feeling better."

"Are you here to see Bob, then?" Avelot asked.

Harriet sighed. "I'm here to beg for mercy," Harriet said. "My cat knocked the biggest bag of herbs off my kitchen bar and into his dish. And it broke open. I was hoping I could purchase another bag from you."

Avelot threw her head back and laughed. She picked up her cat, stood, and set the cat back in the chair.

"Mr. Moonbeam here has done his fair share of mischief on my worktable. Come in and have some tea while I mix up a batch of herbs for you."

Avelot picked up her water kettle, set it on her woodstove, and then walked into her screened porch to gather stems of herbs. She returned to her workbench and efficiently crumbled herbs into a bag, then sealed it and brought it to Harriet.

"Here you go. You might consider putting it into a jar so your cat can't try to get into it."

"Will do," Harriet said.

Mavis took a deep breath. "Gosh, it smells like we'll get a little rain."

Avelot picked up her mug of tea and sipped. "Hopefully, my animal beds will dry before it starts." She glanced out the window at a wire strung between two trees in the backyard. Small threadbare squares of fabric flapped in the breeze.

"Are those your animal beds?" Mavis asked.

"They are. I wash them so often they tend to fall apart. I'll have to get to the thrift store and see what I can find to make more."

"I think we can help you with that if you don't think we're being intrusive," Beth said.

"You don't need to go to any trouble," Avelot told them.

"It's no trouble at all," Beth countered. "We make bedding for our veterinarian friend from fabric and batting left over from making our quilts. We could easily make some for you. What sizes do you need?" Beth followed Avelot out to the makeshift clothesline.

"Gosh, you have a little of everything," Beth commented. She noted that the bedding was made from worn shirts, tablecloths, and bits of toweling. They all had been neatly hemmed by hand. She must spend hours making them, Beth mused.

"I really appreciate you taking care of my niece's wound. I wish she'd go to the clinic and get it checked." She glanced at Avelot. "No offense."

"None taken," Avelot said. "I told her the same thing, but I understand her not wanting to be exposed to a norovirus."

"Thank you again. We need to go back to the bird festival. We're scheduled to work with kids making educational posters about endangered species."

"Heavens, you can't miss that."

The children waiting to start posters were grouped by age around tables at the community center. Paper Chase donated crayons and markers for the younger children, and colored pencils, watercolor pencils, and artists' chalk for the older kids.

Much to Harriet's relief, the Seattle chapter of the Audubon Society had sent several members who were artists to teach the kids. The Loose Threads only needed to refill the water dishes for watercolor painting, and sharpen colored pencils. Connie spent her time with the youngest children, mainly trying to keep them in their chairs and quiet.

The Audubon teachers stayed for two hours and, surprisingly, most of the children wanted to stay longer to continue working on their posters.

"Do we ever get to be done?" Lauren whispered to Harriet.

"Let me see what I can do." Harriet went to her aunt's table. "The kids at our table are about to be picked up," she told Beth, indicating the lineup of parents in the hallway peering in through the windows. "Would it be okay if Lauren drives me to the Steaming Cup so I can get started on my cups of tea?"

Beth looked at Harriet over the top of her half-moon reading glasses. "Even though this sounds like the creative use of an injury, we can do without you two. With one hand to work with, I'm unsure how much help you've been."

"Hey, I tried. I gave the kids lots of advice."

"We'll see you at the Cup when we finish cleaning up."

Harriet ordered a large mug of peppermint tea and added Avelot's herbs. "Would you like a manuka honey stick?" The barista asked. "They are supposed to be healthy for you. These are from New Zealand. They're antimicrobial and antiviral. The owners give away the sticks for a couple of months, and then when people are hooked, they bring them in to sell. They'll have the sticks and jars, and I don't know what else."

"Sold," Harriet said. "Even if it doesn't cure my hand, maybe it will make the herbs Avelot's got me taking taste better."

"Here, take two," he said and handed the sticks to her. "Sounds like you'll need them."

Harriet slowly stirred the honey into it.

"Apart from Arinda, do you know anyone who uses opioids or fentanyl?"

Lauren thought for a moment. "I'm pretty sure one of my clients is addicted to opioids. She was in a car accident a few months ago, and her doctor gave her opioids but then cut her off after a few weeks. She went downhill for a week and then was unavailable for another week, and then suddenly, she was better. A lot better. She threw away her cane and almost danced in the aisles."

"What was her injury?"

"She broke a couple of vertebrae. I suppose she could have found some magic cure, but nothing she's admitting. I commented on how much better she seemed when she returned to work, but she ignored my comment and kept redirecting me to the task."

"Sounds like it's not too likely she'd tell you her source."

"I think not."

"Hmmm," said Harriet.

"This looks serious," Beth said. "What are you two fretting about?"

"Pondering the drug problem in Foggy Point," Harriet told her.

"Did you figure it out?" Mavis asked as she sat down with her latte.

Lauren sighed. "We did not."

"Besides Arinda and Carrie, we don't know who in town is using," Harriet added.

Beth slid her chair out and sat down, setting her iced coffee on the table along with a bag holding a blueberry scone. She broke the scone in half and gave the bigger half to Harriet. Harriet broke her half in half and gave it to Lauren.

Lauren smiled. "Thanks," she said.

"If you girls are hungry, I can buy you scones. These things are so big, I figured we just needed a little bite."

"We're not complaining," Harriet said. "We're worrying about fentanyl. We know lots of people are overdosing, so we know it's in our community; what we don't know is how it's getting here."

Mavis sipped her latte and set her mug down. "I watched a documentary about fentanyl, and it said the chemicals come from China to Mexico. They're processed in Mexico, then transported up the I-5 corridor to Seattle, being distributed along the way."

"Seems like the only way to figure out who is selling in town is to buy some fentanyl." Harriet mused.

Aunt Beth stood up. "Don't you even think about it," she scolded Harriet and Lauren, wagging her finger at them for emphasis.

Harriet held her hands up. "I didn't say I was going to. I just made an observation."

"We need to talk to Detective Morse," Lauren said. "I'll bet the FPPD has got undercover people out there all over the place."

Mavis shook her glass to redistribute the ice. "I'm sure you're right. We could also ask Robin if we can ask her kids. I'll bet they know, or at least they know someone who knows."

Beth sipped her latte again. "I think we need to just say no and stay out of things."

"On another topic," Harriet said as she stirred her tea with the second honey stick. "I've got to go with a mixed group of adults and teens looking for owls tomorrow morning, and after lunch, I'm going to try to make beds for Avelot's animals."

Beth laughed. "Exactly how are you going to do that?"

Harriet sipped her tea. "They don't have to be perfectly square. I can use my electric scissors with my left hand and get close enough."

"I'm free in the afternoon," Mavis volunteered.

"I'll come too and call Connie as well," Beth said.

"I'll call Robin and DeAnn and Carla," Lauren said.

Mavis drained her coffee. "I'll see you all there, then."

CHAPTER TWENTY

"Where did you get all these flannel cuts?" Aunt Beth asked Harriet as she entered the studio and set her bags down on the central table.

"It pays to have friends in high places," Harriet said, laughing.

"What's that supposed to mean?"

"Marjory needed a baby quilt stitched on short notice a couple of months ago. As it happened, my machine was free, so I quilted it for her. Since she lets us meet in her store and always gives us discounts when working on charity projects, I told her I wasn't charging her for it. When I took my flannel up to the counter to have it cut, she took one look at my hand and asked how I would cut it. I told her what we were doing and then told her my plan was to cut my yardage into fat quarters and then hem them using the rolled hem attachment on my sewing machine."

"So, she cut your fat quarters?" Beth asked.

"As a matter of fact, she did."

"That was very nice of her. Mavis and I figured we'd need to do your squares from whatever fabric you had. I didn't know you were going to Pins and Needles. I just pulled scraps left over from other quilts from my stash."

"I was going to do the same thing," Harriet told her aunt, "But Lauren didn't have anything suitable, so we stopped by after coffee yesterday."

"I suppose the little animals won't care if the fabric is new or not."

"What aren't they going to care about?" Mavis asked as she came through the door into the studio, just catching the last part of their conversation. "And where did you get all those flannel fat quarters?" she asked.

Harriet and Beth looked at each other and laughed. Harriet was saved from having to tell her story again by Connie and Carla walking in.

"I brought some homemade gingersnaps," Connie said, setting a plate piled high with cookies on the table.

"The tea water is heated," Harriet told them, referring to her constant heat electric kettle.

"Do you need help setting up your machine?" Lauren asked when she joined the group.

"I suppose I do," Harriet replied. She went to her sewing area and started opening little drawers in the small chest that held all the specialty feet for her machine. "Ah, here it is," she said, pulling the rolled hem foot from a drawer.

Lauren carried Harriet's machine to the big table and plugged it into the power strip under Harriet's chair.

"The foot screws on ..." Harriet started to say but was interrupted by Lauren.

"We have the same machine with the same feet. I just put the very same foot on my machine that's out in the car."

Harriet smiled. "Sorry, I knew that."

A half-hour later, Robin and DeAnn joined the group. Both were carrying plates of food. Robin held a platter of cut-up vegetables, and DeAnn a bowl of hummus surrounded by pita chips.

"You can be late anytime you want if you bring snacks like that," Lauren said and set the hummus and chips from DeAnn in the center of the table.

Harriet stood up. "I'll go get paper plates from the garage."

"You sit down," Beth said. "I can get them."

"My legs aren't broken, and I can lift the paper plates one-handed," Harriet laughed.

Beth sighed. Lauren patted Beth on the arm. "Don't worry, I'll go with her and get napkins."

"Okay, let's take a count of what we have finished," Mavis said. The group went around the table, and they had sixty-five cloths in the end.

"I know this seems like a lot, but Avelot has a lot of little creatures in her refuge center, and I'm sure many of them get their bedding changed multiple times per day. This should give her a good restock."

"On a slightly different topic," Robin said. "Has anyone heard if Maylene's family is planning a memorial service?"

"I haven't heard anything," Beth said. "I don't know where her family is." No one else had any information either.

"There's one thing I don't understand," Carla said. "If drug dealers are selling drugs to make money, why do they sell something that kills people the first time they use it?"

"That's a good question," DeAnn said.

"I've read that some people build up a tolerance to fentanyl," Lauren said. "That assumes they start with a low dose, and therein lies the problem."

"I read something that said that the drug dealers put it in other drugs to give the users a higher high," Harriet said.

"We had a speaker at our PTA meeting last year," Robin said. "They told us that the first time people use meth, it's the highest high they'll get from the drug. Users are seeking that first high, so dealers make combinations to try to get them there. Unfortunately, they often kill them in the process."

Mavis leaned back in her chair. "You know, I read some radical periodicals, but one of my magazines suggested that our foreign enemies are trying to reduce our population of young men who could potentially defend our country."

Beth shook her head. "You can't really believe that. The young people in America who are using drugs like Fentanyl were never going to join the military and protect anything, much less our country."

"We need to talk to Detective Morse," Harriet said. "Journalists can say anything they want, online or in print."

"Morse might know what's happening regarding Maylene's memorial service," Beth said. "At least she can tell us if Maylene's body has been released."

"If she will," Connie added.

"I've got to deliver food to the homeless camp tomorrow," Harriet said. "I could go up and deliver our animal beds to Avelot after that."

Lauren raised her hand. "I'll go with you," she said. "Fortunately for Harriet, my current job requires running test programs at night, so I'm free to chauffeur her during the day."

"That will be great," Beth said. "I've got to make juice carton bird feeders tomorrow, again."

Harriet and Lauren were sitting in the kitchen, Harriet with her cup of herb tea from Avelot and Lauren drinking a cup of coffee from the pod coffee maker, when they heard someone knocking on the studio door.

"I'll get it," Lauren said. "You've got a lot more herbs to go."

"Detective Morse," Harriet heard Lauren say by way of warning. "We're in the kitchen."

"How's the hand?" Morse asked and sat down.

"Coffee?" Lauren offered, holding up a mug.

"Sure," Morse replied. "Dark roast if you have it."

"As for my hand," Harriet said, holding her injured appendage, "It's healing slowly. It's early days, though."

Lauren handed Morse her mug of coffee and then slid the leftover cookies from today's stitching party to Morse. When detective Morse was sufficiently fortified, she set her mug down.

"I stopped by to see if you or your group knew if Maylene had any relatives around here. So far, we haven't found anyone to release the body to."

"We were just talking about calling you to see if you'd found any family," Harriet said.

"We've never heard Maylene talk about living relatives," Lauren added.

"Is it possible for us to see if she has an ancestry account?" Harriet asked.

Morse smiled. "Not legally," she said, looking at Lauren. "And you didn't hear that from me. I just hate to see her cremated and scattered behind the police station," Morse told them.

"Let us ask around," Lauren said. "Maybe we can find someone."

"We heard Maylene died from a fentanyl overdose," Harriet said. "Do you know how she got it?"

Morse shook her head. "You know I can't talk to you about the case. I've read articles, though, that suggest that middle-aged women don't usually overdose on purpose. They can accidentally OD if they've been cut off from pain medication by their doctor."

"I don't know of any injuries or joint replacements Maylene has had that would require pain medication," Harriet said. "She was hiking all over Fogg Park, checking trails."

"It's an open case," Morse said.

"I hope you figure it out," Lauren said. "She drove us nuts, but she deserves better."

"Unfortunately, she's not the only case we've got open where someone's OD'd, and we don't know where they got the drug or how they ingested it," Morse said with a sigh. "I have a feeling if we solve one of them, we'll solve a bunch."

"What about Ta'sean's mother, Arinda? We could find out where she gets her drugs pretty easily," Harriet suggested.

"We know about that bunch," Detective Morse said. "There has always been a certain level of drug dealing and using in Foggy Point, but there's been an explosion in fentanyl. I think we have a new set of players in town; we just haven't been able to identify them."

"We're all very sad that Maylene somehow got caught up in it," Harriet said.

"Maylene did provide us with one bit of information. She died in the woods, which implies she ingested the drug in the woods, which gives us a focused place to look for our new dealers," Morse said.

"I imagine it will be a little difficult with all the bird people tromping through the woods this week," Lauren observed.

"That it will," Morse said and got up to take her now empty cup to the sink. "I better get back at it. If you find any family for Maylene, let me know."

"Will do," Harriet said.

CHAPTER TWENTY-ONE

Beth, Mavis, and Connie were sitting in Harriet's kitchen when she came in from a long walk with her dogs, Cyrano and Scooter. She wasn't up to running yet, with her hand still healing—she tried, but it throbbed as soon as she got started. She figured if she was going to walk, she might as well give the little guys some exercise. Cyrano was in good shape, but Scooter only made it halfway before she had to pick him up and carry him the rest of the way home. They'd only gone three miles, but Scooter had a rough start in life and was still building his strength.

"Lauren is on her way," Beth said when Harriet had unleashed the dogs and made fresh water for them both. "She said she made a few more beds after she went home last night, so she's bringing them over.

"We're all going to work with the kids in a little while, but we decided to see if you needed help loading the food for the homeless and the beds," Mavis said.

Harriet laughed. "I'm pretty sure the cook and his helper can load the food at the restaurant, and Lauren can handle the dog beds."

"Okay," Connie said, "I ran into Jane Morse at the grocery store last night, and she said she'd been up to visit you. We're nosey and wanted to find out what she wanted and what you learned if anything."

"The truth comes out," Harriet said. She relayed the information she and Lauren had learned—mainly that Morse wanted them to try to find Marlene's family.

"It didn't take much reading between the lines to figure out that Morse wants Lauren to hack the ancestry website to see if Maylene has an account and, if yes, if she has a living family."

"Is Lauren going to do it?" Aunt Beth asked Harriet.

"I didn't ask, and she didn't tell," Harriet said. "And yes, I'll tell you if she tells me anything."

"Speaking of the devil, here she comes," Connie said.

Beth stood up. "We better get a move on," she said. "Connie and I've got milk carton birdhouses to make.

"I have to work with the kid's making posters about endangered species," Mavis said. "It turns out that it was more popular than the organizers expected. The kids that worked on them the other day want to make more."

Harriet grabbed a last breakfast cookie someone had made from the serving plate before loading the rest back into the bag they'd arrived in. "Who do we have to thank for these?" she asked, looking from Connie to Mavis to Aunt Beth.

Connie raised her hand, and Harriet held the bag toward her. "Keep them," Connie told her. "You and Lauren can take them with you on your adventure this morning. "I've got more in the car for us," she added.

Lauren drove Harriet's car since they were going to Avelot's Wildlife Center. They stopped at the restaurant and discovered the homeless camp was getting a large pan of macaroni and cheese that had barbecued pulled pork mixed in. It smelled delicious.

Harriet smiled. "I wonder if we can have dinner at the homeless camp tonight."

Lauren looked at her. "Can we just go to the restaurant?" she asked.

"We can if they saved any," Harriet told her.

"Can we make a special request?"

"James doesn't quilt, and other than driving food to the camp, I don't interfere with the running of the restaurant. I can ask James when he comes back, though."

"Do that."

Joyce was sitting at the big table in the central clearing of the homeless camp.

"We have a real treat for you," Lauren told her and set the big pan on the table.

"Barbecue pork mac and cheese," Harriet told her.

"How could they possibly have leftovers of that?" Joyce asked.

"The Bird Festival had food events the last two nights. One was a big picnic, and the other was a fundraising dinner. The restaurant catered the fundraiser, which was good. Still, the cook overestimated how many people would skip the fundraiser and come to the restaurant."

"We appreciate the gift. Max is down helping the kids draw their posters. I may have to try some before he and the others return for dinner. I suspect our heartier eaters will dive into it as soon as they return to camp."

"Maybe you can scoop some into a different container before they see how much there is," Harriet suggested.

"Good idea," Joyce agreed. "Can you stay for tea?"

"Unfortunately, no," Harriet answered. "We made a bunch of small beds for the wildlife center, and we need to deliver them."

"Thank you for the delicious dinner," Joyce told them as she walked with them back out of the homeless camp.

"You're very welcome," Harriet said. "I'll tell James. He's happy to have his overages put to good use."

"Things look pretty quiet around here," Lauren commented as she and Harriet bounced and jounced up the last stretch of the driveway leading to the Wildlife Center and Avelot's home.

Lauren parked, and each took an armload of animal beds and headed for the door. The door wasn't latched, so Lauren pushed on it, and it swung wide open.

"Avelot?" Harriet called.

A small bird flew at her face, and she quickly shut the door behind them and then looked around.

The cages and enclosures that previously sat on shelves around the front room had all been opened and turned over. Birds were perched on the cages or lying on the floor. Mice and rats scurried around the space below the shelves.

"Avelot?" Harriet called again.

She and Lauren stepped carefully through the front room and into the kitchen, which was equally trashed. At last, they noticed Avelot lying face down on the floor in front of the woodstove. Harriet collapsed to her knees and felt for a pulse with her functional hand.

"She's alive," she told Lauren. "Call 911, and then call Paper Chase and see if you can find Bob."

"Can you see the landline?" Lauren asked.

They both looked around but neither found the phone. "You stay with Avelot," Harriet said. You might need two hands, but I can call with one hand."

"I think you'll have to walk up the driveway to get a signal," Lauren told her.

She was right. Harriet jogged at least a quarter mile before her phone finally connected. She called 911 and explained the situation, warning them of the difficult terrain.

It took Paper Chase a few minutes to find Bob, who was receiving a delivery of papers at the loading dock.

"What's the emergency?" he asked when he reached the phone. Harriet explained about his mother.

"I think you should meet your mom at the hospital. Lauren and I can start cleaning up the animal area and recapturing some patients. Do you have any hints as our best approach?"

"There's a clipboard that's usually at my mom's workbench that lists all the current patients, their food and medicine schedule, and which cage they were in. The cages are numbered. Just do what you can. I've got to go see my mom." He hung up and Harriet returned to the house to report what she'd learned from Bob.

Lauren had covered Avelot with a blanket. "I was afraid to turn her over," Lauren explained. "I don't know the rules about moving people when injured. Especially when they're bleeding from the head, which she is."

The all-terrain ambulance arrived along with a smaller fire engine. Harriet met them on the porch. "You have to go through the front room, where the little animals are all running loose. I know taking care of Avelot is the most important priority, but if you can move her out without letting all her little patients loose, I know Avelot would appreciate it."

"Where is she?" The paramedic asked. It turned out it was Philippe Jalbert.

"Oh, hi," Harriet said. She's in the back room, which is her living quarters. If you can, try not to step on the little animals, or let them out."

"Will do," Philippe said and followed her to the back of the cabin.

ARLENE SACHITANO

Philippe and his partner stabilized Avelot's neck and then rotated her over onto a backboard. As soon as she was on the board, they began bandaging her head and assessing her other wounds.

"I think we'll carry her out on the backboard and put her on the gurney out on the porch," Philippe told them.

Lauren cleared a path through the cabin, particularly the animal area, while Harriet searched for the clipboard with the list of animals. The paramedics managed to get Avelot out of the cabin with only two birds escaping.

"I think if they can fly that well, they're probably going to be okay," Harriet said as she and Lauren watched them fly away.

Lauren found the small numbers etched into the bottom edge of the cages so she could set up the shelves. A few cages were damaged, but most were still functional. Harriet finally found the list of creatures and deciphered Avelot's code to determine what sort of bird or animal they were looking for.

Lauren came across the house phone and was rewarded with a tone when she reunited the receiver with the base. Without consulting Harriet, Lauren called Aiden. She quickly explained the situation and asked if he could help them. He said he'd be right over.

"I made an executive decision," she told Harriet. "I found the phone, called Aiden, and asked him to come help. I didn't want to have an hour-long debate."

"I don't have an issue with Aiden helping us. It's a good idea. He can rebandage the patients who need it."

"Well, that was easier than I expected."

"I don't have a problem with Aiden. He's been going to therapy, and I think it's helping."

Lauren shook her head. "Whatever," she said, more to herself than Harriet. She went back to putting cages on the shelves.

CHAPTER TWENTY-TWO

Harriet and Lauren had yet to make much progress by the time Aiden arrived. He came in carrying a hinged box of medical supplies. "What have we got going on here?" he asked.

"Unfortunately, not much yet," Harriet said. "We aren't sure where to begin. Avelot said she needed beds, so the Loose Threads made them some and we were bringing them to her when we found this." Harriet spread her arms around to indicate the trashed room.

Lauren held out the clipboard. "We have this list of which cage the animals were in and what they were being fed. Other than that, we know nothing."

Aiden looked around the room. "Okay," he said. "Lauren, you put a layer of clean bedding in each cage as we need them. Harriet, I'll pick up the animals from the floor and see if you can find them on the list and locate their cage as I take each one. I'll set up an exam table here."

He picked up a table on its side and set it in the middle of the room. "I'll rebandage the little guys that need it and Harriet can put them in the cage that Lauren has prepped. Oh, and you'll need to find their water dishes or water tubes or whatever she uses."

They began their tasks, starting with a squirrel that had a broken tail. Aiden had put on a pair of leather gloves from his toolbox and Harriet was glad he was the one picking up the animals, as the squirrel was scratching and biting at his hand.

"Settle down, little guy," he said softly to the injured animal. "I know your tail hurts. Harriet, can you find me some stir sticks or tongue depressors from Avelot's workbench? I don't know if his tail had been splinted, but I think he'd feel better if it was stabilized."

Harriet found the requested splint, and Lauren put the squirrel in the prepared cage when he was bandaged. The next patient was a rabbit that had a gash on her side. Dirt had gotten into the wound, so it had to be cleaned, and Aiden decided to put in a couple of stitches to close her wound. He had some topical anesthetic to keep her from feeling it, but Harriet still had to hold her still so he could work.

Lauren searched around the floor for more of the little creatures while Harriet helped Aiden. They worked for several hours until Lauren located the tea kettle, filled it, and set it on Avelot's kitchen stove.

"I'm making tea if you two want some. And we have some cookies in the car.

"I could use a break," Aiden said.

"I'll go get the cookies," Harriet told them. "While I'm out there, I'm going to call the hospital and see if we can find out anything about Avelot."

Harriet called the hospital and, after much discussion with the nurse at the nurse's station, was finally able to speak to Bob.

"My mom is in surgery," he reported. "Her spleen was damaged. Thankfully, her head just has a concussion. She lost a lot of blood, but the doctor says barring any complications, she should recover completely. She was awake before she went to surgery. She doesn't know what happened. And especially doesn't know about her little patients."

"My friend Dr. Jalbert is here helping Lauren and I."

"We won't tell my mom they're getting Western medicine," he said with a brief chuckle.

"We're getting them sorted, but it will be a while longer."

"I appreciate your help. And thank you for finding my mother."

"Let us know how things are going," Harriet said. "I'd better get back to the rescue mission."

"Thanks," he said and hung up.

Harriet relayed Bob's report while they had their tea and cookies. "She's lucky she only got a concussion," Aiden said.

"She doesn't know what happened here," Harriet said.

"Hopefully, we can clean it up enough that she won't be too horrified," Lauren observed. "Maybe Bob can come over and do the final tidying."

Harriet laughed. "She might notice the birds that are missing."

Aiden raised an eyebrow. "A couple of the birds flew out when we first arrived," Harriet laughed. "We figured if they were well enough to fly away, they probably didn't need to be recaptured."

"Can you two help me with the raccoon?" Aiden asked Harriet and Lauren. "I have a second pair of gloves in the box."

"Given I'm the one with two functional hands, I guess I get the gloves," Lauren chuckled.

"Adult male raccoons can be quite aggressive," Aiden explained. "As near as I can tell, he's got an injured front foot."

Helping the raccoon required both pairs of gloves and then some. They ended up wrapping the animal in one of the larger quilted pieces they'd brought for bedding. Aiden was finally able to clean up his front foot, stitching the cut that ran across the top. Lauren carried him, still wrapped, to his cage, which she'd set up in its original position.

"That was a tough one," Harriet noted.

Aiden took off his gloves, went to the sink, washed his hands, and pulled a fresh pair of thin gloves from the box he'd brought in. He looked around the room. "Who is our next patient?"

Harriet picked up a bird net from the floor. "We should put the birds back in their original cages. We have them all on the shelves, and I've identified which birds are which. Once we get them sorted, we can see who needs medical attention and who just needs to be fed and watered."

"Sounds like a plan," Lauren said. "I think you'd better let me wield the net and you can open the cages. Aiden can follow along and see who needs treatment if anyone needs it."

"You two need to put clean gloves on. You must change gloves again if you handle any birds with cuts."

Lauren saluted. "Yes, sir."

The trio had just finished catching and caging the last bird when they heard a vehicle come jouncing up the road. Harriet looked out and was surprised to see Mavis driving an old truck with Aunt Beth in the passenger seat.

Harriet met them on the porch. "What are you two doing here? And where did you get that truck?"

Mavis laughed. "Maurice there belongs to my middle son. I didn't think I should attempt this in my car, and Beth's was out of the question."

"James wants you to call him," Beth told Harriet. "He's been trying to call you, but you didn't answer."

"Do you know what he wants? Are they all okay?"

Beth smiled. "Everyone's fine. The social worker called him and asked if he could keep Ta'sean out of town for a few more days. Apparently, Arinda is causing trouble in her efforts to get the baby back and has made noises about Ta'sean helping her."

"I'll go call him," Harriet said. "You two can go in and see how it's going with cleaning up Avelot's rescue center."

"I'm curious," Mavis said. "Your text was brief. I take it someone attacked Avelot and tore up her place."

Harriet came off the porch and started up the road. "I have to go up the road a bit to get a signal. Lauren can give you a tour of the "hospital" and tell you what happened. She called Aiden to come help us and we need every bit of help he could give." Lauren came to the door and ushered Mavis and Beth into the refuge room.

"James, what's up?" Harriet said when he answered.

He explained his call from Jennifer Green. "I called the restaurant and they're doing okay. With all the events the bird people are putting on, our regular restaurant business is slow, and we've got all the banquet needs covered, so I can be gone. The social worker checked with Luke's school, and he's clear to be gone for a few more days. Ta'sean's on an individual plan, so it doesn't matter for him. I mean, they can make it up when he gets back."

"Luke's got an appointment with the dermatologist, but I can change that; otherwise, I think they're fine with staying a little longer."

"How are things going there?" James asked. "Mavis and Beth were both evasive when I called them."

"It's been interesting," Harriet told him. "We came up to the Wildlife Center, I told you about. We'd made bedding for Avelot's enclosures and found her unconscious, and all her little patients scattered about the cabin. We've spent the day capturing them and returning them to their cages. Lauren called Aiden in so he could rebandage the animals who had escaped their dressings. So far, two birds flew out when Lauren and I arrived, but we don't seem to have lost any others that we can detect, anyway."

"Sounds like you've got your hands full. Are you staying safe?"

"We don't seem to be on anyone's radar."

"Okay, then. I'll see if I can get tickets for a few more games, and we'll stay out of your hair."

"I miss you," Harriet said.

"I miss you, too, babe."

CHAPTER TWENTY-THREE

Harriet had just started putting clean beds in the remaining animal cages when the house phone rang. Aunt Beth answered. "Yes, she's here, hang on," Beth covered the mouthpiece. "Bob wants to talk to you."

Harriet greeted Bob and then listened, looking at Lauren as she did. "Don't worry, we've got it covered," she said and hung up.

"What do we have covered?" Lauren asked her.

"Avelot isn't in recovery yet from her surgery, so Bob doesn't want to leave, but his big birds need to be fed. He said he lives in the white single-wide trailer with his birds farther up the hill. They're in the bedrooms in cages, and Bob has frozen chicken in a refrigerator. He says the spare keys are in a jar marked "stinging nettles" on his mom's herb shelf and recommends we put on gloves before reaching in to get them. He also said a trail goes up from behind the cabin. He says to follow the main trail and then branch off to the left on a deer trail connecting to his driveway."

"Sounds simple," Lauren said, putting a clean glove on her left hand.

Harriet went back into the animal room and stood by her aunt. "Can you and Mavis stay here and help Aiden until we get back," she asked.

"We can do that if you and Lauren are sure you will be okay by yourselves," she replied.

"It sounds pretty straightforward," Harriet told her.

"When has that ever proved to be the case," Lauren said with a chuckle.

Harriet and Lauren headed for the front door. "Hopefully, this won't take more than an hour," Harriet told her aunt.

"You two be careful," Mavis said.

Avelot had beds of herbs that led around to the back of the house. She'd put flat stones through the middle of the herbs, creating a path. They quickly found the trail leading up the hill when they exited Avelot's herb beds.

The trail was rocky, and the going was slow, but eventually, they saw what looked like an animal trail off to the left. Lauren pushed a leafy branch to the side, allowing them to start up the trail. They'd gone a few yards up the trail when it turned sharply back to the right and steeply uphill. Lauren took Harriet's arm to steady her.

"Stop," Harriet said. "I hear someone or something."

"It's only me," Max said, coming into view as he descended the steep trail.

"What are you doing here?" Harriet asked him.

Max held his finger up to his lips, shushing them, and then leading them to a narrow path on the right side of the trail. They followed him deeper into the woods until, finally, he stopped. "What are you two ladies doing up here?"

"We're on our way to feed Bob Solace's hunting birds," Harriet told him.

"Avelot's wildlife center was broken into, and she was beaten badly," Lauren added.

"My aunt and Mavis are at the center with Aiden Jalbert, caring for all the little animals. Whoever broke in, ransacked the animal enclosures, and reinjured a bunch of the patients," Harriet said.

"Avelot is in surgery right now," Lauren told him. "Bob called and asked us to feed his big birds. He lives in a trailer farther up the hill."

"That's interesting," Max said thoughtfully. "I'm up here because I've noticed the park ranger Gregory Lewis frequenting our part of Fogg Park, which isn't typical. I also observed him going up to the top boundary of the park and into the woods beyond. Today, I was checking the trails that circle our camp and saw him, so I followed him. We ended up at a white, single-wide manufactured home. I hid and watched while he did everything he could to break into the place, all the while being serenaded by unholy screaming. I assume that was the eagles."

"Is Ranger Lewis still up here?" Harriet asked.

"I haven't seen him go back down the hill," Max said. "We can watch from this trail. Max pulled a branch to the side. We can see the trail I followed him on through here.

Lauren pulled a bandana from her pocket. "Here, you can tie the branch out of the way since this might take a little time."

Max took the bandana and tied the branch. The three of them sat down and watched the trail below them. They heard banging in the distance for a few minutes, and then the forest was silent. After about ten minutes, they heard footsteps sliding along a trail, and a few minutes after that, Ranger Lewis came into sight. His face was red and sweaty, and his pants were dusty.

The trio watched him go down the trail and out of sight. They waited a few more minutes, Lauren untied her bandana, and the trio started back up the trail toward Bob's place.

"I hope we don't have to stick our bare hands into the enclosures with the birds this agitated," Harriet said as they walked.

"Bob wore leather gloves when flying the birds, so I imagine he'll have a pair in his house," Lauren commented.

Lauren pulled Bob's keys from her pocket and slipped one into the lock on the door. It didn't work, so she moved on to the second key. This one worked. As soon as she opened the door, they could hear a hawk screaming and wings flapping.

"Anyone know how to soothe a riled-up hawk or owl?" Harriet asked and headed for the kitchen. The refrigerator-freezer unit held human food. "The bird food must be in with the birds," she told the others and headed to the hall that led to the bedrooms.

The first door she opened was clearly Bob's bedroom. A simple bed was opposite the door, with a nightstand and lamp at one end and a dresser at the other. Stacks of books about raptors were piled around the room. She backed out and shut the door.

"No birds behind door one," she said. "There must be a bathroom somewhere."

"It's off the kitchen," Lauren said.

Harriet opened the next door after Bob's bedroom. She turned the knob, but the door didn't open.

"I think we know what the other keys are for," she said. Lauren brought the key ring over and tried the first one on the doorknob. Thankfully, it opened.

Harriet stepped inside. This room held a large cage with Helen the owl in it. Next to Helen's cage was a freezer that held packages of chicken parts with a small microwave on top of it. Harriet picked out a frozen package and put it in the microwave. Helen sidled along the tree branch that was her perch and started making owl noises in her throat.

When Helen's dinner was thawed, Harriet slipped the leather glove she'd found on her injured right hand and picked up the chicken in her left hand.

"Close the door," she instructed.

There was only one door into the cage, so Harriet took a deep breath and stepped in. Helen immediately flew down and landed on the leather glove covering her arm. Thankfully, Helen sat and waited politely for Harriet to hand her chicken pieces.

"There's a little shelf behind you," Lauren said. "Set the big dish down and hand her a gob of chicken."

Harriet did as suggested, flinching only a little as Helen took the chicken from her. Helen politely ate her chicken, and when it was mostly gone, she flew back to a higher spot on her large tree branch.

Harriet stepped out of the cage and locked it behind her. She removed the leather glove and handed it to Lauren.

"Okay, you get to do the hawk and the falcon." Lauren rolled her eyes and took the glove.

CHAPTER TWENTY-FOUR

L auren was able to feed the other two birds without problems. Harriet carried the empty chicken wrappers to the kitchen, where she found Max poking around in the cabinets.

"What are you doing?" she asked him.

"Just snooping," he said with a grin. "I haven't seen how the other half lives in quite a few years."

"I'm not sure Bob is a representative of the other half," she said, pushing the wrappers into the kitchen waste basket.

"I think Bob probably recycles those wrappers," Max observed.

Harriet sighed. "Fine." She pulled the wrappers back out and set them in the sink.

"Here, let me do that," Max said. "I think it's a two-handed job."

Lauren had just stepped out of the hall to the bedrooms when they heard knocking on the door. She started for the door, but Max stopped her and gestured for the keys. She handed them over, and he took them back to the kitchen and dropped them into the garbage grinder.

When he returned, he nodded to her, and she opened the door. A man none of them knew stood on the little porch. He wore torn jeans and a dirty white T-shirt.

"Can we help you?" Harriet asked as she stepped up behind Lauren. The man pulled a machete-sized knife from behind his back as he pushed his way in.

"You can help me by keeping out of my way while I look for something."

Lauren and Harriet looked at each other and then at Max. "Do as the man says," Max said. The trio backed up until they reached the sofa, where they sat down.

The man started in the kitchen, pulling dishes from one cabinet and salt, pepper, and other condiments from another, slashing the packages open, and dumping their contents. Fortunately, Bob didn't keep a lot of food in his trailer. Harriet guessed he probably ate at his mother's house.

He opened the refrigerator and pulled out several bags of food, tearing them open. When he'd thoroughly torn the kitchen apart, he stormed to the bedroom hallway. It only took him a few minutes to tear Bob's bedroom apart. He kicked over the stacks of books but clearly believed whatever he was looking for wasn't in the books.

The man glared at Harriet, Lauren, and Max as he crossed to the bathroom. Bob kept the bathroom tidy, with only towels, soap, and shampoo on shelves and spare toilet paper and Kleenex under the sink.

The searcher went to Helen's bedroom door and tried to open it. When it didn't give, he shook it harder, twisting the knob. His face turned red, and he whipped around, storming back to the living room and standing before the trio on the sofa.

"Which of you can open these doors?"

Harriet looked at the other two. Meanwhile, the raptors began screaming. "None of us," Max finally said. "We came up here to pick up some food for the homeless camp that Bob left for us, and you've now ruined it."

The man smacked Max across the face. "Try again, old man." Max rubbed his cheek.

"You can beat us all up," Harriet said, "But that won't cause keys to appear."

"How did you get in here, then?" he demanded.

"Bob left the door open for us," Harriet told him.

"He did not."

"His door sticks. You have to lift and push at the same time. If you don't, it doesn't open."

"I don't believe you." He towered over Harriet. "Hand over the keys."

Harriet shook her head. "If I had the keys, I'd give them to you," Harriet told him.

He pulled his hand back and punched her in the face. She crumpled over onto her side, leaning into Max. Max tensed.

"Don't," she whispered to him.

"Let's be reasonable," Max said. "We're just here to pick up some food. Bob has a garden behind his trailer. He told us he had left a few things in the refrigerator and that we would pick up the rest from his garden. He said he had early peas that were ready."

Max was clearly stalling, but Harriet wasn't sure why. "Maybe Bob has a set of keys hidden under the pot of herbs out front."

"And maybe you're trying to get me out of the trailer so you can lock the door behind me." He looked down at Harriet. "You—come with me." He grabbed her arm and pulled her up, holding the knife to her side. You and I are going to check the herb pot. And you two …" He pointed the knife at Max and Lauren. "Don't try anything, or your friend here is going to have a new hole in her side. On second thought…" he said as he pulled a couple of zip ties from his back pocket, strapped their hands together, and then strapped Lauren's ankle to Max's.

The man jerked Harriet roughly through the door and down the three steps to the walkway. He pushed her at the herb pot. She searched through all the plants, knowing there wouldn't be any keys.

"Maybe they're underneath the pot," she suggested.

"So, check," he said.

She tried to push the pot over with one hand, but it was too big and heavy to budge.

"Use two hands," he growled.

She did, but she couldn't protect her injured hand. Feeling the stitches pop as she did her best, she finally slid it a foot or so to the edge of the path, tilting it on its side when it fell off.

"Nothing," she reported.

He poked her in the side. "Try again."

She rolled it onto the grass. She poked at the dried roots that were under the pot. The man came over to Harriet and pressed his knife into her injured hand. "Give me the keys," he shouted in her face. It was the last thing she heard as he put more pressure on the knife, and she passed out as the knife slid into her wound.

When Harriet woke up, she was flat on her back in Bob's front yard and Lauren and Max were standing over her. Bob was standing by the intruder, who was looking a little worse for wear. His hands were tied behind his back, blood dripped from his nose, and his left eye was swollen shut.

"How did you get here?" Harriet asked Bob when she was conscious again. Bob held his phone up.

"I have cameras outside and inside my house. I was in the waiting room while my mom was in recovery, so I thought I would check and see how you three were doing. I watched you arrive and go in, and then I saw this character come walking up the drive. When he pushed his way in the door, I ran for the parking lot and headed this way. I'm just sorry I didn't get here sooner."

"You got here," Max said. "That's the important part. And your feathered friends are fine. They've eaten and are safely locked in their rooms."

"I called 911 as I drove up here," Bob said. "They should be here any minute to pick up this guy and hopefully take Harriet to the hospital. They needed to come up with a rig that could make it up here."

"Who is this guy?" Lauren asked Bob.

Bob turned the man toward him. "I haven't a clue. And I have no idea what that guy was looking for." Bob punched the man in the stomach. "That's for my mother," he said. "I assume he was part of the crew who beat my mother up."

"Now, now," Max said. "Let's let the police take care of him. We don't want you getting into trouble."

"How was your mom doing when you left to come here?" Harriet asked.

Bob let out a breath. "She was in recovery. She wasn't awake yet, but the doctor said that was normal with her sedation. He says you can never anticipate complications, but at this point, he doesn't expect any."

A strange-looking vehicle bounced up Bob's driveway, and a blue light flashed on its roof. "What on earth is that?" Lauren asked.

"I'm pretty sure that is an off-road ambulance," Bob replied.

Two paramedics jumped out of the vehicle and grabbed their equipment boxes before coming to the group in the front yard. The first paramedic kneeled beside Harriet. He grinned. "We've got to stop meeting like this," Philippe Jalbert said. "Now, tell me what happened."

Harriet held up her bleeding hand and explained what had happened. Philippe gently held her injured hand, cutting the torn dirty bandage from her hand. He flushed her wound with sterile water and put clean bandages over it. The other paramedic worked on Harriet's other arm, inserting an IV line and starting a fluid drip.

When Harriet was in the ambulance, they checked the stranger's eye. They were finishing when the police rumbled up.

"What have we got?" Harriet heard a voice she didn't recognize ask.

"I'll stop by Avelot's and tell your aunt what's happened. I'm sure she'll meet you at the hospital."

"Thanks," Harriet said, dozing off as Philippe closed the ambulance door, and they took off down the hill.

CHAPTER TWENTY-FIVE

The Loose Threads agreed to meet for lunch at Harriet's house the following day. Fortunately, Harriet's hand was not as damaged as everyone feared. The intruder's knife slid through her hand an inch to the left of her existing wound, and it didn't do any major damage to her tendons. Her hand had to be cleaned, and then her existing wound was restitched. All the work was able to be done at the county hospital.

Aunt Beth brought the flip chart from a storage closet and tore off the previously used page. "Just so you all know, I invited Bob to meet with us during his lunchtime." Robin started to say something, but Beth held her hand up.

"Before you say anything, I don't think we can solve whatever this is—Maylene's murder, Avelot's attack, and the attack on Lauren, Max, and Harriet—without Bob and Avelot."

"I wasn't going to argue with him coming; I just wondered if you wanted to separate their information onto their own pages or combine it all on one page by topic."

Mavis set a platter of lemon bars in the middle of the big worktable in Harriet's studio. "I think we're going to need to do both," she said. "I think we go in chronological order. Start with Maylene and what happened to her, leading to Avelot. From there, we can put together anything that seems to relate."

Harriet sat at the table, placing a bed pillow on her lap before gently positioning her injured hand.

"Okay, let's get Maylene's information on the chart before Bob arrives. My first point for her chart is that her job for the bird festival was to check out the trails on the maps the attendees were to be given." Robin wrote an abbreviated version of that down on the chart.

"I don't know if we need to note her encounter with the "aliens" near Fogg Park, but I think we should put down her stumbling across the "witch" who we now know to be Avelot. We can double-check with her when she can talk to us, but if she met Avelot, there's a good chance she had gotten off the trails at that point," Lauren said. "She definitely was off the marked route when we found her body. I'd like to know how she got maps on both those days that indicated trails in Avelot's area. There weren't supposed to be any birders on trails by the wildlife center. If I remember right, there were lively debates about whether people could take tours of the center. Avelot said people shouldn't be unescorted on the trails around her place."

Robin paraphrased that and put it on the chart. "I don't know where we put this if we put it at all, but there was that girl that OD'd on my owl walk," Harriet said.

"We should note that to the side," DeAnn said. "We don't know its relevance."

"Seems like we've transitioned into the Avelot/Bob set of facts," Mavis noted. Robin made a dotted line across the paper.

"The next event was Bob's hawk coming back to his bird show with parts of a drone in tow," Beth said.

"And injured," Connie added.

"And carrying a bag of what looked like pills," Lauren added.

DeAnn let Bob into the room while they were talking. "Before you ask," Bob said. "Red did come back with a package of pills. Unfortunately, she's feeling quite possessive of her bag of pills. She's made a nest in her enclosure and is guarding them with her life. She hasn't ripped open the bag, and since her wing is still healing, I don't want to upset her by trying to take them from her. She can't go out and fly until her wing heals, but when that happens, and if my mom's better, we can get them out."

"Does that mean someone is delivering pills in Foggy Point using drones?" Mavis asked.

Lauren sipped her cup of tea. "I don't know why else someone would send a drone out with a bag of pills attached," she observed. "Clearly, dealers are becoming more sophisticated."

"How would Maylene dying from an overdose connect with a high-tech drug supplier?" Connie asked.

"Seems like there are only two possible explanations—Maylene acquired and ingested the fentanyl herself, or someone she encountered on the trail forced her to swallow a fentanyl pill or powder," Beth said.

The group waited while Robin made a note about the hawk and her pills and then the two options for Maylene. While they were waiting, Jorge came in carrying two insulated bags.

"Beth said you, ladies ..." He glanced at Bob. "... and gentlemen ... were meeting and needed some refreshment. I've got pork tacos and chicken burritos in this bag." He set one bag on the table. "And in this bag ..." He set the second bag down. "...we have guacamole, chips, and dulce de Calabasas or pumpkin candy for those who don't speak Spanish."

"Thank you so much," Beth said, her cheeks turning pink.

"Yeah, thanks," Lauren said.

"Your container of guacamole is marked with your name, Blondie," Jorge said with a smile. "And your salad is also marked with your name, Robin."

"Thank you," Robin said.

Jorge looked over at their flip chart. "Be safe, all of you," he said. "Now, I have to get back to the adoring masses at the restaurant." He kissed Beth on the cheek, causing her cheeks to go from pink to red. He laughed as he went out the door.

"Who knows Red has a bag of pills?" Harriet asked Bob.

Bob took a bite of his taco. "Until I told you all here, the only people I know for sure knew about the pills are me and my mom. Anyone could have seen them, but they'd have needed binoculars. The bag of pills was tangled with the pieces of the drone."

"Have you told the police?" Beth asked.

Bob sighed. "I haven't. I wanted to wait until I could get the pills from Red without injuring her further. I fear the police will want to tranquilize her, or worse. Will you tell them?"

Robin took a bite of her salad and chewed thoughtfully. "Robin's the attorney of our group," Harriet explained to Bob before Robin could speak.

"Did any of you besides Bob see the bag of pills?" she asked the group. Harriet, Lauren, Beth, Mavis, and Connie shook their heads. "Then none of you have first-hand knowledge. You only have the hearsay that Bob said his bird has a bag of pills. And he doesn't know what they are or where she got them. At this point, I'd say none of you have anything to tell the police, including Bob."

"Don't you think the fact that both Bob's and Avelot's homes have been broken into, suggests someone thinks they have something of value?" Harriet asked.

"It suggests someone thinks one of them has something of value, but it's anyone's guess what that could be," Robin countered.

"You're sure you didn't recognize the guy who attacked us at your house?" Harriet asked Bob.

"I've never seen him in my life," Bob replied. "Other than the people in the falconry group and the people at Paper Chase, I don't know anyone else in Foggy Point."

"Do you know Gregory Lewis? The park ranger?" Harriet asked.

"I know who he is. He told me where they wanted me to fly the birds when that woman asked me to put on the show," Bob said.

"You mean Betty Ruiz?" Harriet asked.

"Yes, that's the one."

Bob glanced at his watch. "I've got to get back to work," he said and stood up. "Thanks for lunch."

"Okay," Robin said when he was out the door.

"Can you put down Gregory Lewis's name?" Harriet asked.

"In what context?" Robin asked her.

Harriet sighed. "I'm not sure how to put it. Max observed Lewis trying to break into Bob's place before we arrived. He also said Lewis has been walking the trails through Fogg Park and into the forest beyond. He says this isn't typical. He says the park people generally leave their section of the park alone."

"I could imagine the people putting on the bird festival wanting to be sure all the areas their attendees might hike through were pristine," Beth said. "They wouldn't want any used condoms or other detritus on the trails."

Robin held her marker. "So, what do you want me to write?"

Harriet pressed her lips together. "Could you just put his name up there for now?"

"I wonder if we could put a little camera on one of Bob's birds. Maybe we could catch a picture of the drone flying around," Lauren said.

"That assumes they had more than one drone since Red broke the one she encountered during the show," Harriet said.

"We'd also have to determine if Bob's other birds are less likely to attack a drone," Beth said.

"We can at least ask Bob," Mavis said.

Robin made a note on the board. "What else can we do in the meantime?" Robin asked the group.

Carla had been sitting quietly at the end of the table. "What if we try to follow the drugs?" she asked.

"Explain," Lauren said.

Carla's cheeks turned pink. "Well, Maylene died from a fentanyl overdose. One of Harriet's owl-walk kids OD'd but was saved. Bob's bird is hoarding a bag of pills that could be fentanyl. And I don't know how Arinda fits in, but she also OD'd from fentanyl. Seems like Foggy Point has a drug problem."

Harriet leaned back in her chair. "That's a thought," she said. "I wonder if Maylene took the fentanyl herself or if someone gave it to her?"

"We could talk to Maylene's dry cleaner friend," Lauren suggested. "He might know if she had a pain issue that would cause her to seek pain relief from illegal sources." Robin wrote that down on their chart.

"I can go talk to the high school and junior high counselors," Connie volunteered. "They could tell us how much of a problem they have with drugs at school. And maybe who is supplying the kids if they know."

"Beth and I can talk to Detective Morse," Mavis suggested. "I'm not sure how much she'll be willing to share, but we can try."

Lauren ate a scoopful of guacamole from her personal container. "I can do a background check on Gregory Lewis," Lauren said.

"Good idea," Harriet told her. "I'd like to know why he was trying to get into Bob's trailer the other day. And I don't want to suggest Arinda yet, but if we think this a viable track to pursue, I can try to talk to her. I'm not sure we can believe anything she says, and I don't want her coming after Ta'sean, but like I say, if we have to, we can try to talk to her."

"I wonder if Philippe Jalbert would know anything?" Beth mused. "The EMTs are the people who have to pick up the OD victims. He might know some of the drug people because of that. Mavis and I could go talk to him."

Robin was writing on the flip chart as fast as she could. Finally, she set her pen down and turned to the group. "Seems like we all have tasks to do."

"I don't," Sarah said. "I can talk to my neighbors; several isolated cabins are on our side of the hill. If there are people repackaging drugs and distributing them, I wouldn't be surprised if they live on my hill. I pass some pretty sketchy people on my road these days."

Robin picked her pen up and added Sarah to the list of tasks. "Okay, now are we good?" she asked with a smile.

"We left Jenny out," Lauren said, "But I guess that's okay since she isn't here."

CHAPTER TWENTY-SIX

Harriet picked up the empty mugs, took napkins from her big table, and carried them to the kitchen. Lauren took a mug from Harriet's good hand. "Let me do that. One at a time is going to take you forever."

"Do you have to work this afternoon?" Harriet asked Lauren, who was the only person who hadn't left.

"My project can wait until later. Besides, I'm sure everyone left so quickly so that they could do their tasks from the list. We don't want to be left behind."

Harriet laughed. "I don't think talking to the dry cleaner is going to take much time."

"Assuming Bill Park is available."

"Unless he has a worker, he'll be there," Harriet said, picking Scooter up. She rubbed his ears.

"You behave yourself while we're gone," she instructed.

"Does he listen to you?" Lauren asked her.

"Not really. Scooter recently discovered the joy of digging through wastebaskets. We've tried putting them up on the counters, but Fred helps him by tipping the baskets over, then Scooter drags the contents all over whatever room they're in."

"Carter hasn't tried that yet. He's taken to emptying the tissue box on my nightstand. He can just reach it from the side of the bed. With my allergies, it's not very convenient to keep the tissues on top of my dresser across the room."

Harriet set Scooter back down. "I'll drive."

Bill Park was pressing shirts when Harriet and Lauren entered his shop. His shirt pressing station sat at a right angle to his front counter so he could keep an eye on any customers who came in. He turned his machine off and approached the counter when they came in. "Do you have any news about Maylene?"

"I'm afraid not," Harriet answered. "We were hoping you could answer a few questions."

"Sure," he said. "Anything I can do to help."

"We were wondering if Maylene had said anything about her back hurting," Harriet said.

"Since she's been hiking the trails," Lauren added.

Bill pressed his lips together while he thought. "No, I don't believe she did," he said. "She mentioned her knee being a little sore, but I offered her some ibuprofen, and she said it wasn't that bad."

"Thanks," Harriet said and turned toward the door.

"Why are you asking?"

Harriet looked at Lauren. "I don't know if you've heard, but we overheard someone say Maylene died from a fentanyl overdose," Lauren said.

The color drained from Bill's face. "I can't believe that. Maylene was opposed to drugs of any sort. She'd never willingly take fentanyl or any other drug, legal or otherwise."

"That was what we thought," Harriet said, "but we figured you might know her better than we did."

"Thanks for letting us know," Lauren said.

"Please," Bill said. "Find out who did this to her."

Harriet sighed as they left the shop. "I guess that was a long shot," she said.

"We had to check it out," Lauren said. "Hopefully, the others are learning something useful."

"Let's go back to festival headquarters and see if they've made any new copies of the trail maps," Harriet suggested. "Maybe we could even see a copy of the originals."

Kath was in the office when Harriet and Lauren arrived.

"If you're looking for Mason or Gregory, they're in a meeting and won't be out until after five, so they'll probably go home after."

"We were actually looking for fresh trail maps," Lauren said.

Kath went to the mail slots set up for the festival workers. She brushed her hand across the ends of papers sticking out from several of them and stopped and pulled a group of papers from one.

"Mason seems to have some maps I've not seen before," she said, handing them to Harriet.

Lauren looked over Harriet's shoulder as she flipped through the pages.

"Could we possibly get copies of these?" Harriet asked Kath.

Kath took them back and looked at them. "They don't appear to be state secrets, I don't see why not. Are you still taking tours through the woods with the kids?" she asked.

"Yes," Harriet and Lauren said in unison. Harriet wasn't sure she had any more hikes scheduled, but she wouldn't lose the opportunity to study the maps. The lines she saw in her brief examination seemed different than the trail maps they'd seen before.

Kath went to the back of the reception area and photocopied the requested maps. She put them in a manilla envelope and handed it to Harriet.

"Do you feel like a beverage from the Cup on our way back to my house to study our maps?" Harriet asked. "A little hot chocolate will help my hand feel better."

Lauren looked at her and shook her head. "Whatever."

Harriet had spread the new maps on the ottoman in the upstairs TV room at her house when her phone rang. "Sarah, what's wrong?" she asked and then listened.

"Uh-huh … uh-huh …" she said. Alright, we'll be right there."

Harriet hung up and turned to Lauren. "Call Robin and tell her to meet us at the police station—Sarah's been taken in for questioning."

Fortunately, Robin was available and would meet them there as soon as she made childcare arrangements. Harriet and Lauren took Scooter and Cyrano out, gave them treats, and headed for the Foggy Point Police Department.

Harriet and Lauren arrived first and asked to speak to Sarah. Their request was denied, but Detective Morse joined them in the waiting room a few minutes later. Morse looked tired. She sat on a plastic chair and indicated the other two should do the same. She'd taken them to the far corner of the room, making it difficult for the desk sergeant to hear her.

"Sarah was found near her cabin with a dead man. She'd called 911, but the guy was dead by the time the EMTs reached them."

"Can either of you tell me what's going on?"

"Nothing specific," Harriet said. "She told us some questionable people were moving onto her hill, and she was going to talk to her neighbors and see if they knew anything."

Lauren walked over to the visitor coffee station and poured herself a cup. "Anyone else?" she asked, holding a cup up. Harriet and Morse shook their heads. "Sarah did say she'd encountered some sketchy people on the trails going to and from her neighbor's cabins."

"Yeah," Harriet added. "She said they didn't look like the typical hikers, either." Robin arrived before they could discuss Sarah's encounters any further.

"What's going on?" she asked, looking at Harriet instead of the detective.

"Sarah didn't have your phone number handy, so she called me," Harriet said. "She told me she was walking on one of the deer trails near her house when a guy came up from behind and attacked her. Sarah was fighting back when her attacker suddenly collapsed. She told me she didn't attempt CPR as she was afraid he'd consumed illegal substances. She didn't want it to contaminate her. She called 911, and by the time the EMTs found her, the guy was dead. They called the police, and here we are."

Robin turned to Detective Morse. "I'd like to speak to my client now, please." She stood up, and Morse did the same.

Harriet and Lauren called Beth, Connie, Mavis, and Jenny, and by the time Robin and Sarah came out an hour and a half later, they were all in the waiting room with Harriet and Lauren.

"DeAnn is picking up Robin's kids, but Carla doesn't think she should bring Wendy to the police station," Connie told the group.

"Sarah is free to go for now," Robin told the group. "I suggest we reconvene at Annie's before Sarah tells you what happened." The group agreed, and they gathered their coats and bags and left.

CHAPTER TWENTY-SEVEN

Sarah wore gray sweatpants and a gray sweatshirt with FPPD printed on the front. Her long, curly hair was wet and pulled back in a bun at the nape of her neck. "You sit down, honey," Beth told Sarah. "What would you like to drink?"

Beth went to the coffee shop counter and ordered Sarah's latte and two chocolate chip cookies. Mavis brought Harriet a small mocha and sat down beside her.

"Beth and I don't need to meet with Detective Morse. I'm pretty sure Robin learned as much as we were going to," she said.

Lauren carried her coffee to the big table and sat down next to Harriet. "Don't start without me."

Sarah sipped her latte quietly while everyone else got their drinks and gathered around her at the table.

Beth reached across the table and put her hand on Sarah's. "Okay, are you ready to tell us what happened?" she asked.

"I'm not sure I know what happened. As discussed at the meeting, I planned to ask some neighbors what they knew about the strangers walking on our trails. I was on my deck looking out over the valley and saw part of a roof that I hadn't noticed before. It looked like it had a big metal can where the roof vent would be, so I thought I'd walk a little way down the hill and take a closer look. I was walking along when someone grabbed me from behind. I haven't said anything about this, but since my 'bad boyfriend' episode, I've been taking self-defense classes and martial arts. As soon as I was grabbed, I went limp, slithering from his grip. When I was free, I twirled around and elbowed him in the nose. I guess I hit him harder than I thought, but his nose sort of exploded and started bleeding all over the place. He put both hands to his face and then collapsed and stopped breathing. I didn't want to try CPR with his face a bloody mess. I called 911, and I think you all know the rest."

"Tell them about the gloves," Robin prompted her.

"The guy was wearing those black disposable gloves," Sarah said. "They looked like they had talc on the fingers. I assumed that was the stuff they powder them with to make them easier to get on."

"Did you touch the gloves?" Mavis asked her.

"No. When the guy made a grab for me, his hands went into my hair." Sarah had thick, full hair that hung past her shoulders, so Harriet could see how that could happen.

"I told Detective Morse about it, and she had a forensic person come in and wipe a special cloth all over my hair. They told me not to touch it until I'd showered and washed it wearing rubber gloves. She said it probably was nothing but talc, but you can't be too careful. They kept my clothes, sent me to a shower room, and gave me this lovely ensemble when I was done." She gestured to the sweat suit.

"Morse is assuming that if I played a role in this man's death, the DA would conclude it was self-defense." Sarah twined her fingers together.

"In my martial arts class, they taught us that the idea that you could kill someone with one strike upward on the nose is a myth. Given that, I'm pretty sure my elbow to the nose couldn't have killed the guy. There's a spot on the side of the skull where the bones originally knit together that, if you hit it just right, can kill a person, but I wasn't anywhere near that spot."

Beth patted her hand. "I'm sure when they do the postmortem, they'll figure out he died from a heart attack or an aneurysm or something like that," she said. Sarah picked up her mug with two hands and sipped. "I never thought I'd be that close to a dead body again after what happened with Seth."

Harriet and Lauren made eye contact when she mentioned Seth. He was Sarah's abusive boyfriend, who had been killed in Sarah's bedroom while she was sleeping. She had called Harriet on that occasion, too.

"Do you want to go back to your house tonight?" Mavis asked Sarah.

"Or would you like to stay with one of us?" Connie finished for her.

Sarah looked up from her cup. "I need to go home for Rachel. She'll worry if I don't come back and feed her dinner." Rachel was Sarah's cat. She doted on the animal ever since Seth injured the cat.

Robin stood up. "I'm getting a refill. Does anyone else need anything?"

Sarah held her empty mug up. "Could I have a small refill?" Robin took Sarah's mug to the counter.

"Sarah," Mavis said. "Once your attacker fell to the ground, did you recognize him?" Sarah thought for a minute, then shook her head.

"The only place I'd see someone like that would be my martial arts class, but he didn't seem like a martial artist. He was sort of grungy."

Mavis sighed. "Maybe Detective Morse can identify him."

Beth turned to Harriet. "Did you and Lauren learn anything before this all happened?" Harriet sat back in her chair.

"We learned a couple of things," she said. "First, Maylene's dry cleaner was a dead end. He said she didn't touch drugs of any sort. When we finished talking to him, we stopped by the festival headquarters. We got some new trail maps from Kath in the office. We'd just started looking at them when Sarah called."

"Let us know if the maps lead anywhere," Mavis said.

"Will do," Harriet said, and she and Lauren left.

While Harriet and Lauren were gone, the dogs had scattered the maps, but fortunately, they didn't damage them. Lauren bent to pick up the papers. "You get settled with your pillow while I straighten these."

Harriet did as instructed, and Lauren brought the maps over and set them on the ottoman in front of her. They each picked up a map and studied it. Harriet set hers down and picked up another.

"These don't look like hiking trails," she said. "Look," she said, pointing to a square on the map she was looking at. "If I'm not mistaken, that's the restroom building in Fogg Park, the one by the homeless camp."

Lauren came around the ottoman and looked where Harriet was pointing. She used her finger to trace the trail that crossed over the restroom and out into the park. She finally straightened up. "These aren't hiking trails."

"What are they?"

Lauren blew out a breath. "I could be mistaken, but I've done some programming for a company that uses drones to do land surveys. Not the detailed surveys, of course, but just to locate plots. Anyway, these look like the maps they used. My client marked the drone flight path with those pink dotted lines."

Harriet traced her finger along the pink dotted lines. "These seem to crisscross over the park and off the edge." She set the map she was looking at down and picked up another page. With a little turning and swapping out of pages, Harriet was able to connect the pink dotted lines. "Can you get the tape from the drawer under the bookshelf?" Harriet asked.

Lauren handed it to her and watched as she struggled to tape the pages together before taking the tape from her and finishing the task. Harriet scooted to the front of her chair and watched over Lauren's shoulder as the map grew bigger.

"These paths cover almost all of Foggy Point," she said as Lauren finished the final page.

"These must be the drug delivery routes, don't you think?" she added.

"It could be a delivery route for almost anything," Lauren said. "And there is no start or stop point that I can see, so that doesn't help us any."

They both sat back in their chairs. Harriet's cell phone rang. "This is Mason Sanders," the caller said. "I just wanted to let you know that the police told us about a woman being attacked on Miller Hill that ended with a man dying. In lieu of that, they strongly suggested we hire security for our activities in the woods. You have an owl walk tomorrow, so I just wanted to let you know there will be a security person with you and ensure you don't leave without him or her."

Harriet thanked him for the heads-up and rang off. "I don't know how much of that you heard," Harriet said.

"I could hear it all. Mason has a loud voice. I wonder who the guards will be."

"The guy who attacked Sarah is no longer a threat. I'm guessing whoever his cohorts are won't be coming down the hill where we will be hiking. Especially not with the homeless camp in the area."

Lauren folded up the taped-together map and set it on the coffee table. "How do you feel about going to check on how Avelot's doing?"

Harriet sighed. "That's probably a good idea. Bob probably doesn't know about Sarah's dead guy, and that's up in his neck of the woods."

"Good point," Lauren said. "I'll drive," she said.

CHAPTER TWENTY-EIGHT

B ob was coming out of his mother's hospital room when Harriet and Lauren arrived. "How's your mom doing?"

"The doctors think she'll start waking up tomorrow. They've lightened her sedation and say she's sleeping now."

"We won't disturb her," Harriet said. "We mainly were hoping to talk to you, in any case."

Bob furrowed his brow. "Has something happened?"

"Sarah was walking down a trail to check out a building she saw from her deck, and someone attacked her," Harriet told him.

"Is she okay?" Bob asked.

Lauren chuckled. "She's fine, her attacker, not so much." She explained Sarah's response and the attacker's subsequent death.

Bob put his hands in his back pockets and looked down. "That's crazy."

"Sarah's been taking self-defense training after she was involved in an incident a while back. But it's not clear her skills were such that she could have killed a guy," Harriet told him.

"Clearly, he was trying to harm Sarah," Lauren said. "We figured you should know bad people were roaming your hill."

Bob laughed. "I think we'd figured that out already. That's why we're here, and my mom is in there."

"We knew that," Harriet said. "Lauren and I just thought you should know you might run into somebody on the trails."

"Not that guy, of course," Lauren said.

"I can take care of myself," Bob said. "But thanks for the warning. Since my mom seems to be doing a little better, I was going to go feed Red and take Helen and Pere out to hunt for their own dinner."

"Let us know if you see anything when you're at the top of the hill," Harriet said. "Sarah thought she saw a cabin that had been modified with a new roof and some sort of filter unit on top of it. That's what she was trying to get a closer look at."

"I'll let you know, but I think the birds will be hunting above Fogg Park. I try to keep them away from areas where there are cabins."

"I'm glad your mom is doing better," Lauren said.

"Me too," Harriet said. "Let us know if she needs anything."

"Will do," Bob said. "Thanks." They parted ways, Bob going in the opposite direction from Harriet and Lauren.

Harriet's phone rang as they reached Lauren's car. "What's up?" she answered when she saw her aunt calling. She listened and then turned to Lauren.

"Jorge is trying a new Mexican soup recipe. She wants to know if we can come eat."

"We have to take care of our dogs first, but if that works, I'm in. Did she say who else will be there?"

Harriet turned back to the phone. Her aunt had heard Lauren's reply, and Harriet listened while her aunt spoke. Harriet assured her they would be there, and ended the call.

"She says the Threads are all invited," Harriet told Lauren. "And she also invited Detective Morse."

"I wonder if she'll show up," Lauren said.

"One way to find out," Harriet said, struggling to buckle her seat belt.

Morse joined them, but no one spoke about Sarah's situation while eating. "This is amazing," Connie told Jorge.

"It's a good way to use leftover chicken, beans, corn, and whatever else didn't get used that day. And you can use canned beans, corn, and tomatoes if necessary."

"I'm with Connie," Lauren said, "It's amazing."

"Anything I don't have to cook is amazing," Morse said. "But this is exceptional."

"Thank you, everyone," Jorge said. "Now, did you leave room for some churros?"

Everyone said they had, and Jorge retreated to the kitchen.

Morse sat back in her chair. "You've all been very patient, not asking me about Sarah's situation. I still can't tell you much, but here's what I can say—Sarah's attacker appears to have died from a drug overdose."

"What?" Beth said.

"The medical examiner said that's a preliminary finding. She has to wait for the toxicology results. She said it will also take more testing to determine how it was administered."

"That sounds crazy," Harriet said. "The guy was attacking Sarah, right?"

"That's what Sarah says," Morse answered.

Lauren started to protest, but Morse held up her hand. "I know, I can't believe Sarah attacked the guy for the purpose of killing him either."

Mavis shook her head. "That's just crazy."

"We've got a fentanyl crisis in this town," Connie said. "I talked to the counselors at the high school, and they are beside themselves. They've never had overdose problems like this before. They all carry Narcan with them and stock it in their offices."

"Unfortunately, they don't know who is supplying the kids, and the police department hasn't been able to find out who is bringing the drugs in. We arrest very low-level dealers supplying the kids, but whoever is at the top of the supply chain has everyone intimidated. No one will give up the people above them," Morse told them.

Jorge brought in a big platter of freshly cooked churros, ending the discussion of drugs and their dealers.

"I've been thinking," Harriet said when she and Lauren drove back to Harriet's place.

"That's always dangerous," Lauren said with a chuckle.

"Be serious. I was thinking about what Morse said about the police being unable to identify anyone except the lowest level dealers."

"Okay."

"I'd like to get the Threads together tomorrow morning and see what if we can take a crack at figuring out who is bringing the drugs in."

"I take it you have a plan for how we'll do it?"

"I do," Harriet said with a smile.

"Do tell."

"We know Maylene was killed in the woods, and Red tangled with the drone over the woods, and Sarah was on Miller Hill when she was attacked, so I'm thinking Fogg Park and Miller Hill are areas we could concentrate on.

"I'm thinking Connie can talk to teachers at the high school and maybe identify kids she can talk to. There are probably kids in high school now but were in her class when they were in grade school."

"That's a good idea."

"Then, I was thinking we can set up both Sarah on Miller Hill and Max in Fogg Park with night vision binoculars to scan at night, looking for the drones. I assume they fly at dusk or later, or we'd see them."

"What else?" Lauren prompted.

"I thought a couple of people could cruise down by the docks where the drug dealers have traditionally plied their trade. If we set up two or three cars, they can radio each other and cycle through the area—maybe take pictures of anyone they see."

"Someone could drive by the kids club where the at-risk kids hang out," Lauren suggested.

"Good idea. They are supposed to provide alternative activities to keep kids out of trouble, but Luke told me when he was still in the foster home that dealers know the vulnerable kids are there. And they don't have enough staff to watch all the kids all the time."

"That's awful," Lauren commented.

"We should check out the alternative high school, too," Harriet said. "When we were working with the foster kids, one of the teachers told me that most of their students were basically good kids who were living in homes where the parents were users. Like Ta'sean."

"Do you think we could get anything from Arinda?" Lauren asked.

"Someone could try, but I don't want to engage with her. We've been working hard to keep her away from Ta'sean."

Lauren sighed. "Okay, so we've got a pretty good to-do list. Let's call people when we get back to your house. Hopefully, everyone is available."

"Sounds like a plan."

CHAPTER TWENTY-NINE

"**D**idn't we just do this yesterday?" Mavis asked Harriet when she sat down at the big table at the Steaming Cup.

"Did we miss something?" Robin asked before Harriet could answer. She had walked in the door, approached the table, and stood over Harriet.

"Why don't we wait until everyone is here? Then I only have to say this once," Harriet suggested.

Robin spun on her heels and stomped over to the bar to order her drink. "What's wrong with her?" Lauren asked Harriet when she set Harriet's hot chocolate in front of her and then sat down beside her with her own latte.

DeAnn joined them at the table, carrying a cup of tea and a blueberry muffin. "Her daughter has a new boyfriend, and Robin and her husband disapprove. First, they think she's too young to have a boyfriend, especially since he's three years older than her, which is a big gap when she's in middle school and he's in high school."

"And she's going to take it out on us?" Lauren asked.

DeAnn sipped her tea. "She'll calm down after she has some coffee. Her daughter snuck out to meet this boy after Robin told her she couldn't see him anymore. Robin just found out and had a big fight with her daughter and grounded her. Her husband is skipping his pickleball game to stay home with her while we meet."

"That explains it, I guess," Harriet said.

Robin returned to the table, carrying a mug of black coffee and a cheese Danish. "I'm sorry," she said to Harriet. "Problems at home."

"It's okay, DeAnn explained it to us. I'll try to keep this short."

Robin sat down. "Like I said, I'm sorry."

"Not a problem," Harriet said and sipped her hot chocolate.

"I guess you have a new plan," Beth said and sat at the table.

Harriet held up her good hand. "Just hold on. Carla just pulled into the parking lot, and Sarah was right behind her."

When everyone was seated at the table, and Robin had a fresh legal tablet from her tote bag, Harriet set her mug down with a loud thunk. "I know you're all wondering why we're here and Lauren and I will try to keep it brief."

Lauren rolled her eyes. "This was Harriet's idea, but I agree with her." Harriet cleared her throat.

"I was telling Lauren after dinner last night that everyone clearly recognizes we have a problem with fentanyl in our town, and the police are getting nowhere."

"So you think we can do something the police can't?" Beth demanded.

Harriet blew out a breath. "I'm not thinking we're smarter than the police or anything. I just think they don't have enough resources to look everywhere for the next level in the chain of dealers."

Lauren sipped her latte. "Harriet has a point." She pulled her iPad from her messenger bag and handed it to Robin. "Here, I wrote down what we were thinking."

"We were thinking Sarah and Max could watch with night vision goggles," Harriet said. "They would be looking for the drones. If they can see them flying, maybe we can figure out where they are coming from or going to.

"We were thinking Connie could approach some of the high school students she knows from when she was their grade school teacher and maybe squeeze a little intel from them about who the next level of supplier is."

"Here's where the rest of you come in," Lauren told the group. "We all know the traditional drug trade in Foggy Point uses the docks at the waterfront to meet and do business. We thought that if we had at least three cars and drove random patterns, we would likely see a drug deal or two. And there are a few legitimate businesses opposite the docks, so perhaps we could go to some of them to give ourselves extra time in the area."

"There's a shop that rechromes items," Jenny said, "I have a piece from my antique stove that needs to be rechromed. I meant to take it, but I was waiting until my husband could go with me. We could do that."

"That's great," Harriet said. "Maybe someone else can think of something like that, too."

"Harriet and I are going to talk to Kath again in the festival office and see if we can get her to reveal why they have maps with what look like drone routes marked on them."

Carla cleared her throat. "I hope it's okay that I told Terry about Maylene's murder and the dead man who attacked Sarah," she said.

"That's just fine, honey," Mavis assured her. "What did Terry say?" Terry was Carla's boyfriend. He worked for the Naval Criminal Investigative Service and was based in Bremerton, Washington.

"When he was working undercover, he stayed in the Foggy Point Motel. He said it looked to him like a lot of drug people stayed there and did business there. He said he and I could stay there and observe who comes and goes. He also said he knew the manager from when he was there for his work, and he was sure they would let him put his security cameras back in place outside the building so we could watch who came and went."

Lauren took her pad back from Robin and typed in Carla's activity while Robin wrote it on her legal pad. Harriet sipped her hot chocolate while they wrote. "Lauren and I are going to the kids club, also," she said when they were finished. "We're going to talk to the program manager and see how much they know about the drug dealing that goes on among their population."

"Hopefully, none if they're meeting their mission statement," Aunt Beth said.

"But they probably know who is trying to infiltrate their groups or who they've had to ban due to drug use," Harriet countered.

"I suppose," Mavis said.

"Can anyone else think of anything?" Robin asked.

"Seems like we've got a lot covered," DeAnn said.

Connie looked across the table at Carla. "Wendy is welcome to stay with Grandpa Rod and me while you and Terry are at the motel."

Carla's cheeks flushed. "Thank you," she said. "I was going to ask you, but I didn't want to be a bother."

"Honey," Connie said. "Wendy is never a bother."

"Before we go," Harriet said, "could everyone available to spend some time driving around the docks get together and pair up in teams?"

"Also," Lauren added, "you probably should set up a schedule of some sort and also make sure you all have each other's cell phone numbers."

"I've got a typed list of all our numbers if anyone needs it," Harriet volunteered, but no one did.

"When are we going to meet to report our results?" Beth asked.

"The festival ends tomorrow," Lauren said. Maybe after the closing would be an excellent time to compare notes."

"Where?" Lauren asked.

"I vote for Harriet's sewing room," Beth said. "We don't want to be seen meeting as a large group every day."

"Let's wait until the day after," Mavis said. "Some of us have final activities before closing, so it will be hard to do much. Let's meet on Sunday afternoon. If we go to the early church service, we can spend a few hours on our various tasks and then compare notes."

"That sounds like a plan," Lauren said.

"See you all then," Beth said, picking up her purse.

"Want to stay for tea?" Harriet asked her aunt.

"Sorry, Jorge is waiting. We're watching a movie tonight. You could come watch with us if you want," she offered.

"No," Harriet smiled. "I don't need to be a third wheel at your movie date."

"I'm not as fun as your aunt," Lauren said, "but I'm available for a cup of tea and a British mystery."

"What about your dog?" Harriet asked.

"He's visiting with my neighbor. She makes him homemade dog biscuits."

"Lucky him," Harriet said. "Let me walk my pair and give them a snack, and then we can go upstairs."

"I'll start the tea."

CHAPTER THIRTY

Harriet and Lauren stopped by the bird festival offices Saturday afternoon. They needed to turn in the attendance reports from their final classes, which gave them a perfect excuse to talk to Kath again about the maps. Kath was sitting at her station, arranging papers on the tabletop.

"Hey," Harriet said. "We have our class lists and also our lists of supplies we used."

Kath took them and put them on one of her piles of paper. A strand of hair fell over Kath's left eye, and she blew a breath to move it out of the way. "Are you ready to be done with all this?" Harriet asked her.

"You don't know the half of it. Gregory, Mason, and Betty are enjoying galavanting around to all the activities, glad-handing all the out-of-town folks. Meanwhile, anyone with a complaint or a problem with their schedule or anything else gets sent right here."

"That doesn't seem fair," Lauren said.

Kath shook her head. "Tell me about it."

"At least it's almost over," Harriet sympathized. "We'll get out of your hair, but before we go, can you tell us if the park services use drones for anything?"

"I wouldn't know if they did. They don't tell me what they do when they aren't in the office, and Gregory is rarely in the office. He'd be the one to ask if they were using drones for anything. Mason is more of an administrator. He spends his time going to meetings and networking with other organizations."

"Thanks, Kath," Harriet said and turned to go.

"Anyone who flies a drone bigger than fifty-five pounds in weight has to have a drone pilot's license, and their drone has to be registered, and if they are going to fly in Foggy Point, they need an additional permit. People have to provide copies of all three of those things to our forestry office before they can fly in our area," Kath told them. "I assume if we have any drones, we'd also have copies of those three things. I can look in the office for you when I return next week if you'd like."

"That would be helpful," Harriet told her. "I don't know if you knew, but one of the hawks that did the demonstration ran into a drone when she was flying over the forest. We were just wondering if the drone belonged to the forestry people."

"There aren't very many people in our county that have drone permits. I could give you a list of all the people who have permits. I don't think it's a state secret. Even if it is, I don't care now," Kath said.

"We don't want you to jeopardize your job," Harriet said.

"I don't care anymore," Kath said. "This week has just done me in."

"Maybe you should think about it," Lauren said. "We'll stop by the forestry office next week. If you've changed your mind, it will be fine."

"Now, we will leave you in peace," Harriet assured her.

"We don't care?" Harriet said when she and Lauren were back in Lauren's car. "We don't care if she can tell us who is flying drones around, possibly transporting fentanyl?"

"Of course, we want to know, but we don't want that poor woman losing her job because of us. We can figure out the information another way," Lauren told her.

"In the meantime, let's swing by James' restaurant and see if anyone's taken any leftovers to the homeless camp lately. They usually put stuff in the big freezer in case no one is free to take them up there. We can talk to Max and see if he agrees to the task we've signed him up for."

Lauren unlocked her car and opened Harriet's door. "Let's swing by the outdoor store and pick up some night vision binoculars for Max before we go. If we tell Vern we're trying to help get rid of fentanyl in our area, he'll probably sell the bino's to us at cost."

"Good idea," Harriet said. "I'll call Sarah and see if she needs us to pick up a pair for her while we're there."

"Hey, Siri," Lauren said in a loud voice. An Irish man's voice answered over Lauren's car speaker. Lauren told the car to call Sarah.

"Sorry," she said to Harriet. "Watching you try to dial one-handed is too painful—and probably is painful for you, too."

Sarah answered, and Lauren determined that Sarah did not have the required binoculars and had planned to go to the Outdoor Store the following day. Lauren told her they would take care of it and bring them to her in a few hours.

"Okay," Lauren said. "Outdoor Store, restaurant, homeless camp, and then Sarah's?"

"Sounds good."

"I wish I could donate the binoculars," Vern said when Harriet explained what they were doing.

"Our sales are down this year. Between big box stores and online shopping, it's been tough. I can let you have them at cost."

"We're happy to pay full price for them," Harriet said.

"No, no, I'll give them to you at cost; you'll save a few dollars, and it won't hurt my bottom line."

"We appreciate your help," Harriet assured him.

"And this might be a fool's errand in any case. If the police haven't been able to find the supplier, I'm not sure what we think we're doing," Lauren said. "We should try to do something before anyone else dies."

Vern patted Lauren on the back. "I understand your sentiment. Hopefully, these binoculars will help you."

The shopkeeper took two boxes from the shelf and carried them to the cash register at the back of the store. Harriet got her wallet from her bag but couldn't get her card out one-handed. "A little help here, please," she said to Lauren.

Lauren chuckled and took Harriet's debit card from its slot in her wallet, handing it to Vern when she'd extracted it. "Sorry, I keep forgetting you're disabled."

"What happened to your hand?" Vern asked.

Harriet explained her two injuries while Vern rang up their purchase and slid the two boxes into a handled bag. "Are you sure you gals should be out hunting for those drug people? Seems like they're dangerous."

"We'll be careful," Harriet assured him. "We're limiting ourselves to surveillance at this point. If we see anything, we'll call the police."

Vern walked them to the door when they were finished. "You two take care," he said with a wave.

Harriet had Lauren summon her husband's restaurant on her car's phone. She quickly determined they had food to pick up and take to the homeless camp.

"Does every restaurant have this much food waste?" Lauren asked Harriet.

"You'd be amazed. I think James does better than most at food planning. He told me that one restaurant in America can produce twenty-five thousand to seventy-five thousand pounds of food waste per year."

"So, if everyone gave their leftovers to the homeless and food insecure, we wouldn't have hungry people in this country. Is that what you're telling me?"

"Simplistically, yes. Making that happen is harder than you think. James, Luke, and I have talked about this for hours. Mostly, it comes down to money and desire. People like James create excess food, but someone has to collect it from him in a timely fashion, figure out who it needs to go to, and then deliver it to them. That involves having a census of how many hungry people there are and where they are. If the people aren't where the food is, someone has to transport it safely. It goes on and on. It's a complicated problem."

"I'm glad James can directly give his leftover food to our local homeless camp," Lauren said.

"Me too."

Lauren unloaded the food while Harriet carried the binoculars to Max and handed them to him. She explained what the Threads were doing and his part in the scheme.

"If I'm understanding you correctly, you want me to see if I can catch sight of a drone or drones flying over our airspace."

Harriet nodded. "Yes, that, and if you catch sight of one or more, see if you can tell where it's coming from and where it's going."

"That should be easy enough. I know just the observation spot I'll use. There is a rock outcropping just uphill from the Fogg Park boundary. It will keep me away from lights in the parking lot."

"That sounds good. I think the binoculars do work best in total darkness."

"Can I pay you for the binoculars?" Max asked.

"No, we got a deal from the Outdoor Store."

Max smiled. "Just because I live in the woods doesn't mean I have no money. I get social security and a small pension."

"It's okay, Max. You're contributing by sitting on your rock in the dark watching for drones."

"Well, thank you."

"Okay," Lauren said when she brought the second box of food to the table and set it down. "These are pot pies. According to the chef, they are completely cooked and just need to be warmed over your fire. They're wrapped in foil and have either a 'c' or a 'b' scratched into the wrapper, indicating chicken or beef."

"Would you like to stay and eat with us?" Max asked as Joyce unloaded the first box."

"Thank you, but we've got to take Sarah her binoculars. She's our other spotter. She lives in a cabin on Miller Hill."

"Thank you for bringing dinner," Joyce said.

"You're very welcome," Harriet said. "And Max, we'll check back in a day or so to see what you've observed." Max gave them a salute, and they left to go find Sarah.

Sarah was waiting at her open door when Harriet and Lauren stepped onto her porch. "Come on in," she said and then shut the door when they were in.

"Rachel has been meowing so loudly I was afraid I wouldn't hear you knock. I watched your car lights drive up the last part of the hill."

"What's bothering her?" Harriet asked.

Sarah sighed. "I don't know. Maybe she can tell I've been tense since my episode with that guy. I've had to talk to the detectives twice, and it only happened yesterday."

"What did they want?" Lauren asked.

"I just heated water. Would you like some tea?" Sarah asked.

"Do you have peppermint tea?" Harriet asked, thinking she could get some of her Avelot-prescribed tea out of the way.

"I do," Sarah told her. She got out three mugs and a selection of tea bags, including peppermint. Sarah delivered the mugs, tea bags, and a plate of gingersnap cookies to her kitchen table. She smiled and looked at Harriet. "You've given us gingersnaps so many times, I've become addicted."

"They do keep well," Harriet said with a shrug.

Lauren stirred a spoonful of honey into her tea. "What did the police want the second time. I assume they were just asking the basics the first time."

Sarah sipped her tea. "They asked me a lot of questions about fentanyl. I had nothing to tell them. They don't dispense it at the senior care home. My parents have been firm from the get-go that any opioid drugs or anything like that have to be dispensed by outside nurses, PAs, or doctors. They don't allow anything like that to be kept on our premises. The providers must bring it and take anything they don't use away. Signs are posted so people who enter the main doors can see the policy. They want to keep people from getting any ideas about breaking in.

"They asked me if I'd taken opioid drugs when I was hurt a while back. They asked me if my doctors would back me up when I told them I didn't take anything like that. I told them to live it up. They can grill my doctor and the pharmacist. They tried to give me opioids, and I refused. I'm sure they'll remember."

"Why were they so intent on asking about fentanyl? Is that what the guy died from?" Harriet asked.

"Apparently. Morse had said she thought he'd died from an overdose. After the first detectives grilled me for an hour, Morse came in to tell me I could leave, and she told me she thought the dead guy had fentanyl powder on one of his gloves and was going to dose me with it. If he'd gotten it in my mouth or eye or maybe even my nose, it could have killed me. I had my hair loose that day, and I guess when the guy grabbed me, he only got my hair with the poison hand. When I bashed his nose, he grabbed it with both hands and Morse thinks he forgot about his poison glove and got the poison in his nose or mouth or eye or something."

Lauren took a bite of a gingersnap and chewed thoughtfully. "Is the powdered fentanyl that powerful?" she asked.

"I saw a commercial on TV that showed a quarter with three or four grains of fentanyl on its surface and warning that it only took a couple of grains to kill a person," Harriet said.

"Yikes," Lauren said.

The women sat in silence for a few minutes. Harriet finished her tea and set her mug down. "We better get going."

Sarah got up and went to a sideboard and reached into a china bowl, taking out a stack of bills. She handed them to Harriet. "Here's for the binoculars."

Harriet counted the bills and gave half of them back to Sarah. "Vern gave them to us at cost."

"That was generous," Sarah said and put the returned bills back in the china bowl.

"Hopefully I'll have something to report tomorrow."

"Let's hope everyone does," said Lauren.

"See you at my house," Harriet said, and she and Lauren left.

CHAPTER THIRTY-ONE

"**D**on't tell your father what we're having for dinner," Harriet instructed Cyrano, Scooter, and Fred as she poured a bowl of cereal and added milk. Harriet sat at the kitchen table, and the animals sat in a semicircle at her feet.

"I know your father left me a whole selection of dinner options in the freezer, but after all the tea, hot chocolate, and cookies I've had today, I'm not sure I could eat a real dinner. I know you would like something better for your leftovers, but this is as good as it gets."

When Harriet had finished her cereal, she put a spoonful of cereal dregs in each of their bowls. The two dogs inhaled theirs, and the cat sniffed his. The cat looked up at Harriet with a look of disgust, turned around, and headed upstairs.

"You can't win them all," she told the dogs. She picked up the bowls and put them into the sink. Her phone rang as she turned the water on to rinse them. "Lauren," she answered. "What's up?"

"I was looking at our assignments list. We can't go to the alternative school tomorrow since it's Sunday, but do we want to try the kids club?"

"Sure," Harriet replied, "But we need to check when they open. What time are we meeting with the Threads?"

"That's what I was going to ask you. I don't have a time written down."

"I think we just said afternoon. What if we go to early church, go to coffee somewhere, and then drive by the kids club."

"That sounds good to me," Harriet agreed.

"Okay, I'll come get you at seven-thirty."

"I'll be ready."

Harriet called James and was happy things were still going well in Arizona. "I'm getting a little tired of my dad's stories of my baseball days, but the boys are eating it up," James told her.

"That's good, I guess. Things are fine here. We survived the bird festival." Harriet chose not to tell James the negative stuff until he got home. She was sure the goings-on in Foggy Point wouldn't make a significant newspaper, so she wasn't worried that he'd find out about Maylene and the guy Sarah killed until he got home.

"I haven't heard anything else from the social worker, have you?" James asked.

"I have not, and I haven't heard from or seen Arinda either."

James sighed. "I'll assume we can come home on Tuesday, then."

"I'll be counting the minutes," Harriet said.

"Me too, babe. Love you."

"Love you, too."

Harriet had just crawled into bed when her phone rang again. "Hello," she answered. Her phone display showed a string of numbers she didn't recognize.

Harriet was surprised to hear Carla's voice on her phone. The young woman explained that she and Terry needed help at the motel and would hand him the phone to explain.

"Sorry to call so late, but we have an interesting situation. An hour ago, we noticed the park ranger check into a room two doors down from our room," Terry said. "Just now, a second person arrived. The figure looks like it could be a woman, but they are bundled up, with their face mostly covered with a wool scarf. He or she walked up, so we can't get a license plate. Can you possibly get a partner and drive by here? It would be good if you could see who it was and even better if you could get a license plate number and make of their car."

"Let me call Lauren, and we'll get there as soon as possible." She hung up and speed-dialed Lauren, explaining what Terry wanted.

"Can you drive well enough to come get me?" Lauren asked. "It will be the quickest route if you get me, then we go there." Harriet agreed and hung up.

"Keep the beds warm," she told the pets. She knew Fred would get on her pillow while she was gone. The dogs wouldn't leave their beds for anything short of a fire.

Lauren looked around the pickup truck Harriet drove up in. "Okay," she said. "We're going undercover, I see."

"Aunt Beth keeps Uncle Hank's old pickup in the garage row behind my house. I figured no one would recognize us in this thing."

"That's for sure. And you do realize Greg Lewis could be having an affair that has nothing to do with drugs or drones or anything else other than him being an unfaithful jerk."

"I do realize that, but I also realize that he could be in cahoots with Betty Ruiz or some unknown woman."

"Why do you think it would be Betty Ruiz?" Lauren asked as Harriet eased the pickup into a concealed spot behind a dumpster across the street from the motel. They could just see over the top of the dumpster.

"Only because they worked together on the bird festival, and I don't know any other women he knows. Besides, I don't like Betty. She's so mean when you talk to her; she seems like someone who could hang out with drug people."

"That's pretty thin," Lauren commented as she pulled out a pair of night vision binoculars.

"When did you get those?" Harriet asked.

"I got them a couple of years ago. Les and I were helping our uncle figure out what was breaking into his chicken house."

"What was it?"

"It was the biggest raccoon I'd ever seen. My uncle used a live trap and relocated it, then he reinforced his chicken coop and chicken yard."

Harriet's phone rang. It was the unidentified number again. "Is that you in the brown pickup?" he asked. She affirmed that it was, and he identified which room the subjects were in.

"How did you know we were in the pickup?" she asked.

"There haven't been any vehicles on the road in the last hour," he told her. I watched you drive past and circle into the parking lot across the street. We can just barely see the top of your truck behind the dumpster. I'm pretty sure no one else will notice it. And if they do, they'll assume you're doing things you don't want anyone else to see."

"What should we do if we see who it is?" Harriet asked.

"If you can follow them without being seen, do it. If not, see if you can identify them."

"Lauren brought night vision binoculars, so we should have a good chance to ID them. How should we get hold of you?"

"If you can follow them, do that. If not, call Carla's cell. We should be able to tell if you're following them. We're going to stay put and watch Greg's room. Maybe someone else will show up."

"Okay, got it," Harriet said and hung up.

Lauren propped her elbows on the pickup dashboard and held the binoculars up to her eyes. After twenty minutes of silence, Lauren sat back and stretched her arms. "Want a turn?" she asked.

"Sure," Harriet said, focusing the binoculars on the target room.

"I saw a couple go into the end unit, three doors down," Lauren said. "They stayed about fifteen minutes and then left on foot."

"She just came back with a guy," Harriet said.

"I can tell without binoculars that it's not the same guy," Lauren told her.

"I guess we know what happens in that room."

Lauren let out a breath. "Not our concern."

Ten more minutes passed, and finally, Harriet saw the door to Greg's room open. A figure stepped out, turned to speak to whoever was in the room, presumably Greg, and then turned around and walked away. Harriet was able to see the person's face when she turned. As suspected, it appeared to be Betty Ruiz. Looking through the night vision binoculars at the distance they were observing from made it impossible to confirm it was Betty with one hundred percent certainty. Still, it had to be a close relative if it wasn't Betty.

"I think it's her," Harriet said and handed the binoculars to Lauren.

"You're right," Lauren said after taking a long look. "What should we do. It will be hard to follow her if she doesn't get in a car."

"Let's call Terry. We know who it is and can find out where she lives. It would be useful to see if she meets anyone else, but I don't know if we can do it without being seen."

Lauren found Carla's name on her favorites list and pressed the button. Carla answered and handed her phone to Terry. Lauren explained the situation, and he advised them to go home.

"You know who she is, so we can find her. Trying to follow her on foot when you're in a vehicle would be difficult," he said. "Following her on foot in the dark is too risky. If she makes you, she could call someone else to ambush you. You've both done enough. Good job," he said.

Lauren ended the call. "Well, that was fun," Harriet said. "Do you need us to stop anywhere on our way home?"

Lauren laughed as she looked at the time on Harriet's phone. "It's almost one o'clock. "I'm not sure what you think would be open."

"Hey, I was just asking."

"We need to get home and try to sleep before it's time to get up and go to early church."

Harriet turned the truck on and guided the vehicle away from the dumpster. She drove through the parking area until she found a driveway onto the street behind the building. She drove out onto the street behind the derelict building they'd been in front of.

"Do you know how to get home from here?" Lauren asked her.

"We're only a block from the motel."

"Yeah, but it's dark."

Harriet chuckled. "Foggy Point isn't that big," she said. "You can open your phone's navigation program if you're worried."

Lauren shook her head and looked out the side window. Harriet had her home in another ten minutes and then drove another fifteen minutes to return to her own house. "It's going to be a short night," she told Fred when she returned to her house. The dogs were sound asleep, and the cat was only awake because she had to move him off her pillow. As soon as she slid into bed, the cat settled next to her and was asleep again in moments.

CHAPTER THIRTY-TWO

Harriet woke at five the following day. She had tossed and turned all night, dreaming of Betty Ruiz handing pills to Arinda. At the same time, Ta'sean sent his video game star ships after her while the baby crawled under everyone's feet.

She had startled awake when Fred slapped her cheek. When the cat saw she was awake, he rubbed his head against her face and meowed. She assumed she must have made a sound.

"Let's go downstairs and make some tea and kitty kibbles." Fred jumped off the bed and waited at her feet while she picked up her robe and slipped her arms into the sleeves. He followed her down the stairs to the kitchen while the two dogs snored on.

The Loose Threads met on the church steps after the early service. "That was a good sermon," Connie commented. "Do you think he gives the same sermon three times in a row?"

"I suspect he changes his delivery depending on the group, but the theme is the same," Aunt Beth replied.

"I will provide coffee and tea at my house," Harriet told the group, but Lauren and I are going by the Cup and getting hot chocolate and lattes. Then we'll see you back at my house for a report.

"We probably shouldn't follow one after the other up Harriet's hill in case anyone is watching us," Mavis said. They had all decided to meet right after church and then take up their tasks.

"Do you think we've attracted that much attention?" Sarah asked the group.

"I hope not, but if they were willing to kill Maylene and attempt to kill Sarah, we can't assume anything," Harriet said.

Sarah cleared her throat. "By the way, I invited Bob Solace to join us." Harriet raised her left eyebrow. "Bob was coming home from flying his owl, and he apparently noticed the reflection on my binocular lens. He knew where my cabin was, so he drove on up. He wanted to ask if we had a short-term space for his mother in the nursing wing in the senior center, but then he asked what I was watching, so I told him, then he had a few things to say, so I invited him. I hope that's okay."

"That's fine," Harriet told her. "He's as involved in all this as we are.

"Beth and I are going to swing by our houses and change out of our church clothes," Mavis said. "That will spread out our arrival times."

An hour later, the Loose Threads sat around the big table in Harriet's studio. "Does anyone need anything else?" she asked.

Beth removed the plastic wrap from a platter of brownies, while Mavis did the same with a platter of lemon bars. "We thought we'd bring a little snack," Mavis said and slid her platter to the middle of the table.

Harriet got up and went to the kitchen, returning a minute later with a stack of paper plates and paper napkins balanced on the back of her injured hand. "You should have let one of us do that," Beth scolded her.

"I'm fine," Harriet muttered. Bob Solace knocked on the studio door, and Carla got up to let him in. He carried a to-go cup from the Steaming Cup. Mavis slid a wheeled chair toward him, and Robin and Carla made space for him at the table.

Harriet sipped her hot chocolate. She was sure she would need it to get through this meeting. "Who wants to go first?" she asked the group. No one spoke.

"Okay, Carla and I will start," Harriet said.

Carla's face turned red. She cleared her throat. "Terry and I were at the Foggy Point Motel. He's still there, keeping an eye on things. He also put up some video cameras outside. We were watching who was coming in and out of the motel. We suspect the end unit is rented by a sex worker. Terry says he's not sure she and her clients are doing anything with drugs at the motel. He said they probably have another location where their procurer stays and provides drugs for the girls.

"We were watching for a few hours, and we saw the guy from the forestry place—Greg Lewis, I think. He had some food delivered, and then a person who looked like a woman arrived. The person had a watch cap on and a coat with the collar turned up, but they were small. We called Harriet and Lauren to come look from across the street when she went inside." She looked at Harriet who took up the story.

"I called Lauren, and we took Aunt Beth's pickup and parked in that abandoned strip mall parking lot behind the dumpster. We watched the door Terry identified. Lauren has night vision binoculars, so we could see clearly."

"What time was this?" Aunt Beth interrupted.

"Around midnight," Lauren answered. "We left around one in the morning."

"Anyway," Harriet continued. "We're ninety percent certain it was Betty Ruiz. We were going to follow her when she came out, but she was on foot. She might have been parked somewhere nearby, but the streets were too quiet to try to follow her to her car without being spotted."

Lauren sipped her latte and took a bite of brownie. "She was in the room long enough that she and Greg could have been having a tryst, or she could have been buying drugs or receiving drugs for distribution. We couldn't tell."

"She carried a large enough purse that could have concealed quite a few bags of pills in it," Harriet added.

Robin had set up the flip chart and started making notes on a new page. 'Betty Ruiz meets Greg Lewis,' she wrote. She turned back to the group. "What else?"

Bob Solace leaned forward and put his elbows on the table. "Sarah and I spotted a drone coming over her hill and headed down toward Fogg Park." Robin added that to the chart.

"Also," Bob continued. "For what it's worth, my owl tangled with someone or something. I send my birds out one at a time from the top of the hill, and they go down into the woods to catch their dinner. Helen is usually pretty efficient. She's a great horned owl. They eat primarily rodents but will eat other stuff, such as reptiles, birds, and anything. They don't lay eggs until around Christmas, but maybe she's scouting for a nest. They reuse other birds' nests, like red-tailed hawks or big birds. It's a little early to be looking, but you never know.

"Anyway, Helen flew down to the forest like usual and, after a few minutes, started squawking. She's not normally noisy, so I think she encountered someone or something. If it was a person, I wouldn't be surprised if they're hiking around with claw marks on their head. Usually, an owl wouldn't attack someone unless they had a nest nearby, and we know that's not the case, but something excited her."

Robin made a note about the owl's behavior. "Nothing happened when DeAnn and I did our drive around the docks. We saw a few people standing in front of a warehouse sort of building, smoking, but that was it."

"Mavis and I saw a boat come in. It appeared to be a fishing boat," Beth told the group.

"It was strange," Mavis added. "There isn't a fish processing plant at that dock. Beth and I looked up the property tax information and couldn't find anything that sounded like they were fish processors. Glynnis from the' Small Stitches' has a daughter who works at the Foggy Point PUD. She asked her daughter if any businesses along the docks used excessive electricity. We figured if someone was processing fish, they'd have refrigerators or freezers which would pull power, but she came up empty."

"I went to the rechrome shop," Jenny said. "I asked the proprietor, Tom, if there was any increased drug action in the area. He said not any more than normal. It's always been the drug dealer's area. Tom says it used to be just marijuana, then it was heroin coming up I-5 from Mexico. Then it was meth labs. After that, the police cracked down on the labs, and the necessary chemicals got hard to get. He said things have been quiet since then—until recently. He says he thinks something is being trafficked, but whatever it is, the usual dealers aren't doing business around the docks."

Harriet sipped her hot chocolate. "So, I wonder what that means."

"I don't know," Jenny said. "I did see Mason Sanders. He was coming into the chrome shop. He was having some award plaques chromed for the next event that was being held in Foggy Point. Some sort of car rally that was starting and ending here. It sounded like it was a couple of weeks from now."

"Thank heaven they didn't want quilts for that event," Lauren muttered.

Sarah laughed. "Amen, Sister," she said.

"Did you get anywhere with the students?" Harriet asked Connie.

"I talked to a group of friends that have been together since grade school. I laid it on thick. Some of them have younger siblings. These are good kids, so I don't think they're directly involved in drug use, but they know who the players are. They didn't tell me anything useful today, but I asked them to think about what I said and that I'd like to meet with them again tomorrow. I told them I'd buy them all ice cream at Rime. I figured that would take them far enough from school and other places the drug users hang out so that they might feel more comfortable talking. It may take a couple more talks to get what we need, but I'll keep working it." Robin made a note under the category of school kids and labeled it "ongoing."

"What else do we have?" Beth asked.

"Lauren and I haven't been able to talk to the kids club or alternative school yet, but we will get on it tomorrow," Harriet reported. "I'd like to take a crack at the fishing boat if it's still at the docks. I can use the excuse of the restaurant to ask them about the fish."

"Are you sure that's safe," Mavis asked.

"I'm only going to ask them if they have fish for sale. I hope I can get close enough to the boat to see what's happening."

Robin made a note on the board and then turned to the group. "I went by the homeless camp and learned that most were gone all day at a church program. They all get haircuts, get their feet looked at and treated if needed, and they are given new socks if they need them, and toiletries if they need those. Also, a spa comes and gives massages to anyone who wants one. A group of doctors, physician's assistants, and nurses provide them with a once-over. Dr. Joe Hall brings his staff, and they check everyone's teeth. In any case, Max couldn't miss that."

"How often do they do this?" Harriet asked.

"Apparently, every other month. If they have some ongoing issue, the various practitioners will make appointments and even provide transportation," Robin told her. "Max was already gone when I got there. They always leave one person to guard the camp. Max had left a message with that guy. Carl said Max wanted us to know he had seen something, and if someone came up to the camp tomorrow, he'd give a full report."

"Aunt Beth," Harriet said. "Did you and Mavis have a chance to talk to Philippe Jalbert?"

"I called him," Mavis answered. "He wasn't available to talk to us. He was at a swim meet with his kids, and it was noisy. He said he could talk to us tomorrow, also."

Lauren chuckled. "Sunday isn't the best day to start our investigations."

"We've set up a cruise-the-docks schedule," Jenny told them. "Those of us who have more than one car at our disposal will change cars after each cycle we do."

"Don't forget to take lots of pictures," Lauren reminded them.

"I'm going to sit with Sarah on her deck," Bob said. "If and when we see a drone, I'm going to go hike the trails where it goes out of our sight and see if I can see where they are going."

"Be careful," Mavis cautioned him.

"I can take care of myself. Don't worry."

"Take your phone and call Sarah when you're safely finished and home again."

"I'll be leaving my truck at Sarah's, so I'll see her when I return to get it."

"Do we have anything else to talk about?" Robin asked. "I've got the first rotation at the docks."

"I'm going to see Wendy at Connie's," Carla said. She ducked her head. "If that's okay," she said, looking at Connie.

"Dios Mio," Connie said. "She's your daughter, and you can come anytime. That's why we gave you a key."

Carla's face turned red. "Thank you," she mumbled.

"Okay, I guess we're done here," Harriet said.

"Keep the leftover brownies and lemon bars," Aunt Beth said. "I'm guessing we'll need to meet tomorrow evening, and we can eat them then."

"See you all then," Harriet said, carrying the brownies to the kitchen. Aunt Beth and Mavis followed, carrying the lemon bars and paper dishes.

CHAPTER THIRTY-THREE

"Ineed to go check on Carter and spend a little time with him before we go check out the fishing boat," Lauren told Harriet when everyone else had left.

"Good, that'll give me time to call James and run a load of laundry before we go out again."

"I'll come get you in a while, okay?" Lauren confirmed.

"I'll just be here," Harriet told her. Harriet walked Lauren out and then returned to the kitchen. "Let's go for a walk before we call your dad," she told Scooter and Cyrano.

She took them into the woods at the end of their street. Both dogs immediately put their noses to the ground and started sniffing everything in their path. Harriet let her mind wander as the dogs slowly descended the path.

Harriet tried to imagine Betty Ruiz as a drug moll. It was hard to imagine, but she found it equally hard to imagine her having an affair with Greg Lewis at the Foggy Point Motel. At the least, she'd think they'd go out of town.

It was equally hard to imagine Betty dealing drugs, although Harriet wasn't sure what a real-life drug dealer was supposed to look like.

She let the dogs sniff their way through the forest, marking their territory until their little bladders were empty, and then she turned around to head for home.

"James," Harriet said when he answered his cell phone. "It's so good to hear your voice."

"What's wrong?" he asked her.

"I just miss you," she said, not wanting to alarm him.

"We'll be home in two days. Our flight arrives in Seattle at five p.m., and we'll drive home. Undoubtedly, we'll stop for food along the way, so we'll probably get in between eight and nine."

"That sounds good," Harriet said, wishing it was earlier.

"I'll tell my dad to have my mom pick him up at our house. The boys will want to leave the car as soon as possible."

"And the little boys here are anxious to see them, too. Fred's been sleeping on Luke's bed during the day."

"Tell them it'll be two more days, then they can have all the boy time they want."

"Okay, speaking of the boys, I owe them a treat. We just got back from a long walk in the woods."

Harriet heard a knock on the studio door and the sound of it opening. "I've got to go; Lauren is just arriving."

"All right, I'll talk to you tomorrow."

"Love you," she said.

"Love you more," he replied. Harriet knew her cheeks were pink, even though Lauren hadn't heard James's words.

"How are we going to do this?" Lauren asked as they got their coats on.

"I think we go right to the dock the fishing boat is tied to and see if we can find someone. I'll identify myself as being with the restaurant and looking for fresh fish."

"Sounds good."

"If we don't find anyone, we'll walk out on the dock and see what we can see from there." Harriet parked at the curb across the street from the sidewalk that led down to the docks where the boats were tied up. In past years, boats were at all the docks along the water, but now, just a few had berths for boats. The rest were rented out for their warehouse spaces.

"Do you know anyone who rents warehouse space down here?" Lauren asked Harriet.

"Tom Bainbridge had a workshop down here when he made storage boxes and tables for the homeless camp. I don't know if he still has it," Harriet said.

"Maybe I'll call him tonight," Lauren said. "He might know what's going on down here."

"We should have done that last night," Harriet said. "The more we know, the better."

"We're here now; shall we forge ahead?"

"Might as well."

Harriet locked the car, and she and Lauren walked across the street and down the side street to the dock area. They walked along the wooden dock area, looking for the boat Mavis and Beth had described. Lauren pointed down the dock. "That's the only boat that looks like it could be a fishing boat. See the poles and nets sticking up?"

Harriet started down the dock in that direction. "I still don't see any people." They reached the boat, but Harriet couldn't help noticing that fish were lying about the deck. "That's weird," she said to Lauren. "Shouldn't they be on ice?"

"You'd think, but maybe these are rejects. The rest must be in the holds on ice."

When they reached the boat, a man came through a cabin door. "Can I help you ladies?" He asked.

Harriet stepped forward. "Hi, I'm Harriet Truman, and my husband, James, owns the restaurant on Smugglers Cove. I heard a fishing boat had docked down here, and I thought I'd see if you were selling fresh fish."

The man stepped closer, wiping his hands on a red rag. "This load of fish is already spoken for, but I could maybe give you a sample fish, and you could see if your husband is even interested. Come on board, and I'll take you below to choose a fish." He looked at Lauren. "The passage is too narrow for two to come at a time. I'll take Harriet down, and my deckhand can take … what was your name, miss?"

"Lauren," she said, purposely omitting her last name.

"Okay," the first man said. "Here, ladies first, he told Harriet, and she started down the steep stairs. Lauren followed with the deckhand behind her.

No lights were in the hold, only the slightest shadow from the deck above. Moments later, the space went completely black.

CHAPTER THIRTY-FOUR

Harriet felt something sharp poking into her side. She smelled a faint whiff of ether or something similar and realized she'd been unconscious. She was on her side, her hands secured behind her back.

"Lauren?" she called out. She heard a moan somewhere to her left. "Lauren?" she called again.

"Where are we?" Lauren groaned.

Harriet tried to sit up and hit her head on something above her. "I think we're in the boat. Are your hands tied behind your back?"

She heard rustling sounds. "No, but my arm and leg are shackled to something."

"Can you untie yourself?"

"I didn't say I was tied, I said shackled. There are big metal cuffs around my wrist and ankle. Like they used on slave ships."

"I guess they didn't want to sell us any fish," Harriet said with a strained chuckle.

"And we broke one of my mother's cardinal rules."

"Which one?" Harriet asked her.

"The one where Les and I were always supposed to leave a note before we left, saying where we were going and when we would be back."

"Yeah," Harriet said. "That's a good one. We were supposed to go to the kids' club, but did we tell anyone about the dock?"

"We did when your aunt and Mavis talked about the boat. We didn't say when we were going, though."

Harriet sighed. "We've got several teams doing drive-throughs, and someone is bound to notice that my car is parked on the street a block up from the dock."

"Let's hope so."

"Can you move around at all?" Harriet asked.

"Not much. I've got a little range with my leg, but my arm is pinned at what would be waist high if I stood up. It's above my head currently since I'm sitting."

Harriet scooted around a little to see if she could move out from under whatever was above her head. To her surprise, she was not attached to anything. Her hands were tight behind her back, and her ankles were tight to each other, but that was all. She tried to roll over and, after three tries, made two rollovers. She gently raised her head and discovered she had rolled out from under whatever was over her head.

"Say something, and I'll try to roll over to where you are," Harriet asked Lauren.

"Row, row, row your boat, gently down the stream, merrily, merrily, merrily, merrily, life is but a dream." Harriet rolled over a few times toward Lauren's voice. "Second verse, same as the first," Lauren sang and began the song again.

"Move your free leg around. I think I'm near you." Lauren did as instructed, and Harriet scooted on her side until she ran into Lauren's foot.

"Now what?" Lauren asked.

Before Harriet could answer, they heard clunking noises above their heads, and the hatch opened, letting weak light into their area. The deckhand came down the ladder carrying a bundle wrapped in a dark blanket. He took the bundle to the opposite side of their hold and peeled back the blanket, exposing a dark-haired person. He quickly tied the person's hands behind their back, followed by securing their legs together. He flipped the blanket back over the person, preventing Harriet and Lauren from identifying whoever it was.

The deckhand looked over at Harriet. "You've been active while I've been gone," he said, dragging her back to the table she'd been under when she woke up. "I don't know where you think you're going. The hatch is bolted shut, and your friend isn't going anywhere with those shackles. Besides," he added, "you're going to want that blanket I put you on when we get out to sea."

With that, he went back up the ladder and shut the heavy hatch cover, and they heard the bolt slide into place. "If whoever that is was drugged like we were, they'll be out for a while," Harriet said.

"Maybe you can roll over there and see who it is," Lauren suggested.

"I was thinking I'd roll back over to you and let you use your legendary manual dexterity with your one free hand to untie my hands."

"Ohhh, I like a challenge. What sort of rope is it? And you can answer as you roll." Harriet took a deep breath and started rolling.

"I can't tell what sort of rope it is since it's behind my back, and my wrists aren't very sensitive as far as identifying fiber types."

"Do I have to do everything?" Lauren said. "I'll tell you what it is when you get here."

Harriet groaned as she rolled over and over with a few sessions of scooting in between. She finally let out a breath. "I'm here, I think."

Lauren swept her free leg back and forth until she found Harriet. "You're going to need to come a little closer. You might even need to sit across my lap. With my right hand in the air, I don't have a lot of slack."

Harriet slid up against Lauren's thigh. "I wasn't kidding when I said you needed to sit across my lap. It's dark here, and no one can see us, so don't worry about the optics; just get up here."

It was easier said than done. Harriet got up to her knees and launched herself at Lauren. Lauren groaned as Harriet landed. "Sorry," Harriet said.

"No problem," Lauren assured her. Harriet could feel Lauren's hand on her wrists. "Squeeze your wrists together as much as you can," Lauren said.

"I'll try, but they're roped pretty tight to each other."

"Anything will help."

"This is going to take a while. This rope is some sort of nylon or synthetic." Lauren picked at the rope for what Harriet guessed was fifteen minutes. She let out a sigh. "I've got to rest a minute; my fingers are cramping."

Harriet smiled, although Lauren couldn't see it in the dark. "I'm not going anywhere."

"You know," Lauren said, "I'd never been kidnapped before I met you."

"This may come as a surprise to you, but I'd never been kidnapped, stabbed, knocked out, or had any other violence perpetrated on my person before I moved to Foggy Point, Washington and that's saying a lot since I moved here from California."

"Do you think all this violence in the last few years is why we've become such good friends?" Lauren asked.

Harriet laughed. "I'd like to think we're friends because we both like to quilt, like dogs, watch mystery movies, and like to go to the local coffee shops."

"There is all that, plus the fact that I tend to work in a male dominated industry, which doesn't lend itself to making lots of girlfriends," Lauren observed.

"Hello?" A weak voice came from across the hold from Lauren and Harriet.

"Connie?" Harriet asked in a loud voice.

"Harriet?" Connie answered in a weak voice. "Where are we?"

"We're not really sure, but we think we're in a hold in a fishing boat," Harriet told her.

"We were invited onto a fishing boat when we were drugged with something."

"Lauren? Is that you? Is anyone else here?" Connie asked.

"I don't think anyone else is," Harriet said. "How did you get here? Weren't you talking to a group of kids at the ice cream shop?"

"I was. I'm not sure exactly what happened. I bought the kids their ice cream, and we talked at a table. They hadn't revealed anything yet. They were afraid of whoever was on top of the drug distribution chain. One of the boys who had come along with one of the kids I know slipped me a note and asked if he could meet me by the restrooms. When there was a lull in the conversation, some of the kids went to the counter to get water, and I went back to the hallway where the restrooms were. The last thing I heard was the boy who had given me the note say, 'I'm sorry', and suddenly I couldn't breathe, and I blacked out."

"How did they get you out of the ice cream shop?"

"There's an emergency exit at the end of the hall the restrooms are on," Connie said. "I assume they carried me out the door and into a waiting car."

"Are you bound in some way?" Harriet asked her.

"I think my hands are handcuffed behind my back, and my legs feel like they are duct-taped together."

"Huh," said Lauren.

"What?" Asked Connie.

"Well, I've got one arm and leg shackled to the wall, and Harriet is tied with fishing rope, hands behind her back and legs together. I'm trying to pick the rope off her wrists, one-handed."

"Hush," Harriet said, and they all fell silent. They could hear thumping on the deck above them.

"I'm going back to my spot," Harriet whispered. She was becoming efficient at rolling across the space. "I'd play unconscious," she quietly told Connie.

They heard the bolt slide on the hatch cover, followed by the weak light shaft as the hatch opened. "Help me with the bigger one," a gruff voice said.

"Let's wrap her in a blanket and slide her down the ladder," a second voice answered. "And hurry up, Sketch and G-dog were right behind us."

Harriet heard something bump down the ladder. She could hear one of the men climb back up the ladder. A few moments later, he returned with something over his shoulder—presumably another person wrapped in a wool blanket.

"Let's go move the car," the gruff-sounding man said.

"It stinks like fish in here," the other guy said.

"We can leave the hatch open," Gruff said. "They're all secure, and we don't want anyone kicking it before we're outta here."

Harriet heard the two men climb the ladder, and their footsteps faded as they walked away. As soon as it was quiet, Harriet rolled over to the new arrivals, who had been dumped unceremoniously in the middle of the hold. She quickly scooted herself until she was parallel with the first person. She used her teeth to pull the wool blanket away from one end of the person.

"Yuck," she said and made a spitting noise. "I think this blanket is from World War II."

She pulled again and uncovered a shoe. "I'm at the wrong end," she told Lauren and Connie. "But I think I recognize this shoe. I'm pretty sure this is Mavis, which means the other lump over here must be Aunt Beth."

She heard the faint sound of footsteps again. "Back under the table for me," she said, rolling away from the two new arrivals and returning to her spot.

CHAPTER THIRTY-FIVE

A few minutes later, they heard someone at the hatch. "I can throw this one over my shoulder," a new voice said. Presumably, this was either Sketch or G-dog.

Harriet caught a glimpse of the man in the shaft of light that shone in through the open hatch. He was taller than the others. The man had a bundle over his shoulder as he descended the ladder. When he reached the bottom, he dropped the bundle on top of the two already in the middle of the floor. He went back up the ladder and returned a moment later with a second bundle, dropping it on the pile.

"Help," they heard Mavis call from under the bundles. Harriet rolled over to the pile and twisted around until her feet were against it. She pushed on the new arrivals to get them off Mavis.

"Help," Mavis said again.

"I'd help if I could," Harriet told her loudly. "My hands and feet are tied, so I'm limited."

"Harriet?" Mavis said. "Where are we?"

"As near as we can tell, we're in the hold of the fishing boat you saw. Lauren and Connie are here, too. I'm guessing my aunt is there beside you. The weight I just pushed off you is probably two more Loose Threads. I don't know who yet. My guess is Robin and DeAnn. I assume they were driving around down here."

"They were," Mavis said. "We were taking turns circling around."

"Let me unwrap your blanket. And see if I can do the same with the other three. Help if you can."

Harriet twisted around and rolled on her side, using her bound hands to grasp Mavis's blanket. Finally, she grasped it and rolled away from Mavis, taking the blanket.

Mavis let out a big breath. "Thank you," she said. "That blanket is full of dust."

Harriet scooted over to the next bundle and repeated her maneuver, uncovering her aunt. After a few minutes more of scooting, sliding, and rolling, she was able to locate Robin and DeAnn, who were still unconscious.

"How are your hands and feet bound," Lauren asked Mavis.

"I can't see, of course, but it feels like duct tape."

"We can work with that," Lauren told her. "I'm shackled with metal cuffs. One arm and one leg. I'm not sure how I get out of these."

"I'm going back to Lauren," Harriet said. "She's trying to pick the rope around my wrists loose."

"While I'm working on Harriet's rope, if you are bound with duct tape, try wiggling your wrists or ankles back and forth to see if you can loosen the tape."

The group remained silent for the next thirty minutes or so. Harriet was sure she could hear the water lapping against the side of the boat. "Let me try to move my hands," Harriet told Lauren. Lauren let go of the now shredded rope. Harriet rubbed her hands back and forth against each other, pulling hard. Finally, her left hand came free.

"I'm free," she said. "My wrists may never be the same, but my hands are free. Let me see if I can get my ankles free."

"Before you start that," Beth said, "why don't you scoot over here and see if you can tear the duct tape from my wrists? Then I can work on some of the others."

"Good idea," Harriet said and scooted over to the center of the space. It only took a few minutes for Harriet to peel the duct tape apart and free her aunt. She immediately ripped the tape off her ankles.

"You finish working on your ankle ropes," Beth told Harriet. "I'll get Mavis and anyone else who is taped."

The hold was quiet again while people helped each other break free from their bonds. All the Loose Threads bound with duct tape were free within a few minutes. Robin approached Harriet and took over, trying to shred the braided rope. It took a few more minutes, but Robin got the rope loose, and Harriet could pull her feet out.

"Now we need to figure out something for Lauren," Harriet said. She crawled over to Lauren, grabbed the chain attached to her leg, and followed the length of it to the side of the boat.

"Anything?" Lauren asked her.

"I'm not quite sure how it helps us yet, but your leg shackle chain is not bolted to the outer part of the boat itself; it's attached to a board. If any of you can move around, see if you can find anything we can use as a tool," Harriet said to the group.

"I've got a small multitool in my jeans pocket," Mavis said.

"Bring it over to Lauren. That could be helpful. The shackles have a bolt holding them in place."

"Where is Lauren?" Mavis asked.

"I'm bolted to the side of the boat. Carefully step toward my voice."

"Keep talking," Mavis told her.

Lauren started singing again, and Harriet groaned. Lauren stopped abruptly when a bright light illuminated the area. Robin chuckled. "I forgot I had this light in my jacket pocket. I use it when I walk the dog at night. It's supposed to blind an attacker if they try to kidnap you at night."

"Okay," Lauren said as Mavis approached her. "Everyone check your pockets and see if we have anything else that might be useful."

"I've got a couple of protein bars," Connie said.

"Sadly, I just have a couple of dog waste bags," Harriet offered.

"I've got some mints," DeAnn told them.

"I think we need to save the food items until we get a sense of how long we'll be stuck here," Harriet suggested.

"Hopefully not too long," Lauren said. "Didn't they leave the hatch cover open?"

Robin flashed the light beam over to where the ladder they'd all been carried down had been.

"Ummm, we have a problem," Robin announced. "Apparently, our captors pulled the ladder up after themselves."

"But the hatch is still open, right?" Lauren asked from her dark corner. Robin flashed her light up to the open hatch. "Well, that's something, anyway," Lauren commented.

"They said something about not wanting us to die too soon or something like that," Harriet said. "I assume that means while we're at the dock."

"Let's look around and see if we can find anything that can be used to propel at least one of us up to the hatch," DeAnn suggested.

Harriet started looking at the table she'd been stashed under. She attempted to pull on it, but it seemed attached to the wall. She felt the slimy top surface; when she pulled her hand back, she held it to her nose. It smelled of rotted fish.

"Robin," she called. "Can you bring the light over to the table?"

Robin joined her and shone the light on the surface of the table. Among the fish slime were small blue tablets. She started to reach out to touch one, but Harriet grabbed her arm. "Don't touch them," she cautioned. "If I'm not mistaken, there's a good chance these tablets are fentanyl."

"What?" Beth called from across the room.

"Fentanyl?" Mavis asked.

"We have to assume they are until someone tells us otherwise," Harriet said. "I volunteered at a zoo in California a few years ago. I worked in the nursery. When we got harbor seals in and needed to give them vitamins, we put them in their smelt and then fed the fish to the seals. I think our savvy drug dealers put bags of fentanyl into fish to bring them here from international waters. That could be why they were anxious to not sell the fish and to get us away from this boat."

"If that was the case, why are we here?" Lauren said from across the room.

"First, they've already moved the fish-anyl," Mavis pointed out. "Second, they wanted us to quit looking until they can vacate the area."

"That's optimistic," Connie said. "They wanted us to quit looking permanently. Speaking of that, I'm thinking the clock is ticking. They must figure that people will be looking for us, and with some of our cars parked near the dock, it won't take long before someone checks this boat. I don't think our kidnappers are going to let anyone find us here."

"Okay," Harriet said. "Let's take one thing at a time. First, we must see if we can get out of this hold. If we can and no one is guarding us from the dock, we go to the nearest open business and call the police. If nothing's open, we walk until we find something."

"Harriet's right," Beth said. "And so far, I've found a piece of fishing net. It looks like it's a piece from a larger net."

"I've got a couple of two-by-fours over here," DeAnn said.

"Okay, let's keep looking," Beth said.

Fifteen minutes later, the pile of collected items was under the open hatch.

"Let's see what we've got here," Harriet said.

CHAPTER THIRTY-SIX

The most valuable items they found were the fishing net, the two-by-fours, several pieces of fishing rope Harriet had been tied with, and a partial roll of duct tape.

"How far up do you think that is?" Harriet asked.

Robin stood up and reached her arms over her head. "Ten, maybe twelve feet?" Robin guessed.

"Do you think we could reach the top if one of us held another on our shoulders?"

"Maybe, but I don't think we can boost anyone high enough to hoist themselves out of here," Robin answered.

The clinking of Lauren's chains interrupted them.

"I've loosened the bolt in my leg shackle. Can anyone come help me?" Harriet stepped carefully over to where Lauren was still attached to the side of the boat.

"Robin, can you bring the light over?" Robin joined them and illuminated the leg shackle Lauren had been working on.

"Here, give me that," Harriet said, holding her hand to Lauren, who handed her the multitool.

Harriet slid the side of the bottle opener blade into the slot on the bolt's head. She wrenched on it, and it moved slightly but elicited a groan from Lauren.

"Would hand lotion help?" Beth asked. She brought it over to Harriet.

"Does anyone else have undeclared items in their pockets?" Lauren asked.

"Sorry," Beth said. "I forgot about it. It's in a smaller inner pocket of my jacket. And we're all stressed about our situation. There's no reason to get snippy."

Harriet patted her aunt's arm. "She didn't mean anything," she said. "She's still attached to the wall, so she's bound to be a little more stressed than the rest of us."

"What she said," Lauren mumbled.

Harriet pulled Lauren's sock off, squirted a generous dollop of lotion onto her bare ankle, and spread it around the shackle. Getting Lauren's sock off helped loosen the shackle. Harriet gently wiggled the metal cuff from side to side, adding more lotion.

"Hold the cuff steady," Lauren said. "I think I might be able to wiggle my foot out."

Harriet did as instructed, and with a few groans, Lauren's foot slid free of the shackle. She rubbed her ankle with her free hand.

"Robin, can you shine the light on her wrist?"

Robin moved the light, and Harriet used the bottle opener on the bolt head of her wrist shackle.

"This thing is not moving," Harriet said.

"Squirt some of that lotion on it. And help me stand up. My arm is asleep."

Harriet helped Lauren up, and Lauren leaned against the ship's side. "Whew, that was a head rush," Lauren said. She reached with her free hand to the one still shackled. "This cuff feels different. Squirt some more of the lotion on it."

Lauren wiggled the cuff back and forth. "Let me see," Harriet said. She scratched on the cuff. "I think you're right. This feels like it might be leather or something like that."

Harriet closed the bottle opener and opened one of the blades in the multitool. "Hold very still," she instructed Lauren, sliding the blade between Lauren's arm and the cuff. She sawed back and forth. Slowly, a notch formed on the edge of the cuff.

"I'm going to move to the other side of the cuff," she announced. She repeated the sawing on the opposite side.

"Let me see if that's enough to pull my hand through," Lauren said.

"Squirt more lotion," Robin suggested.

Harriet added lotion, and Lauren held the cuff in her free hand and pulled on her bound hand, wiggling the cuff as she did so. After one final hard pull, Lauren's hand slid free of the shackle.

Lauren slid to the floor, rubbing her shoulder. "I need to rest a minute here before I can try to help with our escape." Harriet patted Lauren's shoulder.

"You just rest a few minutes. The rest of us will work on the escape plan."

"I have an idea," Mavis said. "I'm not saying I can do what I'm going to suggest, but if you younger, slimmer people are willing, I think it will work."

"Let's hear it," DeAnn said.

"Okay. One of you will be the base, and another will get on her shoulders. The rest of us will have used the rope to tie the fishing net to the six-foot-long two-by-four. The person on the shoulders will angle the two-by-four through the hatch opening and then lay it across so the net hangs down." Mavis paused. When no one argued with her plan, she continued.

"If the shoulder person can reach the hold edge, they might be able to crawl up and out."

"May I suggest one amendment to the plan?" Harriet asked.

"What is it," Beth asked.

"I think it might be easier for climbing out if we handed the shoulder person a plain two-by-four to lay across the opening before she puts the one with the net up. Then, when the first person up is trying to maneuver through the hold, they'll have one more place to put their hands for balance."

"It can't hurt," Connie said.

"I volunteer to be the base," Harriet said. "Since I still have a wounded hand, I don't think I'd make a good climber."

"Anyone have a problem with that?" Beth asked. No one did.

"All right," Harriet said. "Who is willing to get on my shoulders? And among those willing volunteers, who weighs the least?"

"I vote for Robin," Lauren said. "With all her yoga, she's probably the most flexible and probably has the most arm strength, too."

"Works for me," Harriet said. "Are you willing, Robin?"

Robin laughed. "You guys catch me if I fall."

"We'll try," Connie said.

"Maybe we should pile those nasty blankets we were wrapped in around my feet," Harriet said. "If we fall, we'll have a little padding."

The group gathered the blankets while Connie and DeAnn started attaching the netting to the two-by-four they had determined was the strongest. Robin sorted the two-by-fours, choosing the second strongest looking one to take up to the hold opening.

When everything was ready, Harriet positioned herself below the hatch opening. She bent her knees, giving Robin a place to put her foot as she grabbed Harriet's outstretched hands and sprang up to her shoulders. Harriet immediately crumpled to the ground. Connie and Mavis broke their fall.

"Okay," Mavis said. "For our second try, Connie and I will brace Harriet, and Beth can help boost Robin into position. DeAnn can hold the two-by-fours at the ready so Robin can position them as soon as she's ready."

"Let us know when you're ready," Connie told the group.

"There is no time like the present," Harriet said and looked at Robin. Are you ready?"

Robin gave her a nod, and everyone got into position. The second try went better. Robin got the two-by-four into position before wobbling and jumping off Harriet's shoulders.

"Everyone okay?" Beth asked.

Harriet stretched her wrists back and forth but didn't say anything as pain shot through her injured hand. "Let's go," she said.

It took two more tries to get the two-by-four with the fishing net up to the top of the hold. Robin again slid down as soon as she got the board in position, so there was no chance of her climbing out.

"Shall I try to climb up?" DeAnn asked.

"Go for it," Robin said.

"Let's hold the bottom edges of the net while she climbs," Mavis said to Beth.

DeAnn climbed up the net and, with a bit of maneuvering, got a leg over the lip of the open hatch. As soon as she caught her balance, she froze in place.

"What's wrong?" Harriet asked.

"Foggy Point, we have a problem," DeAnn said in a fake voice.

"What is it?" Mavis and Beth said at the same time.

DeAnn finished crawling out of the hatch opening and leaned her head back in. "You guys need to come up here and see for yourself."

It took the group at least fifteen minutes to climb up the fish net and onto the deck. Harriet was the last one up. She got to her feet and stood beside Lauren.

"This is a whole different problem," Harriet said.

CHAPTER THIRTY-SEVEN

Harriet turned in a circle. All she could see was water. "So, the water we heard lapping at the sides of the boat wasn't the wake of other boats as we sat at the dock," she said. "We were being towed out into the shipping lane."

"I don't suppose any of us know how to operate a fishing boat," Lauren said hopefully. They all looked at each other, and they shook their heads one by one.

"I'm going to go to the bridge and see if I can radio for help," Harriet said.

"I'll come with you," Lauren said.

"Let's go see if we can find the galley," Beth told Mavis and Connie.

Robin looked over at DeAnn. "I guess that leaves us to find the ladder."

Harriet paused before heading up the stairs. "Let's meet back here when we've finished our tasks." Everyone agreed and went about their assigned tasks.

Harriet and Lauren returned first. DeAnn and Robin returned a few minutes later, dragging a ladder. "Did you get hold of anyone?" Robin asked.

Lauren laughed out loud. "All the wires have been cut, and the electronics have been destroyed."

"Can you fix it?" Lauren laughed again.

"I'm good, but not that good," Lauren said. "It's an ancient system. I'd need old-school parts." She held her hands up. "Before you ask, I did try a few things, but whoever destroyed it did a good job."

"Looks like you had better luck," Harriet said to DeAnn.

"Yes and no," DeAnn replied. "We found *a* ladder, not *the* ladder. I'm not sure this one will reach all the way to the hold floor, but someone can climb down and jump the rest of the way. If we're not rescued before nightfall, we'll need the blankets from down there."

Connie, Mavis, and Beth finally arrived, carrying bottles of water, a box of lunch-sized corn chips, and a handful of granola bars.

Mavis handed out water while Beth and Connie distributed snacks.

"Do we need to ration these?" Harriet asked, holding up the food she'd been given.

"No," Beth said. "There's more in the galley, and besides, I don't think we're going to be out here that long."

"She's right," Mavis said. "It's not like we're in a rubber raft. Someone will notice a drifting fishing boat."

"I hope so," DeAnn said.

"Let's think about what we can do to make ourselves more noticeable," Harriet suggested.

"What are you thinking?" Lauren asked.

"I'm not sure yet. We ought to search the boat and see what we have to work with."

"I need a little rest period before we search," Connie said. "I don't think I've recovered from being kidnapped yet."

"I'm with Connie," DeAnn said, "I've got a headache. I think a little shut-eye will help."

"Okay," Harriet said. "Let's stay in pairs or trios, especially when we wake up again."

Lauren and DeAnn climbed the short ladder, jumping the last few feet. They gathered the blankets everyone had been wrapped in when they were delivered to the hold, and each wrapped a few over their shoulders. Lauren boosted DeAnn onto the ladder, then DeAnn reached down and helped Lauren onto the first rung.

"Here are the disgusting blankets," Lauren announced as they piled them on the deck. "Maybe we can use them as bedding and put our coats or sweaters on top of them."

Mavis, Beth, and Connie went to one end of the boat with their blankets, made a large mattress from their three blankets, and settled in. DeAnn and Robin made their beds on one side of the fish hatch while Harriet and Lauren went to the back.

Harriet put her blanket down but stood at the side of the boat, looking out at the water. She turned back to Lauren, who was sitting on her blanket. "I don't think I can sleep," she said. "I'm going to go exploring. There must be bunks somewhere. They might have better blankets. And if they didn't remove them, there might be flares."

"Good thought. I'll tag along with you."

"Let's start at the bridge. If signaling devices exist, they'll probably be there," Harriet said.

They climbed the stairs to the bridge and, on the way, noticed a door opposite the opening of the wheelhouse. Harriet looked in. "Here's the bunk room," she said and put her hand up to her nose. "Phew, it smells like sweat and fish."

"I guess we won't be using the bunks."

"Why don't you look around here in case there is anything useful." Lauren gave her a mock salute and stepped further into the bunk room.

Harriet continued into the bridge. Lauren wasn't kidding about the electronics being trashed. She grabbed the boat's steering wheel and moved it back and forth. It was completely loose. It had been disconnected from whatever it was supposed to be attached to. She stepped to the front window. There were miscellaneous parts and pieces on the edges of the wheelhouse framework. She picked up a box wrench and set it down. A six-inch piece of hose and a small coil of wire were next to that. All the items were covered with a thick layer of dust.

She looked around the cluttered floor. It was hard to imagine how they could steer the boat with all the junk strewn about. Finally, she sat on the swiveling chair, where the captain probably sat. If he had a flare gun, it would be within reach. She stretched her hand out and brushed it along everything she could reach. When she reached overhead, her hand touched what she was looking for. A dust-covered flare gun. She pulled it from the clamps that held it in place.

Lauren came in as she was examining the gun. "Does it have a flare?"

"Looks like it." She looked at the ceiling again. "I don't see any spares where the gun was."

"They probably kept a box of flares somewhere."

Harriet stood up and started searching through all the junk in the wheelhouse. Lauren did the same, but neither of them found anything. There was a small table with charts, but they didn't yield anything useful.

Harriet sighed. "Come on, let's try the galley. Maybe we'll find something useful for making a signal."

Whoever cooked in the galley, they were the exact opposite of the ship's captain. The galley was spotless. A small grill was shiny, and the grease trap was clean. A single propane burner sat next to it. Harriet opened a cupboard and found two bowls, a ziplock bag with a whisk, a rubber scraper, and a flipper. No box of flares.

A pantry cabinet was opposite the grill. It contained bottled water, powdered eggs, cans of chili, a package of tortillas, and a box of instant rice. A box at the back of the pantry held spices and oils. Next, was a large box of tea and a one-pound can of grocery store coffee.

Lauren opened a small cabinet and found dishes, dishtowels, sponges, and two saucepans. She blew out a breath. "This guy was cleaner, but he didn't keep a stash of flares so far. How about you?"

"Nothing here either," Harriet said. "And they must have fished nearby, or there'd be more evidence of food."

"Maybe they'd just come in from a long voyage and eaten all the food."

"Okay, let's check out the decks and fishing gear," Harriet said. "When we're done with that, we can wake the others if they're not already up."

A thorough search of the outer parts of the boat didn't yield anything useful. "I'm going to go make some tea," Lauren announced. "I'll leave the awakening to you."

"Gee, thanks," she said and headed to the front of the boat, where Aunt Beth, Mavis, and Connie were sound asleep.

"Wakey, wake, sleeping beauties," she called as she approached their nest.

Aunt Beth sat up and stretched. "Have we been rescued? I'm ready to be done with our three-hour tour."

Harriet chuckled. "No such luck, but Lauren is making tea in the galley."

Mavis stood up. "Did someone say tea?" She picked up the box of snack chips and granola bars and headed for the galley.

DeAnn and Robin joined them. "Are there places to sit?" DeAnn asked.

"I noticed what look like fold-up tables and stools against the walls outside the bunk room," Harriet told them.

Lauren had found mugs and utensils, plus sugar and powdered creamer, and had arranged everything next to the pan of hot water. "I couldn't find a tea kettle, so I made do with a large saucepan. I did find a ladle we can use to dip the water out," Lauren told the group.

It took a lot of maneuvering, but eventually, everyone had tea, a snack, and a place to sit near the galley. Harriet sipped her tea and set her mug on the little table. "We need to make a short- and long-term plan. First, we need to take it in teams and stay awake to watch for lights in the distance or other boats. If each team does two-and-a-half to three-hour shifts, that should cover the night. Second, has anyone seen a lifeboat? It might be in a box or a bag."

"I haven't seen anything on the deck, but there might be something in the fish hold," Robin said. And I think we should see if there is another storage hold."

"Good thinking," Lauren said.

"What about our flare gun?" Mavis asked.

Harriet and Lauren looked at each other. "We've only got one flare," Harriet finally said.

"We need to use it carefully," Lauren added.

"I agree," Beth said. "We wait until we see a boat or drift close enough to shore to see people.

"We should bring a couple of pots or pans wherever the lookout is. If she sees someone, we can bang the pots together to make a noise," Robin said. "If we do that first, hopefully, they will be looking in our direction when we set off the flare."

"Good idea," DeAnn agreed.

CHAPTER THIRTY-EIGHT

Harriet and Lauren sat on the ship's deck, sipping tea and watching the sun rise. Harriet pointed to her left. "Is that shoreline over there?"

Lauren looked where she was pointing. "It's hard to tell with all the mist on the water."

Harriet stood up. "They must have a lifeboat somewhere; we just need to find it. I'm going to look for a storage hold."

"While you're doing that, I'm going to come with you and look for life jackets. They seem to have cleared the most useful stuff from this boat, but I think they didn't have enough time to take bulky items—and they couldn't throw floatation devices overboard. Someone could see them."

"Let's go," Harriet said, heading toward the fish hold. She figured if she started at the hold and walked toward the other end of the ship, she'd find the second hold.

It took two passes, but finally, she found the door under a stack of canvas. Apparently, this hold wasn't used much. If the fish were being used to transport drugs, they probably didn't need the extra storage space.

"I found the hatch to the second hold," she called to Lauren, who was poking around in some piles of netting. It took both of them to clear away the junk covering the hatch and open the heavy cover.

"I'm glad the ladder is in place," she added. "I'm going down."

When Harriet reached the bottom and stepped onto the floor, she put her hand out for balance and found she was touching a flashlight.

"Please work," she whispered to herself. She had to push the switch several times, but ultimately, it moved, and the light came on.

"Let there be light," she hollered up to Lauren. "I found a torch, and it actually works."

"Here I come," Lauren called. Harriet stepped aside to make room for her. She shone the light at the bottom of the ladder until Lauren arrived and then moved the light around the hold to see what was there.

"Okay," Harriet said, "Let's start at the ladder and go clockwise around the hold." Lauren saluted and began touching the wooden boxes stacked against the wall.

"This stack of boxes seems to be fishing nets and ropes," she observed.

Harriet had gone to the following stack beyond Lauren's. "I've got oilskin pants and coats and rubber boots over here. I'm moving along."

Lauren brushed past her to another set of stacked boxes. She took the top off the first one. "This is dried food."

"Good to know in case we get washed out to sea," Harriet said as she moved past Lauren.

"Ahhh," Harriet said, shining the light into a big container. "Here are the life jackets."

"I feel much safer," Lauren said dryly.

Harriet turned slowly, shining the light along the walls. A larger container was on the wall opposite where they were standing. She crossed the room and looked in the container. "Jackpot," she said.

"Life raft?"

"Yes, indeed," Harriet replied. "It's going to be tricky to get it up the ladder and through the hatch, but it must fit, or it wouldn't be down here."

"Unless there's another way in or out of this hold."

"If you see one, feel free to say so. In the meantime, can you help me get this thing out of this box?"

Lauren returned to the box of nets and ropes, selected two longer ropes, and brought them to Harriet. "How do you want to do this?"

"Let's tie a rope around each end and then tie them together," Harriet said. "One can go up the ladder and pull; the other can push and guide from down here."

"Let me go see if Robin or DeAnn are awake yet," Lauren said, heading for the ladder.

Harriet made a big lasso from one of the ropes and slipped it over the lifeboat package. When Lauren returned with DeAnn, she struggled to hoist the boat up to the top of the container and tip it out.

"I found this one in the galley drinking coffee when I went topside. Everyone else is still asleep," Lauren told her.

"Okay, I've got a rope tied around one end of the lifeboat, but I can't get the package out of this container," Harriet told them.

DeAnn and Lauren came down into the hold and joined Harriet at the big box, and together, they were able to get the boat out of the container and then up the stairs.

"While you get the boat unpacked, I'm going to bring up the lifejackets," Lauren said. "I'm not getting into an antique lifeboat without a floatation device."

Harriet and DeAnn carefully unpacked the boat. "Alright, according to the package, this is a life raft designed to hold ten people," Harriet read. When we're ready to deploy, we turn this lever, and it will self-inflate."

"Here's the lever," DeAnn said. "We need to figure out how big this thing is so it doesn't go overboard or anything when we open it."

"Good point," Harriet said. She scanned the packaging. "It appears this thing is seven feet by fourteen feet. And there are four telescoping paddles."

"How are you coming with floatation devices?" Harriet called to Lauren.

"I've got them all piled by the ladder's base," Lauren said.

"Can you bring some shorter pieces of rope when you come?"

"Sure."

Mavis, Beth, and Connie joined Harriet at the life raft, looking worse for the wear. Beth's hair was standing straight up. "Wow, Auntie, it looks like you had a rough night," Harriet said.

"I had no pillow, satin or otherwise, no hairbrush, and I was cold," Beth grumbled.

"Tell me why we're going from a secure fishing boat to a rubber life raft," Mavis asked Harriet.

"Our 'secure' fishing boat, as you put it, has no steering, no communication equipment, and is uncontrollably headed to the Pacific Ocean."

"And you think a life raft is better than that?" Connie asked her.

"Our lifeboat has four paddles, so we have some chance of steering it to shore. It also has various reflective devices on it. If you three want to stay on the fishing boat, you are welcome to it, but I'm going to take the lifeboat and try to find some land."

Robin came up and joined the group. "I'm going with the lifeboat group. Without any lights on this boat, we're lucky we haven't been run over by a freighter."

"I'm on team lifeboat," DeAnn said. "Now that I've voted, I'm going to help Lauren get the lifejackets over here."

Beth sighed loudly. "If you four are going on the lifeboat, against my better judgment, I'll come with you."

Connie looked at Mavis. "I guess we should stick with the group," she said.

Mavis shook her head. "I'm not staying on here by myself."

"If that's the case," Harriet said, "will you three go to the galley and pack some food and water? And DeAnn, can you gather up all the blankets you can find? See if any of the bedding in the bunk room is usable. I'm going to look for a couple of buckets. I don't need to tell you what they're for."

Lauren and DeAnn brought up eight life jackets and several coils of rope. "Do we have an extra passenger I don't know about?" Harriet asked them.

Lauren laughed. "No, but there were extra jackets, so we figured it couldn't hurt to bring one more along. I don't know if these fail, but you never know."

"All right let's meet at the back of the boat in thirty minutes after we've all gathered what we think we need," Harriet said.

"Sounds like a plan," Lauren said. "Let's drag the lifeboat to the back of this boat," she said to DeAnn.

CHAPTER THIRTY-NINE

DeAnn paced off a space at the back of the fishing boat and cleared everything away. "I think we're supposed to put it in the water first," Robin said.

"I'm afraid if we put this package in the water, it'll sink before we open it," Harriet said. "And if we do get it open in the water, it might disappear. I'd like to get it open, attach a rope to it, and then slide it into the water."

"Okay, let's go for it," Lauren said. In a few minutes, Lauren, Harriet, DeAnn, and Robin had the life raft unfolded on the back deck. Lauren attached a rope to a loop at one end of the raft.

"This CO_2 canister must be the inflation mechanism," Harriet said. "Are we ready to let it rip?"

"Go for it," Lauren said. Harriet turned the labeled lever, and the boat startled them all when it immediately filled the tube that defined the raft. She and Lauren slid the life raft over the end of the fishing boat and into the water. Harriet looked back at the rest of the group.

"Here goes nothing," she said and jumped in. "Hand me a life jacket, and the rest of you each put one on, then hand me the other supplies."

Lauren put on her jacket and joined Harriet in the boat to help receive supplies. Robin joined them and started looking around the raft. "This has a canopy with an inflatable frame. Shall I set it up?"

"Yes," Harriet said. "We can use the protection."

When all the supplies they had gathered were in the raft, DeAnn helped Connie, Beth, and Mavis and joined them. "We should distribute ourselves around the perimeter to keep the boat balanced," Lauren told the new arrivals.

When everyone was settled, DeAnn pulled a bag attached to the side of the raft to the center of the space and opened it.

"Whoa," she said. "Look what we have here." Harriet carefully moved over beside her. DeAnn had found a survival kit. It included three flares, dye that could be put in the water, a signal mirror, a signal whistle, a signal flag, a knife, and multiple other valuable tools.

"This will make it easier to attract attention," Harriet said. "Let's see if we can roll up the sides of the canopy so we can put the oars out and start rowing."

"What direction will we row?" Connie asked.

"Given where our fishing boat was docked and the time the kidnappers had to tow us away," Harriet explained, "we must be in the Strait of Juan de Fuca, and we all know it empties into the Pacific Ocean. All we need to do is go crosswise to the current."

"I suggest you four young people man the paddles, and we three elders will look at all the signal devices and see what we can do to attract some attention," Aunt Beth said.

"Okay, paddlers," Harriet said. "Let's position ourselves two on a side and get this boat turned around to face where we think land is."

They took up their positions and, with a bit of a struggle, turned the raft to point toward shore.

After an hour of paddling, Harriet stopped. "Let's hold up a minute," she said. "Does that look like a shoreline?"

Lauren strained to see. "It's so misty and gray it's hard to tell."

"We'll find out soon enough if we keep paddling," Robin said.

Harriet was about to return to her position when she saw something like a giant bird. As it got closer, she saw it wasn't a bird but a drone. "Guys, look," she shouted. "There is a drone circling over us. Aunt Beth set off a flare," she shouted to the other end of the raft. Beth got up and pulled a flare from the survival kit.

"Where should I set it off?" she asked.

"Up in the air," Harriet told her. "Just get it up before the drone goes away."

Mavis took the flare from Beth. She had pulled a pair of gloves from the kit to protect her hands. Mavis leaned out from under the canopy and quickly removed the cap from one end of the flare. She struck the flare against the cap with her other hand, and it ignited. Mavis held it straight up, letting the flash go into the sky. It burned for about two minutes.

"Look," Lauren said and pointed to the left of the flare. "The drone has come back and is hovering over us."

Harriet walked over to Lauren and looked up at the drone. She waved with both hands. Lauren did the same. "Hopefully, whoever is operating the drone will get the message that we need help," Harriet said.

Lauren turned and looked at her. "Let's hope it isn't the people who put us in the fishing boat."

Harriet sighed. "I'm going to think positive."

"Come on, you two," Robin called from the back of the boat. "Until someone rescues us, we need to keep rowing."

"*If* someone rescues us," DeAnn said darkly.

The drone had departed the area, and the Loose Threads returned to rowing. Fighting against the current made for slow going. The foursome had been paddling for thirty minutes more when Mavis, Aunt Beth, and Connie brought bottles of water to them.

"Oh, thank you," Harriet told her aunt when Beth handed her an open bottle. She drank half a bottle and handed it back to Beth so she could cap it.

"I'll leave this here," Beth said, leaning toward the raft's edge.

A flash of motion caught her eye. "Look," Beth said and pointed.

Harriet stood up and approached her aunt, looking where Beth was pointing. The drone was hovering just above and to the side of the raft. "Something is hanging from the drone," Harriet said. "Hang onto my shirt while I lean out and try to grab whatever it is."

It took three tries, but Harriet finally grabbed the cord. She yanked twice, and the cord with a small square pouch attached to its end came loose in her hand. She opened the bag to find a note inside.

"What is it?" Lauren asked.

Harriet unfolded the note and read what it said out loud. "Harriet et al." she read. "Sarah and I have been looking for you, and if you're reading this, we've found you. The drone will have the coordinates of where it found you so we can find you. The pictures it's sending back are of a life raft in the middle of the water. Before that, it was flying over the forest. Hang tight, and Sarah and I will come find you. Although you're out of their jurisdiction, we'll also let the Foggy Point PD know what we've seen.

"Sarah said to tell you that Jorge and Connie's husband have been to take care of all the dogs that were left alone.

"Stay put where you are, and we'll be there soon. It may take us an hour, so be patient."

Harriet folded the note back up. "It was signed by Bob and Sarah," she told the group.

Lauren dropped her paddle to the bottom of the raft. "Thank heaven we're done paddling. My arms may never recover from this."

"Let's have a snack," DeAnn said. "Now that rescue is coming, we don't need to ration our food."

Mavis dug into the provisions they'd brought and handed out bags of chips and cookies. "It would have been nice if the fishermen

QUILTS OF A FEATHER

had stocked healthier snacks," she said as she handed each person a bag of each.

Harriet sat down and opened her bag of chips. "When I finish my snack, I'm going to nap. I didn't really sleep last night and now that rescue is on the way, I think I'll sleep just fine."

"Good idea," Lauren said. "I think I'll join you."

Robin and DeAnn made themselves comfortable against the raft's side and settled in to wait. Mavis, Connie, and Beth sat together in the middle of the raft. "If we just had a way to make tea, this could be quite comfortable," Mavis said.

"I'd like to have the bag of piecing I keep in my purse," Beth said.

"I just want to be on solid ground," Connie said.

"We will be soon enough," Harriet said in a drowsy voice from her corner of the raft.

CHAPTER FORTY

Harriet was awakened by someone yelling, "Hey, Harriet, Lauren." She sat up and saw Bob and Sarah standing on the shore opposite their lifeboat.

"Man the oars," Harriet called to DeAnn and Robin as she and Lauren grabbed their oars and started paddling toward shore.

It took twenty minutes to bring the lifeboat near the shore so Mavis could throw a rope to Bob. He quickly hauled them onto the rocky beach. Sarah held her arm out to steady Mavis, then Connie and Beth as they clambered off the life raft. Bob secured the raft to a large rock and helped Lauren, Harriet, Robin, and DeAnn off.

"What do you think we should do about the raft?" Harriet asked the group.

"Do we have to do anything?" Mavis asked. "It's not our fishing boat and not our raft."

"I thought we should call Detective Morse and hand it to her. We were kidnapped from Foggy Point. None of us have a phone at the moment," she added.

Sarah pulled her phone from her shoulder bag and handed it to Harriet. Harriet took the phone and realized she didn't know the Foggy Point Police Department number. With a sigh, Harriet dialed 911 and explained that she had been kidnapped from Foggy Point and would like to speak to Detective Jane Morse from that department. After discussing why they shouldn't send the nearest police, the Clallam County Sheriff's Department in this case, the 911 operator eventually connected her to the Foggy Point PD. She was able to explain their situation, including their location.

Harriet finally ended the call and handed the phone back to Sarah. "Morse wanted us to stay here until she could get here, but I told her we'd been on a fishing boat overnight and then a life raft all day, and the older members of their group should probably be seen by a doctor and would prefer that it be their own. Morse agreed and said all of us should be checked out, and we could return to Foggy Point if we promised to go directly to the ER, where she'd have officers meet us to take our statement."

"Sarah and I brought my mom's twelve-passenger van from the wildlife refuge so we can all travel together," Bob said.

A Clallam County Sheriff's car pulled up to the road where they were standing. "You must be the kidnap victims from Foggy Point," a tall deputy said with a smile. "I'm told you people are heading back to Foggy Point, and I'm to secure the raft where you landed."

"It's right down the slope, on the rocks," Harriet told him. "You can't miss it."

"Sounds like you all had quite an adventure," the deputy said.

"I wouldn't call being drugged, thrown into the hold of a fishing boat, and cast out to sea an adventure," Lauren answered.

"Ordeal then?" the depute said with a grin.

"I'm pretty sure I'll see the humor in this when I'm warm, have eaten and slept, but now enough of the humor attempts," Lauren said to him with a scowl.

Harriet took her by the arm and led her to the nearby van. "Ease up," she said. "The guy is just trying to be friendly."

When they reached the van, Bob said, "Okay. Sit wherever you want," and opened the side door.

"Why does your mom have a twelve-passenger van?" Harriet asked as she climbed into the seats behind the driver's seat.

"When my mother first moved up to the wildlife property, she had this idea that she would give wildlife tours for visitors all over

Foggy Point." Bob paused while he helped Mavis up the step and into the van. "Anyway, my mom had her greenhouse built simultaneously and immediately planted it with herbs and medicinal plants. When people in the area found out she had some rare plants, they asked her if they could buy some and if she'd make some tinctures. She did, and pretty soon, she was so busy with the medicinal plants business she didn't have time to follow through with the tours. The van became a delivery vehicle when she got customers all over the Puget Sound area and into Seattle. The medicinal plants pay for her whole operation, including caring for the injured birds and animals."

"That's amazing," DeAnn said.

"My mom has a whole line of herbal salves and remedies now."

"Wow, I didn't realize that," Robin commented.

"Is everyone belted in?" Sara asked from the front passenger seat. The group assured her they were.

"I know we're supposed to go straight to the ER to meet the police," Bob said. "But is anyone interested in going through a fast-food drive-thru?"

"I'm not sure I'm ready for food yet, but could we go through a coffee kiosk?" Harriet asked.

"That sounds like a good idea," Aunt Beth agreed.

The rest of the van voted for a coffee stop, and Sarah used her phone to find the closest option. By the time they reached the coffee shop, Sarah had made a list. "I'm going to go inside," she told them. "You can all wait here, and I'll be right back."

True to her promise, Sarah was back in fifteen minutes. One barista carried half the drinks while Sarah handled the other half. Bob met them at the side of the van and opened it, handing the cups to his passengers. Their names were written on the cups, making the process easier.

Bob handed the barista a five-dollar bill for her help, and within minutes, they were on the road again. The group drove silently for a half hour while everyone sipped their drinks, finally warming up. Bob turned the heat up in the back and middle of the van, and soon, the whole group was softly snoring.

"That worked," Sarah said quietly to Bob.

"They looked beat. And I'm sure they were pretty cold after being in that fishing boat and then the raft. None of them were dressed for that sort of outing."

"I noticed several of them were wincing as they got in, and Harriet's injured hand looked like a mess," Sarah said. "It wouldn't surprise me if the hospital kept some or all of them overnight."

"Do you care if I put on some music?" Bob asked.

"Sure," Sarah said.

He put on a CD titled *The Fifty Greatest Pieces of Classical Music* by the London Philharmonic. Sarah felt the tension of the day leaving her body and hoped that the music didn't put Bob to sleep while he was driving. She glanced at him and saw him take a big sip from his large coffee. She smiled. With that much caffeine, he'd be fine.

The Loose Threads didn't stir until Bob pulled the van into the ER entrance at the hospital. Sarah jumped out and went in to tell the intake people they'd arrived. Several uniformed policemen were in the waiting room, and they came over when they heard Sarah tell the nurse that they'd arrived.

The hospital had set up an area with two beds per cubicle and all side by side at the end of the treatment area. The nurse told them, "Harriet will be in the cubicle with a single bed. Everyone else will be two to a room."

Three more nurses came to escort the group to their cubicles. Each had a clipboard with two files on it. Clearly, they were prepared for the group's arrival. They began calling out names and taking their charges to their assigned rooms.

Harriet had just gotten onto the bed in her cubicle when Officer Nguyen came in. He shook his head. "What have you gotten yourself into now?" He asked her.

She sighed. "Would you believe my friends and I were kidnapped?"

"Do you know …" he started to ask when the doctor came in and interrupted.

"I told you; you were not to question my patients until we'd had a chance to treat them. A nurse will tell you if and when they are ready."

"Thank you," Harriet said tiredly when Nguyen was gone.

"Haven't I seen your hand in the ER once already?" he asked. "I'm Dr. Smith, by the way. Now tell me what happened to you and your friends."

Harriet summarized the adventure, starting with being knocked out by something in a handkerchief held over her face and finishing with rowing the lifeboat to shore. "Am I to understand that you hit your head in the hold, under the table?" Dr. Smith asked.

Harriet reached up with her good hand and winced when her hand found the knot on the top of her head. The doctor moved her hand and examined the goose egg on her head. "Bring in a cleaning kit," he said to the nurse. "She's going to need a staple."

The nurse backed out of the area. "Before we look at your hand, is there anywhere else that hurts?" Dr. Smith asked.

He shook his head as he looked at various scrapes and bruises. "Okay, Betty will bring you a gown, and you can get out of your clothes so we can see where else you might be injured."

Betty came back with the cleaning kit and set it on a counter. She handed Harriet a gown and instructed her to strip and put the gown on. While Harriet did as instructed, Betty took her clothes as she removed them, and put them in a clear bag.

"Whew," Betty said, "No offense, but your clothes stink."

Harriet smiled weakly. "I'm afraid they're a lost cause."

"Dr. Smith is seeing some of your friends. I will call for a couple of aides to give you a sponge bath. I think you'll feel much better." She did just that, and she was right, Harriet felt a little better.

CHAPTER FORTY-ONE

As predicted, the doctor wanted the group to spend the night in the hospital. Dr. Smith assured everyone that if they spent a peaceful night and everyone's vitals stayed stable, they'd be released in the morning. "I think I'd sleep better in my own bed," Harriet pleaded.

Smith laughed. "You're the last one I'd let out. You've got an appointment with the hand surgeon a little later. They need to open your wound, clean it out, and stitch it up again. I'm guessing she will put you in a cast or something else to immobilize your hand so you'll quit opening the wound or contaminating it."

"Are the rest of my group okay?"

"HIPPA says I can't tell you anything, but I can say there are no significant problems. Without being specific, a few people missed a couple of doses of their maintenance medicines, so we'll monitor them after we dose them. There are a few bumps and bruises, but you got the worst.

"I've held the police off as long as I can, plus I've got an anxious bunch of family members waiting to see their loved ones when the police are done with you."

"Send them in," Harriet said.

"You asked for it," Smith said with a laugh and left.

Harriet had dozed off when she heard Detective Morse clearing her throat. "Are you ready to answer a few questions?" she asked.

Harriet scooted up into a sitting position. "Fire away."

"Why don't you start with what happened when you parked your car by the docks."

Harriet recited her story again. She described the men she'd met on the boat and agreed to work with a police artist to create an image. "The Coast Guard is looking for the fishing boat you were trapped in, but it drifted over to the Canadian side of the Strait, so they have to do some paperwork before retrieving it. Unfortunately, it was boarded and searched before they got our notice that we were looking for it, so any evidence may be gone or at least compromised."

"That's too bad. Have you talked to the others yet?"

"Their statements are being taken by other officers."

"You might want to talk to Connie yourself."

"Why is that?" Morse asked.

"All of us were taken from around the docks except Connie. She was at Rime, talking to some of her students. They lured her into the hallway by the emergency exit, and she was drugged and taken from there by car to the fishing boat. Her students should be able to tell you who asked them to lure Connie to the hallway."

Jane Morse made a few notes in her little notebook. "Thanks, that is helpful. How long are you in here for?"

"They're going to do some work on my hand tonight, and if all goes well, I will get home tomorrow morning."

"It's probably not the right time to say this, but you and your friends would be safer if you left the crime investigations to the police."

"We find it difficult when our friends are being attacked and murdered, and nothing seems to be happening to figure out who did it and why."

"As I've explained in the past, we are not obligated to share how our investigation is going."

Harriet hung her head. "Okay, got it."

Morse shook her head. "I've heard that before. I may be back before you check out."

"You make it sound like I've got a choice."

"Better than being in a lifeboat," Morse said.

"This is true," Harriet said and yawned. Her eyes were closed before Morse made it to the hallway.

Harriet woke again an hour later when Jorge came into her cubicle. "Sorry to wake you, Mija."

"It's okay. I'm going upstairs to get my hand cleaned out in a little while. I just thought I'd catch a nap before that happens."

"I just wanted to come by and see if you are okay. Also, I wanted to tell you that your dogs and cat are okay. I've been walking them and feeding them. And lastly, I called your mother-in-law to tell her what's happening. I told her I was sure you didn't want her to tell James until he gets home tomorrow since he can't do anything while he's traveling, and she agreed."

"That's a relief," Harriet said, leaning back in bed.

Jorge gently patted her leg. "I'll let you get back to your nap. I will take care of your animals and let Beth's dog out again, and then I'll be back. Have these people call me if you need anything."

Tears filled her eyes. "Thank you, Jorge," she said, swiping at her eyes.

The hand surgeon decided to sedate Harriet while she worked on her hand. When Harriet woke up, she was in the recovery area with a cast on her hand and arm, and a nurse explained that now that she was awake, she was going up to a patient room on the third floor.

"Do I ever get to eat?" Harriet asked.

"You can't get a four-course meal up here, but I can offer an assortment of fruit juices and crackers."

Harriet selected graham crackers and cranberry juice and ate it like a wild animal when the nurse delivered it. "You weren't kidding about being hungry," the nurse said. "I'll bring you a second round."

Harriet had barely settled in her room when her aunt, being pushed by Jorge in a wheelchair, came in. Jorge shrugged his shoulders.

"She insisted," he said.

"I just wanted to see for myself that you're okay," Beth said.

"They completely numbed my hand, so I'm great right now. When it wakes up, it might be a different story," Harriet told her.

"While I'm mobile, I decided to visit the rest of the group."

"The doctors and nurses don't know she's rolling around. They made the mistake of leaving a wheelchair outside her room."

Harriet laughed. "How are the rest of the bunch?"

"Connie and Mavis have cracked ribs," Beth told her. "DeAnn has a sprained ankle, and Lauren has deep cuts around her ankle where the shackle was, and it appears to be infected from the dirty metal cuff."

"What about you and Robin?" Harriet asked.

"I just have bumps and bruises, and Robin has blisters on her hands from rowing and a scrape on her left leg, but otherwise, she's okay."

Before Harriet could comment, a nurse came into the room, hands on her hips and a stern look on her face. "I thought you might be up here," she said. She came over to the wheelchair, and Jorge yielded the handles. "Let's get you back to your room. It's time for dinner."

Beth looked at Harriet and then Jorge. "I guess I shouldn't miss that," she said, and the nurse wheeled her away.

CHAPTER FORTY-TWO

The following morning, the Loose Threads were all cleared to leave the hospital. Harriet was surprised when Kathy, her mother-in-law, came to pick her up.

"I knew your car was down at the docks, and Jorge is taking your aunt home, so I figured you needed a ride home. If you're up for it, I thought I'd make a meal for when the baseball crew gets home. I'll take you home so you can rest, but I'll come get you again before the men are due back."

"That sounds good," Harriet said. "Could we possibly pick up my prescriptions? I have antibiotics and pain medication."

"Sure," Kathy said. "Do you go to Foggy Point Pharmacy?"

"I do," said Harriet. I'm sorry to be such a bother."

Kathy patted her good arm. "You've been through quite an ordeal this last week."

"For all of that, we still don't know who killed our friend Maylene, who attacked Bob's mother, or who is selling drugs in Foggy Point."

"Shouldn't the police be figuring that out?" Kathy asked.

"You sound like Detective Morse. She says we should leave it to the police, but they haven't gotten anything. We at least know that someone is using fish and a fishing boat to bring drugs in. And we know someone is moving them around Foggy Point with drones."

"Really? I've seen drones fly over our house."

"That's interesting," Harriet said thoughtfully. "We've been figuring out where the drone home base is."

"I thought they were doing package delivery for the Postal Place. I saw they were offering that as a service."

"Bob's hunting hawk tangled with one of the drones and returned with a package of pills."

"Is it fentanyl?" Kathy asked.

"We're assuming so. The hawk wouldn't let Bob take it away from her, and she'd hidden it in her nest in her cage. She also has eggs in her nest, so Bob doesn't want to disturb it."

"Are the eggs fertile?"

"He doesn't know, but he doesn't want to disturb her just in case."

"Do the police have any idea who is involved?"

"Not that Morse has shared with us, but it doesn't seem like it. Carla Salter and her boyfriend did a little surveillance at the Foggy Point Motel. They saw the park ranger, Greg Lewis, entertaining in one of the rooms. We don't know if he was doing drug business or other activities. It looked like Betty Ruiz. Hard to imagine her being involved in the drug trade or having a tryst with Greg, but I'm ninety percent certain it was her."

"I'm surprised, too," Kathy said. "I don't know her well, but my garden club interacted with her about our plant sale, and I'd have never guessed she'd be involved in drugs. I did hear she'd been going through a nasty divorce, though."

"You never know, I guess," Harriet said as they pulled into the pharmacy parking lot.

"I'll help you take the dogs out," Kathy said when she'd parked in front of Harriet's studio. After that, I suggest you take a nap. When Will calls and says they are thirty minutes away, I'll call you and then come get you."

"You haven't told them what's been going on, have you?"

"Against my better judgment, I've not said anything. I understand your desire to not spoil their baseball vacation, but James will be upset when he sees you and hears what's happening."

"Let's not hit them with it all tonight."

"Whatever you say," Kathy said, opening the studio with Harriet's hidden key. Harriet hoped her purse was still in her car's back compartment. She'd like to have her keys and phone back.

The dogs jumped up at Harriet, one on each side, while Kathy attempted to attach their leashes. "I guess they missed me," Harriet said with a smile.

Kathy finally got the dogs contained, and they took them outside. "Don't you have a cat, too?" Kathy asked.

Harriet laughed. "I do, but he'll have to punish me for leaving him with others while I was gone for a few days. He'll come around, though, don't worry."

Harriet went upstairs, took her medicine, and fell asleep before her head hit her pillow. When she woke up, Fred was curled by her side. Apparently, she'd been forgiven.

She looked at her alarm, and by her calculations, she had forty-five minutes or so before Kathy would come to pick her up. She taped a gallon ziplock bag over her cast and then quickly showered. She chose a loose-fitting sweater to wear with jeans. The sweater's loose sleeves came down to her fingertips. She knew it wouldn't fool James, but maybe they could get the story of what was happening told before they had to talk about her hand injury.

Harriet had just come downstairs to feed the animals when her house phone rang. Kathy reported she was on her way and expected to arrive in just over five minutes, so much for the thirty-minute warning.

"Are you ready?" Kathy asked when she'd come into the kitchen from the studio.

"Ready as I'll ever be," Harriet said with a weak smile.

"I know I said I'd call you when Will called me to say they were thirty minutes away, but he forgot until they were ten minutes away. I jumped in the car and immediately headed this way, but I suspect our travelers will be there when we get back."

"I'll just jump in the deep end, then."

Kathy reached over and patted her arm. "It's going to be fine."

Kathy parked in the garage, and Harriet followed her into the kitchen. "We're home," Kathy called. The men and boys were sitting in the living room.

"Aren't you guys tired of sitting?" Harriet asked as James stood up and came to her, pulling her into a hug. She melted into his arms. Everything seemed better now that he was home.

"Are you all hungry?" Kathy asked. "I've made homemade Mac and cheese and green salad."

"We're starving," Luke said, speaking for Ta'sean and himself.

"I'm sure you are," Will said with a laugh. "It's been at least two hours since they've eaten." He had wrapped his arm around Kathy's shoulders and looked at her alone as he spoke. Harriet hoped she and James were that much in love when they were James' parent's age.

Harriet went to the kitchen to help Kathy carry condiments to the dining room table and deliver the main dishes. "This looks great, Mom," said James. "I'm not sure I could handle another ballpark hot dog."

"I was even missing my greens," Will said. He was notorious in the family for his avoidance of anything green.

"Come on, boys," James called the boys who had migrated to the backyard. "You can play catch after dinner. We adults have some catching up to do." He looked at Harriet as he said this last.

"This Mac and cheese is delicious," Will said, preventing James from saying anything else. Harriet looked down at her plate and picked at her food.

"Who wants coffee or tea?" Kathy asked when everyone was finished eating.

"May we be excused?" Luke asked. When Will said yes, the boys carried their plates to the kitchen, picked up their new-looking baseball gloves from a chair by the back sliding door, and went outside.

"I'll get the coffee," James told his mother. "Go sit down with Dad and Harriet."

"Thank you, son," Kathy said, joining Will and Harriet in the living room.

James brought a tray with four cups of coffee, each doctored with the appropriate amendments. "Now," he said when he finally sat down with his mug. "Tell me what it is you've been avoiding telling me for over a week."

"We've had a little trouble while you guys were gone," Harriet started.

James held up his hands to stop her story. "You call being kidnapped and set out to sea a little trouble?"

"What?" Will said. "Kathy, did you know about this?"

Kathy's face turned a becoming pink. "Not at first, but I did find out when they were in the hospital."

"And you didn't think I should know?" James demanded.

"It's my fault," Harriet told him. "I didn't want to spoil your vacation with the boys."

"Lucky for me, Jorge didn't feel so protective. He called and told me the night you disappeared. He also told me several people have died. And you didn't think I'd want to know?"

"I thought things would be safer for the boys if they stayed out of town," Harriet said.

"Oh, so it's all about the boys."

"Ease up, James," Will said. "She was just thinking about the boy's vacation, and we did have a good time."

James sighed and slumped back in his chair. "Okay, we did appreciate the peaceful vacation," James said. "Now tell me everything."

Harriet held her hand up, letting the sweater fall back and revealing her cast. "Jorge did say you had injured your hand. He didn't say your hand was in a cast."

Harriet put her hand on his thigh. "I'm sure Jorge was frantic about my aunt. She, Mavis, and Connie cracked and broke a few ribs, plus acquired a few assorted bruises. Lauren and I could climb the ladder into the ship's hold. Still, our other members were tossed unceremoniously into the hold after being carried down the ladder over the bad guys' shoulder from the deck."

James asked more questions, and Harriet answered them as well as she could.

"I assume there was some reason you couldn't leave this to Detective Morse," James said when she was finished.

"We reported what we knew, but people we know continued to be hurt. Avelot Solace was attacked, and they've not found who hurt her. Sarah was attacked, but since her earlier incident, she's taken advanced self-protection classes. She ended up killing her attacker, but the police have made no headway in figuring out why he attacked her. They did clear her of any wrongdoing. It was clearly self-defense."

"Wow, you and the Threads have been busy while we were gone." Harriet smiled at James.

"Always," she said and kissed him.

CHAPTER FORTY-THREE

Harriet finished telling James and Will everything that had happened in the last week or so. Starting with Maylene's death and ending up with the kidnapping and rescue from the boat by Bob and Sarah.

"Is the case now in the hands of the police, without further help from the Loose Threads?" James asked Harriet.

She grinned. "We do have a little follow-up that needs to be done."

James looked at the ceiling, rolling his eyes as he did so. "Please tell me it's nothing dangerous."

"It is definitely not dangerous. The seven of us who were kidnapped have been asked to meet with a police artist to create sketches of the kidnappers."

James let out a breath. "That sounds safe enough."

"I'd like to go up to the homeless camp and talk to Max and then to Sarah and Bob afterward. They were doing surveillance with night vision goggles trying to see where the drones were landing when they were done flying around Foggy Point."

James ran his free hand through his hair. His other arm was around Harriet's shoulders. "I should have figured the trip to the police station was too simple," he finally said.

"Maybe we should table this discussion until tomorrow," Harriet said. "I'm sure you gentlemen all have suitcases of laundry that need to be done, and the boys will want to get reacquainted with the dogs and cat. The pets are very anxious to see the boys."

"Harriet's had a difficult few days, James," Kathy said. "She could use some rest without being lectured by her devoted and well-meaning husband."

"I'm guessing she wants to check on her aunt, too," Will said.

"She is in the room," Harriet said. "And she does, in fact, want to check on her aunt, but an in-person visit can wait until tomorrow. If I had my cell phone, I could call her, but as it is, I will call her when we get home. And that reminds me that we need to go to the phone store so I can be connected with the rest of the world again."

"Have you tried using 'find my phone'?" James asked.

Harriet laughed. "We were kidnapped, divested of our cell phones, and haven't had a chance to reunite with our pads or laptops, so no, I have not been able to use 'find my phone'. It didn't seem to be an option on the hospital room phones."

James pulled his phone from his pocket. After looking at Harriet's cast, he opened the 'find my phone' app and looked at the result. "Hmmmm," he said. "My phone seems to have lost contact with your phone."

"Chances are, they removed our SIM cards or worse if they are tech-savvy kidnappers," Harriet said. She smiled. "I've had my eye on the latest model of my old phone recently, but I didn't have a good reason to upgrade. Now I do."

James stood up. "I'll go get the boys," he said.

The dogs and cat were delirious with joy when Luke and Ta'sean walked into the kitchen from the garage.

"What am I? Chopped liver?" James complained.

Harriet wrapped her arms around him and hugged him. "I still love you," she said and smiled.

James looked over her shoulder down at the kids and dogs. "I guess I'm yesterday's news," he said with fake sadness. "They can just eat store-bought dog treats if that's how they're going to treat me. No more James specials. You can take them to Carter."

Harriet leaned her head on his shoulder. "They still love you, and as soon as the boys are tired of being licked, they'll move on to you."

"Yeah, yeah, yeah," James said. "In the meantime, I'll bring our luggage in."

"I'm assuming you'll want to go by the restaurant in the morning before we do my chores."

"You're assuming right, but I'll go in early. You can have a leisurely morning, and I'll be back before you miss me."

"I need to go by the school and arrange for Ta'sean to have a different tutor for a few days while Connie recovers."

"Can you call them?" James asked her. I don't think you should be driving with your hand like that. Not until it has had time to heal. If you need to go to the school in person, I'll call my dad and ask him to take you."

"I don't want to bother your father," Harriet said.

"He won't mind. He likes to feel useful."

"I hate being dependent on people."

"That's what families do; they help each other when needed."

As predicted, Will was happy to drive Harriet around the next day. Harriet was feeling much better, having had a good night's sleep since James returned home. As promised, he'd left early for the restaurant. The boys had gotten up and made their own breakfast, walking down the hill to catch the early bus, ready to regale their friends with spring training stories. They were both dressed in new team shirts.

"Are we off to the police station first?" Will asked her when he'd arrived. Before asking, he had a cup of coffee and a couple of cookies from the jar on the kitchen counter, lest Harriet want to leave immediately.

"No, I'd like to visit my aunt and ensure she's okay. I called, and she said to come over. She's planted herself in her recliner. She has two broken ribs and can't really do anything for a few days and is already bored. I think she wants to review our adventure. Her two best friends are also home bound because of their own rib injuries. Lauren and I somehow escaped being thrown on the floor at the base of the ladder into the hold, so no cracked or broken ribs for us."

"That was fortunate for you, although you seem to have re-injured your hand."

Harriet held up her hand. "I'm losing count of how many times it's been restitched. Having my hands tied behind my back in that filthy fish hold didn't help things, and then sleeping on that boat ..."

"Punch her address into that gadget, and off we'll go," Will said. His car had an in-dash navigation system, and it took Harriet a minute to figure out where to put her aunt's location. Still, in a few moments, they were underway.

"This is nice," Will commented as they approached her aunt's bungalow.

"You probably know she lived most of her adult life in the house I'm living in. She gave it to me a few years ago. She wanted to give me her business, and it made more sense to her to give me the whole shebang."

"This seems like a more manageable size for a woman living alone," Will said as he parked in front of her house.

"It is," Harriet agreed. "Her friend Mavis also lives in a cottage on the water not far from here."

Will exited the car, approached Harriet's side, and opened her door.

"Thanks," she said.

"How are you feeling?" Harriet asked as soon as they were in the door. "Have you met James's father, Will?" she asked.

"I think so, but 'hello', just in case we haven't met. This pain medication scrobbles my brain."

"How are your ribs?" Harriet asked again.

"I'll live," Beth said drily. "How is your hand?"

"They should have done a cast sooner, I think. It keeps things from pulling or bumping it or anything."

"Are you on your way to see the police artist?" Beth asked.

"I am, after a couple of stops." She looked at Will as she said this, and he nodded. "They can't expect you to go to the station, can they?"

Beth laughed. "They tried, but I convinced them that Mavis and I saw nothing. The kidnappers grabbed us from behind and knocked us out with something. We were thrown into that stinky fish hold the next thing we knew. Even that was a little vague until you took my blanket off. That was when the pain in my ribs set in."

"Lauren and I talked to our kidnappers about buying fish, so we did see their faces. From the voices of the guys who tossed the rest of you into the hold, I think there were at least four. The guys that threw the last few of you in had on balaclavas, so all someone could tell them about those two is maybe skin and eye color."

"Well, let's hope you and Lauren can tell them enough to get a good drawing."

"Don't hold your breath," Harriet told her aunt. "We were knocked out too right after we saw them, so that may have messed with our memories."

"Can we bring you anything?" Will asked.

Beth smiled at him. "My friend Jorge is bringing me lunch and spending a little time, so he's got me well taken care of."

Harriet realized that was Will's subtle way of telling her it was time for them to get moving. "We better get going, then," Harriet told her. She leaned in and kissed her aunt's cheek. "Give us a text or call if you need anything."

Harriet turned and headed for the door. Will reached around her, opened it, and guided her onto the porch.

"You need to be just a little careful, Missy," Will said with a smile. "I'm here to help, so let me."

She sighed. "Okay, okay. I'm just used to being independent."

"Where to next?" He asked.

"I'd like to talk to Max at the homeless camp in Fogg Park. We should go by the restaurant and see if James has any food we can take to them. I try not to go up there empty-handed if I can help it."

"Do we need to call James and warn him?"

"We probably should," Harriet told him.

Will reached the car's control panel and pressed the restaurant number in the phone book.

"Is James available?" he asked when the phone was answered. "It's his father."

"Yes, sir," the voice who had answered said.

Harriet looked at Will. "You've got them trained."

"They kept me on hold once for a rather extended period. James read them the riot act, so now they jump when I call. As it happened, that was when Kathy sprained her ankle in the garden, and I was taking her to the emergency room."

"Hi, pops, what's up?" James said.

"You're on speaker phone with your lovely wife listening in. We are going to the homeless camp to talk to Max, and I was wondering if you have any food for them."

"As a matter of fact, I do. The crew here didn't get up there as often as we would have liked, so they kept putting stuff in the freezer. Come on by, and we'll load you up. And Harriet?"

"Yes, dear," she said with a smile only Will could see.

"Are you taking it easy?"

"Yes, your father is making sure I don't overdo."

"Good. See you soon and love you."

"Love you too," Will and Harriet both said and laughed.

CHAPTER FORTY-FOUR

As promised, James filled the trunk of his father's car with enough frozen food for several meals, along with bread and cakes. "How will they keep this much food from spoiling?" Will asked Harriet as they made their way to the park.

"They have quite a setup these days. They have a solar-powered refrigerator and other insulated storage boxes."

"That sounds nice."

"They've had several offers to move into houses, but the main group isn't interested. A few younger people stay at the camp and then make use of the services offered, but not so much the main group."

"They're lucky they have you and James to feed them."

"The food James sends would go to waste if he didn't bring it to the camp."

"Here we are," Will said as he pulled into the parking lot and backed the car into a spot close to the trail to the camp.

"Perfect."

"You can carry a bag of baked goods in your good hand, but nothing bigger than that," Will told her.

Harriet took the bag of dinner rolls and headed up the trail. "Anyone home?" she called as she approached the clearing, then set her bag of rolls down.

"We're here," Joyce Elias called out in her lilting British accent.

"James's father is bringing some boxes of food." As she said this, Will arrived, setting his box on the table beside the rolls.

"There are two more boxes," Will said and turned to go back down the trail.

"Max," Joyce called out, and the tall, white-haired man appeared immediately from a side trail.

"Oh, Harriet. I didn't know we were expecting company."

"First, help James's Da carry some food boxes from his car."

"Certainly," Max said and hurried down the trail to the parking lot. A few minutes later, he returned, followed by Will, each carrying large boxes of frozen food.

"James said there's a couple of days' worth of food here. His workers kept putting it in the freezer when they didn't have time to drive up here."

"I'm sure they missed James when he was gone," Joyce observed.

"I hope they didn't let you go hungry," Harriet said.

"The methodist church knew James was going on vacation, so they arranged to bring us food every other day. We did just fine. Didn't we, Max?" Joyce said.

"They aren't the cooks that James is, but their casseroles filled our bellies."

"Before we go, could I talk to you a minute?" Harriet asked Max.

"Why don't I give you a tour of our camp?" Joyce said to Will and led him down one of the trails in the central area.

"Sarah told me you, and she and Bob have continued watching for the drones with the night vision binoculars."

"Yes, we have," Max said.

"And did you see anything worth noting?"

"Indeed, we did. We've gotten together and talked about our observations. As near as we can tell, the drones originate below Sarah's and to the west of Bob's around dusk. They think they leave from a trailer in the woods. The drones cross back and forth around the hill, making deliveries, it would seem. In the middle of the night, often at two or three in the morning, they appear to return to the storage buildings on the other side of our parking lot."

"Who owns the buildings?" Harriet asked although she was pretty sure she knew.

"They belong to the county parks department. I've sat near the buildings to observe what's happening."

"And" Harriet prompted.

"A man comes and catches them and does something to them before opening a set of doors and putting them inside."

"I'd sure like to look inside," Harriet said.

"The man locks it up tight, and I've visited the locks during the day, and they are complex. Well beyond my basic lock-picking skills."

"Could you recognize the man?"

"Unfortunately, no. The man wore a black knit cap pulled low over his brow, a black jacket, pants, and gloves."

"I'll have to think about this. Thanks for your work."

"No problem," Max said. "As always, I'm happy to help."

"Can you handle another unplanned stop before we go by the school and the police station?"

"I am at your service," Will said with a smile. "Where are we going?"

"I'd like to go by the senior care home on Main Street."

"Okay, what are we doing there?" Will asked.

"My friend Sarah's family owns it, and she works there. I'll give her a quick call, and if she's there, we can swing by and ask her a few questions. Otherwise, she lives near the top of Miller Hill."

Harriet realized she didn't have her phone, but Will was already looking up the number on his car phone. He dialed it in, and she could hear the speaker phone dialing. Harriet quickly determined that Sarah was there, and she told them they were welcome to come by.

"How are you doing today?" she asked Harriet.

Harriet sighed. "A little worse for the wear," she admitted. "I was telling Will here that I think I might have been better off if they'd put a cast on my hand and wrist sooner." She looked at Will. "This is James's father, Will, by the way."

Sarah smiled at Will. "We met at a fundraiser last year. Nice to see you again, Mr. Garvin."

"I wish it was under better circumstances," he said.

"We all do," said Harriet. "Sarah, we came by to ask you about your observations with the night vision binoculars. Max told us the drones seemed to be landing at the parks department sheds at Fogg Park. Did you and Bob notice anything else?"

"Max probably told you we're pretty sure the drones take off from one of those trailers back in the woods just below my level on the hill. We didn't observe them flying up the hill. We think they either go up in the morning or someone picks them up and drives them up to have their payloads attached."

"Max also told us he checked out the shed during the day and that it has a complex lock on it. He said it was beyond his picking skills." Harriet said.

"I wonder if Carla's boyfriend could pick it for us."

"I hate to ask him," Harriet said. "I wouldn't want to get him in trouble."

"What am I missing?" Will asked.

"Terry works for NCIS in Bremerton, often undercover."

"We could at least consult him about our next move," Sarah argued. "NCIS may be involved with this drug bunch; they do seem to be transporting their drugs on the water."

Harriet sighed. "I guess it can't hurt to ask."

"What if we took a set of large bolt cutters and broke the lock?" Will asked. "We could say we heard a noise inside and thought someone was in trouble." Harriet had to smile at Will's use of 'We.'

"Can we do that?" Sarah asked.

"If we both say we heard the noise, it would be hard to disprove. We'll ensure we don't carry the bolt cutters to the shed first. We could go to the door and mime listening and trying to get in—just in case there's a witness," Harriet said.

"We need to do your other chores first," Will cautioned.

"I agree. We also need to think a little about this. I'm sure Lauren still has some tools she used with her garden planting activity during the bird festival. We could go by the parks department for permission to return the tools. That would give us a good reason to be at the sheds. Then we can hear the noise and break into the drone shed."

"Sounds like you have a plan," Sarah said. "I'd volunteer to help, but I've got to work here all day."

"It's okay," Harriet assured her.

"Where's our next stop," Will asked.

"Okay," Harriet said with a smile. "Time for us to move on. Thanks for the info."

Harriet followed Will toward the exit. "We need to go by Ta'sean's school to arrange a substitute tutor for a week or two until Connie is better."

Foggy Point Middle School had already heard about Connie's accident and knew that Ta'sean would return today. They'd arranged a tutor for him, and he was already working with the woman.

"That was easy," Will said.

"The school has been accommodating concerning Ta'sean," Harriet told him.

"I'm glad to see our tax dollars are working. Now, are we finally going to the police station?"

Harriet smiled at him. "Yes, on to Foggy Point PD."

Harriet explained to the desk sergeant why she was there. She made a phone call, and an officer Harriet had never met came to get her. He said that Will would have to wait in the lobby.

"You be sure to open all the doors and pull out chairs for her, young man," Will told him loudly. "She's been injured, and we don't want it to worsen."

The officer stiffened, and Harriet thought he might salute, but instead, he held the door for her and led the way back into the office cubicles. The officer handed Harriet off to an artist he introduced as Kari Sullivan.

"Let's go into an interview room so we won't be disturbed," Kari suggested. "Here, let me get the door," she said as they approached the room. "Could I get you a cup of tea or coffee?" she asked.

"A cup of tea would be nice," Harriet answered.

"I'll be right back," she said, leaving the room.

Harriet looked around and wondered if she was being recorded. She knew from Detective Morse that some of the Foggy Point Police interview rooms were wired for video and sound. At least there wasn't a mirror in the room—a sure signal of an observation area on the other side.

"Here we go," Kari said, setting two mugs of hot water on the table. She then pulled several sachets of tea from her pocket, along with sugar packets and powdered creamer.

Harriet picked up a packet of Steven Smith black lavender tea. Kari took it from her, opened it, and put it in a mug before sliding it to Harriet's side of the table. Harriet picked up a sugar packet, and Kari opened it and dumped it into her mug.

Kari repeated the process with her own tea before sitting across from Harriet. They both sipped their tea and set their mugs down.

Kari cleared her throat. "How this works is that we will talk about your day leading up to the incident where you encountered the person we're going to create a picture of."

"Okay," Harriet said. "Where do you want me to start?"

It turned out she wanted Harriet to start with waking up in the morning and ending with waking up in the hold of a fishing boat. Harriet told her everything she could remember. When Harriet got to the men she'd talked to, Kari asked her a few questions about details. She was surprised that when Kari asked questions about the two men, she could recall a few more details than she'd expected.

"I think we're ready to start drawing," Kari said. "Wait here," she said and left the room, returning a few minutes later with two notebooks, a sketch pad, and pencils.

"These notebooks contain many facial features, hair, and ear images. As you attempt to describe features, you can look in the notebooks to help," Kari explained.

It took forty-five minutes to come up with images of the two men.

"Is there anything we should change?" Kari asked when she'd set the two pictures side-by-side on the table.

"No," Harriet told her. "I think that's it."

"Would you like to see the pictures done with our other witness?"

"Sure."

Kari pulled two more pictures from the back of her sketch tablet and set them on the table next to Harriet's images.

"Wow, they are remarkably similar," Harriet said.

"Yes, they are," Kari said. "That's a good sign."

"If we're done, I need to go rescue my father-in-law."

"Sure," Kari said and led her back to the lobby.

CHAPTER FORTY-FIVE

"I'm sorry you had to sit in the lobby for so long," Harriet told Will as they got in his car. "Would you like to drive through the Steaming Cup on our way to Laurens? I'm buying."

"If I can get a muffin along with it, I'm in."

"Sure. I feel bad tying you up all morning."

"Besides the baseball trip, this is the most fun I've had all year. I've never gotten to play private detective before."

Harriet chuckled. "The Foggy Point Police would like it if I didn't do any detecting on their patch."

"If they did their job, you wouldn't have to do their jobs for them."

Harriet was liking James's dad more by the minute. "We could take the time to go inside if you'd rather sit while we eat."

"It's probably my generation, but I don't think we're good at eating in the car as we drive."

"I'm fine with going in. I usually go through the drive-in on the fly as I go from one activity to another, but I think with one hand, I might be better sitting at a table."

"What do you think is going on here?" Will asked as they sat at a table with a drink and a pastry each.

Harriet sipped her cocoa thoughtfully. "We know someone is trafficking drugs, in particular fentanyl, in Foggy Point. We've encountered some rough-looking customers these last few weeks—the man who broke into Bob's trailer, the man Sarah killed, and the men who kidnapped us. But ..."

"You believe someone else is involved?" Will asked.

"I just have a hard time believing that any of the people we've encountered are smart enough to have put together the drone delivery system, the fishing boat, and all the rest. We saw the park ranger at the Foggy Point Motel with women coming in and out late at night. They could have been drug customers, low-level dealers, or sex workers with nothing to do with the drug activities."

"Could he be Mister Big?" Will asked.

Harriet had a hard time keeping a straight face. "It's possible, but he seemed like a weasel, not a Mister Big."

"In Miss Marple's movies, she always said you have to allow for a Mister or Miss X, someone who is unidentified," Will said. "Kathy and I love Agatha Christie," he added.

"I think we're looking for a Mister or Miss X." They finished their treats, each lost in their own thoughts.

With Will's help, Harriet called Lauren and explained what they needed from her. The doctors had told all the kidnap victims to stay home and rest for a few days. It appeared that everyone else was following doctors' orders, so Harriet wasn't surprised to find Lauren at home.

"Aren't we meant to be at home, except for visiting the PD to do our artist sketches?" she asked Harriet when she opened the door to Harriet and Will.

Harriet smiled. "How are you feeling?"

"My shoulder is messed up from hanging from the shackle for so long. Torn ligaments or tendons or something. Since I'm taking pain meds, Detective Morse sent a car to drive me in for my visit with the artist."

"We just got back from there. I'm guessing your pictures were the ones they showed me when they'd finished mine."

"Did we both see the same guys?" Lauren said with a laugh.

"You did," said Will. "I'm James's father. Harriet says your pictures were remarkably alike."

Lauren held her hand out and shook his. "I think we've met before at the stable."

"Probably," he said. "My memory isn't quite what it used to be."

"So, what brings you to my door, looking for garden tools? You have plenty at your house."

Harriet explained their ruse. "Being kidnapped wasn't enough? You want to go for being arrested, too?"

"I'll be with her," Will said. And by the way, do you happen to have a strong bolt cutter? It will save us having to drive back home."

"I have several models you might want to look at."

"Why am I not surprised," Harriet muttered.

Will followed Lauren into a bedroom at the back of her apartment that she used for storage. They came out a few minutes later, with Will holding a large pair of cutters that looked new.

"Have they ever been used?" Harriet asked.

"Not really. They were part of a security operation. I'll tell you all about it another time."

"We should probably go anyway," Will said.

"Call me and tell me what happens," Lauren said.

"Will do," Harriet told her.

Harriet was happy that Kath was the only person in the Parks Department office. "I was wondering if I could borrow the key to the shed where the garden tools are kept at Fogg Park. I have some tools Lauren Sawyer had from the classes we did."

"Technically, you are supposed to be accompanied by Mason or Greg, but they seem to be working from home, although they're never reachable there or who knows where else."

Kath went to a cabinet at the back of the office. She returned with a double handful of keys, which she set on the counter in front of Harriet.

"Take them all," she said. "I'm afraid the tags have become worn and are hard to read. You'll just have to try them all until one works."

"I don't want you to get in trouble. Won't you lose your job if Greg or Mason return and find his keys gone?" Harriet asked.

"I'm pretty sure they each have keys to the sheds they use frequently," Kath said. "And I think I told you before, I don't give a rip. My pension is fully vested with the county, so they can't hurt me now. I'm tired of those two and their demands. Neither one of them does any of the reporting the county requires from this office. I do it. And I never get so much as a thank-you."

Will picked the keys up. "We'll bring these back as soon as we finish," he said. Will waited until they were back in the car to say anything. "That was strange," he said as he backed out of the parks department parking lot.

"Yeah, Kath has been pretty disgruntled every time I've been in that office, but it works to my advantage since she gives me whatever I ask for."

"When we get to the sheds, we still need to put the garden tools away. The keys save us the problem of breaking into the target shed."

Harriet held her wounded hand up over her heart. "Is your hand hurting?" Will asked her.

"My pain pill is wearing off. I don't have my purse, so I didn't bring them."

"Do you want to go home and get your medication?"

"No, I'd like to get on with our investigation of the drone shed. We can go home after that."

"If you're sure ..." Will said and drove them to Fogg Park.

"Would you take pictures of everything we see in the drone shed?" Harriet asked as they got out of the car.

"Sure." He opened the console between the seats, took out his phone, and put it in his pocket.

Harriet opened the car's back door and started to pick up tools. "Just wait a minute, Missy. Put that down. Let's go to the shed door and start trying the keys. I'll carry them over there, and you can take them, one at a time, and try them. I'll bring the tools while you're doing that."

It took four tries before Harriet found the correct key. "We're in," she said to Will.

He brought the hand shovels in and set them on the shelf that was labeled for them. Harriet stepped out of the toolshed. "Boy, it smells bad around here," she commented.

"I noticed that myself. And it gets worse as you approach the drone shed," Will said.

"Let's get this over with and get out of here," Harriet said. Will carried the keys to the drone shed door and tried them in the lock. "Look for one that's different," she told Will. "We know it's more secure than the others."

Will spread the keys out, and he and Harriet quickly picked out a different one. "Okay, here goes nothing," Will said, slipping the key into the lock. He opened the door, and they both stepped back as they were assaulted by the heavy odor of death.

Harriet stepped back into the shed and quickly identified the source of the odor. Gregory Lewis was sprawled in a pool of blood on the floor of the shed. She stepped out of the shed and shut the door.

"What's going on," Will asked.

"Call 911. We've just found a dead body."

CHAPTER FORTY-SIX

"**D**ad," said James as he walked into the lobby of the Foggy Point Police Department. "You were supposed to be keeping Harriet safe."

Will straightened to his full height—two inches taller than his son. "If you would stop yelling at me and look at your wife, you'd see she is safe and sound and was never in any danger. We didn't kill this gentleman after all. We were returning tools to the shed next door to the one the man was in, and we smelled a terrible odor."

"The parks department clerk had given us all the shed keys," Harriet added. "We opened the door and found Gregory. It had nothing to do with us."

"I thought you were coming here to work with the police artist after you delivered the food to the homeless camp. And then maybe buy a new cell phone for you."

Will and Harriet looked at each other. "We forgot the phone," they said in unison. James closed his eyes and shook his head.

"What were you doing all this time?"

"We went to check on Harriet's aunt," Will said.

"I talked to her," James interrupted. "The only reason she wasn't with you is because she couldn't get out of her chair."

"We went by the senior care center and talked to Sarah," Harriet said. "She confirmed what Max told us."

Harriet was about to tell James about going to Lauren's and the parks department, but Will looked at her and then at the desk sergeant. "Maybe we should talk about this at home," he said.

"I'll ask the sergeant if you are free to leave," James said.

The sergeant picked up his phone before James got to the desk and called Detective Morse. "The detective wants to talk to you. Someone will come get you," he told the trio.

An officer came through the door to the back and asked Harriet and Will to follow him to the back. "I'm not going without my husband," Harriet said. The officer looked at the desk sergeant.

"It's okay," the sergeant told him. "If Morse doesn't want him back there, she'll tell him."

As they followed the officer back, she heard the sergeant tell somebody in the back area that Morse wouldn't risk being cut off from James's baked goods. Harriet chuckled as she followed Will and James to the interrogation room.

"Being kidnapped wasn't enough for you?" Morse said as she dropped a folder onto the table James, Will, and Harriet were sitting around.

Harriet sighed. Will cleared his throat. "I'm not sure we've met. I'm William Garvin, James's father. I was escorting Harriet when we smelled a terrible smell and investigated."

"And you two just happened to have the keys to the parks department sheds?"

"Their secretary seems to be having some sort of breakdown. We asked for the key to the toolshed to return some garden tools we'd used at the bird festival and hadn't returned," Harriet explained. "She all but threw the whole group of keys for all the sheds at us."

"I admit," Will said. "With the way she was ranting, we took the keys and ran, lest we be further pulled into her drama."

"We put our tools away but couldn't help but notice a horrible smell coming from the shed next door. I sort of recognized it."

Morse shook her head and looked at the ceiling. "Let's not be coy. Anyone who has ever smelled a dead body will never forget the odor. Go on, you smelled a dead body, and since you had all those keys, you opened the shed, then what?"

"I saw Gregory Lewis lying in a pool of blood. I backed up, and we shut the door, and Will called 911."

"You didn't check to see if he was alive?"

"Oh please," Will admonished her. "Smelling like that? He hadn't been alive for a while. I was in the army in my youth, and I dealt with more than one dead body in Vietnam."

"Okay, so you only touched the keys, the lock, and the door?" Morse asked them both.

"Yes," they both affirmed.

"Do you want to tell me why you returned the garden tools today?" Morse asked Harriet. "I happen to know you and your fellow kidnap victims are supposed to be home recovering. What aren't you telling me?"

"Max from the homeless camp, Bob Solace, and Sarah Ness were not kidnapped with us. While we were tied up," she said with a smile, "the three of them were watching the skies over Foggy Point with night vision binoculars. They all live toward the top of Miller Hill and have observed drones flying back and forth, and we all wonder where the drones' home base is. They discovered they were going to bed at the parks department sheds."

"And you thought returning the tools would give you a reason to snoop?"

"We didn't know we would have the keys to all the sheds when we set out to return the tools. Will and I were just going to look around."

She and Will looked at each other. Morse shook her head. "Somehow, I think there was more to that plan than you told me, but we'll leave that for now. Did you find the drones? I've not been out there yet."

Harriet leaned forward. "I only got a quick glance, but the shed where we found Greg's body was lined with shelves full of drones in multiple sizes."

Morse stood up. "I'll be right back."

She left the door cracked open, and they could hear Morse sending a team of criminalists to the shed to "give the drones the full treatment."

"Is there anything else you've failed to mention?"

"I don't think so," Harriet said. "Our only other activities resulted in us being kidnapped, and you already know about that."

"Tell me anyway. This was a drug investigation at that point. Now it's part of my homicide investigation." Harriet gave her a brief summary of the fish being used to transport drugs and the Threads being gathered up and kidnapped. "Hmmm …" said Morse. "You must have been getting close, or they wouldn't have bothered with such a risky maneuver."

"One more thing," Harriet said. "One of our members checked into the Foggy Point Motel and set up a security camera outside just to see if there was any drug activity going on. She called Lauren and me when she saw Greg receiving visitors in one of the units. They looked like they might be sex workers, except for Betty Ruiz, who stopped by for an extended visit. We tried to follow her when she left but lost her."

"Did you or your 'Threads' see any drugs?"

"No. It may have had nothing to do with the drug problem, but now that Gregory is dead, it does make you wonder," Harriet said.

James took Harriet's good hand in his. "Next time, don't try to protect me from all this." He looked at Morse. "My dad and I took the boys to spring training in Arizona and were gone all week. No one told us anything until Jorge called to tell me she and her aunt had been kidnapped."

Morse chuckled. "I know how you feel."

"Are we done?" Will asked.

"I'd like a written statement from you," she said. "I'll send someone to Harriet's to take her statement tomorrow, and if you'd like, she can take yours then, too."

"Sounds like a plan," said James and stood up. "We need to get Harriet a new phone, and then we'll go home and stay there."

"I'm happy to hear that, although I'm not sure I believe it," Morse said, opening the door and ushering them out.

CHAPTER FORTY-SEVEN

"**I**'ve got to get back to the restaurant," James said as they exited the phone store. His father had left them at the police station and headed home to explain what was going on to his wife.

"Can I trust you to stay home and rest?" he asked.

"I plan to nap with our animals when we get home."

"I'll pick up the boys at school so they can take the dogs out if necessary. After that, I don't know when I'll be home. The team at the restaurant did their best, but a few problems arose, and they didn't get food orders in. I left a chicken casserole in the freezer with instructions on how long to bake it and at what temperature. Luke can handle it."

"I'm not a total invalid," Harriet said.

"I know, but you need to rest for a few days after the ordeal you've been through."

Harriet sighed. "Fine," she said, and when they got home, she went upstairs and collapsed on her bed. Fred was already waiting for her, and the two dogs joined them when they returned from their trip outside with James.

Fred licked Harriet's cheek and then curled up with his head on her shoulder. Harriet barely noticed the two dogs jump up on the bed. She'd planned on reading but was asleep before she could pick up her book.

Harriet woke up to her hand throbbing and the wonderful smell of chicken casserole wafting up the stairs. She went into her bathroom and noticed her next pain pill sitting on a piece of paper with a note in Luke's handwriting, explaining that it was her next dose and that she wasn't to take it until it was after five o'clock. He'd also set a glass of water on the counter. She smiled as she took her pill and drank the water. Luke must have come in while she was sleeping after realizing she couldn't open her prescription bottle one-handed.

She ran a brush through her hair and headed downstairs. "Thank you for setting out my medication," she told Luke when she entered the kitchen.

He blushed. "I figured it would be hard for you to open the bottle one-handed."

"Well, it was very thoughtful."

"Dinner will be ready in about twenty minutes. Ta'sean is making a salad to go with our casserole. He's out walking the dogs right now."

"You boys are spoiling me."

"Well, you were kidnapped," he said.

"Has anyone called?" Harriet asked.

Luke laughed. "The shorter list would be who hasn't called. All your quilt friends have called, plus the guy with the tattoos on his arms."

"Bob?"

"Yeah, him."

"What did they want?"

"Most of them wanted to know how your arm is, and Connie, Mavis, and your aunt all asked about Gregory Lewis."

"Wow, the quilting 'Thread-line' is efficient."

Luke looked at her quizzically. "What's the 'Thread-line'?"

"It's like a grapevine, only it involves quilters. And it's much more efficient."

He laughed. "If you say so."

Ta'sean came back in with the dogs. "Can I feed them?" he asked.

"As long as you don't overdo it," Luke told him.

Harriet smiled to herself. Luke was so responsible. She and James would have to talk again about where Ta'sean should go. Luke was growing up fast, but they'd like him to have what childhood he had left without having to parent his half-brother. That was a matter for another day, she thought. She needed to return phone messages.

"I'm going to the TV room upstairs to return messages," she told Luke. "After dinner, could you help me set up my new phone? I'm not sure I can handle it one-handed, but I miss it."

"Sure," Luke answered.

"Aunt Beth," Harriet said when she'd gotten settled upstairs with the landline phone. "How did you, Connie, and Mavis find out about Greg Lewis?"

Her aunt chuckled. "James's father stopped by Jorge's restaurant to get burritos for dinner and he told Jorge about you and he finding a body. I'm sure you can imagine the rest."

"None of the rest of the Threads who left messages mentioned Greg, so apparently, the word hasn't spread."

"If you're up for it, we could meet with all the Threads at the Steaming Cup."

"Will your ribs allow you to travel?"

"They're getting better. The doctor told me to use a pillow to support them if I need to cough, and he said walking around some is good for keeping your lungs clear."

"How are Mavis and Connie?"

"About the same as I am. We all need someone to drive us, but we can work that out."

"It will have to be in the afternoon. I have a doctor's appointment in the morning, and then I'd like to pick up the boys from school.

James probably will need to work late again. His people did their best, but no one can do things like James."

"Jorge's the same way," Beth said. "He thinks no one can run his place as well as he can."

"Can you help call everyone?"

"Of course. Our phone tree is still in working order. I'll call Mavis and Connie, and they'll call their lists. Could you call Sarah? And Bob, if you want him there."

"I can do that. And I think it's only fair to include Bob. We wouldn't have discovered Greg if it hadn't been for Bob, Sarah, and Max figuring out where the drones were coming from."

"What about Max?"

"They don't have phones in the homeless camp, and I don't think Max would want to come. He prefers smaller gatherings."

"Okay, well, we better get on with our phone calls."

"Love you," Harriet told her aunt, and they rang off.

Sarah and Bob didn't answer their phones, so Harriet left messages and went downstairs, hoping dinner was ready. Ta'sean had just carried his salad bowl to the kitchen table, and Luke had just pulled the casserole out of the oven.

"Is it okay if I serve this up over here?" he asked.

"Sure," Harriet replied.

Luke served the dinner, and the three of them enjoyed it.

CHAPTER FORTY-EIGHT

Harriet drove herself to the doctor. He removed her plaster cast and cleaned her wound. "It's too early to remove your stitches. We'll switch to a soft cast if you promise to keep out of trouble. I'd like to see you in two more days to clean this again. Are you still taking the antibiotics they prescribed at the hospital?"

"I am," Harriet affirmed.

Her doctor looked at her hospital records. "I think I'll add another antibiotic. Your hand being in the Strait and that dirty fish hold have created quite the infection. I'd also like you to go to the lab and have another blood test, and before we put your cast on, we're going to swab your wound."

"Whatever you say, doctor," Harriet said with a smile.

The doctor left, and his assistant came in, swabbed her wound, and put on the soft cast. A nurse brought in a paper with her instructions, a prescription, and her subsequent appointment on it. She gave Harriet a lab order and sent her off to find the lab. It was another hour before Harriet finished at the hospital. She decided a visit to Lauren was in order.

"I know we're going to see each other tonight, but I'm going up to the homeless camp and thought you might like to come along and get a little fresh air."

"Let me walk Carter, and then I'd love to go. I think maybe I should drive."

"Are you still on antibiotics?" Harriet asked. "I notice you're sporting a new bandage on your wrist."

Lauren lifted her pant leg. "And my ankle. Apparently, there was something nasty in that fish hold."

"So I've been told," Harriet said. "Are you sure you should drive?"

"My wrist and ankle together aren't as bad as your hand."

"Okay," Harriet picked up Carter's leash from a hook by Lauren's door. "Here, let's get this guy out so we can see Max." They took Carter out and settled him with a treat before driving up to the homeless camp.

"Is Max around?" Harriet asked Joyce.

"He's here somewhere," she said and called his name.

"Hold your horses; I'm coming," he called as he came into the clearing from the direction of the parking lot. "I was just emptying the trash." He looked up. "Oh, Harriet, Lauren, I didn't realize you two were here."

"Let me make some tea," Joyce said.

"Okay," Harriet said, and Lauren agreed.

"We wanted to come by and see if you had any thoughts about Greg Lewis's death. Our quilt group is meeting this evening at the coffee shop to see if anyone has any ideas about what's happening. I'm guessing you don't want to come to the Steaming Cup with a group of women."

"You guessed right," Max said. "As for thoughts, I'm not sure I have anything new. Bob, Sarah, and I all saw Greg going in and out of the shed with drones that had landed in the parking lot. I never saw anyone else with him.

"Did you ever look during the day?" Joyce asked him.

"I did look a few times. Lots of people go in and out of those sheds during the day."

"Do they go in the drone shed?" Lauren asked.

"No, I can't say I've seen anyone, but that Greg fella go in that one."

"Who goes into the other sheds?" Harriet asked.

"I don't know all of them, but that loud woman, Betty, who signed me up to teach art classes, comes and goes, and so does the head guy of the whole bird thing."

"Mason?" Harriet asked. "I wonder what he's doing going in the sheds. Doesn't he have minions to put things away?"

"There have been other people carrying tables and chairs and things like that. I don't know who they were, but I suspect they are run-of-the-mill volunteers."

"Okay, thanks," Harriet said.

"Do you folks need anything from town?" Lauren asked Max and Joyce.

Joyce smiled. "Thank you, sweetheart, but we're in good shape with all the food James sent yesterday."

"Okay, we'd better get going, then," Harriet said as they walked back down the path to the parking lot. "Do you mind stopping by the pharmacy on our way home?" she asked.

"Can we stop by Annie's on our way?"

"Sure. It's still a few hours before we meet at the Steaming Cup."

"I was thinking of her cinnamon twists. My cupboard is bare, and I didn't want to pay for grocery delivery for a box of cereal, a quart of milk, and a loaf of bread."

Harriet laughed. "That is pitiful," she said. Our freezer is always full of meals and treats between James and my aunt.

"Well, bully for you," Lauren said. "While you're over there in the land of plenty, I'm starving, and my wrist hurts."

"Okay, we'll go to Annie's after that pathetic declaration. After our meeting, the boys and I will assemble a care package for you from our stores."

"Don't tell me you aren't going to have a cinnamon twist."

Harriet laughed. "Only if they're fresh from the oven."

Before going to pick up the boys in front of their respective schools, Harriet had walked the dogs, and took a short nap. She was still tired from her sailing adventure. As Ta'sean got into the car's back seat, Harriet noticed Arinda hurrying along the sidewalk toward them. Fortunately, she was tottering on heels not meant for running, and Harriet could pull into traffic before she reached them.

"Was that my mom?" Ta'sean asked, looking out the back window.

"It looked like her," Harriet said. "The social worker told us she's not supposed to talk to you without one of their people being there."

"Get your seatbelt on," she told him.

Ta'sean did as asked. "I wonder what she wanted," Ta'sean grumbled.

"Nothing for you to worry about," Luke told him. "Can Ta'sean and I go to the coffee place with you and your quilt friends this afternoon?" Luke asked.

"We could take our homework and sit at a different table."

Harriet knew Luke had been worried about her since the kidnap, so she agreed. "You have to stay at your table and promise to work on your homework."

"We will," the boys said in unison.

Harriet and the boys were early. She'd wanted to ensure she could get the table closest to the big table where the Threads were to meet. Luke and Ta'sean had eaten at home, but Harriet knew they were in a perpetual state of hunger, so besides the drinks they wanted, she ordered chocolate chip cookies, Danish pastries, and several muffins.

When the boys were settled, Harriet seated herself at the side of the table closest to their table. She'd ordered hot chocolate and a muffin for herself. Connie, Mavis, and Beth were the next to arrive. Connie's husband dropped them off with instructions to call him when they were ready to be picked up again.

Harriet called James and told him where she and the boys were, and that Arinda had surfaced again. He told her he'd call Jennifer, Arinda's social worker, and let her know that Arinda had attempted contact.

Carla came with Sarah and Bob. She was carrying a small pillow, which she handed to Harriet when they went to the table. "I made you a pillow to rest your injured hand on," she said, her cheeks turning pink as she spoke.

"Thank you," Harriet told her. "This was very thoughtful." She set it on the table and gently put her injured wrist on it.

Robin and DeAnn arrived next, looking none the worse for wear. Robin glanced over at Luke and Ta'sean. "I see your boys came with you," she said to Harriet. "My kids wanted to come, too, but they've been glued to my side since we got rescued. I needed just a little breathing space."

"My husband took our bunch to get ice cream, or they'd be here, too," DeAnn said.

"DeAnn and I are taking all our kids to a group therapy session to help them process the kidnapping," Robin told them.

"Sounds like a good idea," Harriet said.

Jenny arrived last. "Sorry I'm late," she told the group.

"Detective Morse called and asked me to come in for an interview. I told her I wasn't kidnapped, which she already knew, but I guess she wanted to know why not since I was down in the dock area at the same time as the kidnapping."

"I'd like to hear about how you evaded our kidnappers, too, but get your drink and food first, and let's all get settled before you tell us," Harriet said.

"Okay, I'll be back in a minute." The rest of the group chose their seats and settled down at the table with their snacks.

CHAPTER FORTY-NINE

"First, I'd like to hear how Jenny escaped being picked up by the kidnappers," said Harriet.

"It was curious, really. I was in the chrome shop talking to Tom. I'd visited the day before but just popped in to look at some new pieces he'd finished. Tom suggested I go upstairs into his attic to look at some unfinished pieces. I'm looking for a nameplate for my antique stove, and he thought one of his unfinished pieces might be the one. While I was upstairs, some men came into the shop. Mason was one of them, and then a few minutes later, a pair of rough-looking young men came in and asked if Tom had seen me that day.

"Tom was suspicious of them, so he denied my presence. When they were gone, he came upstairs and told me they were looking for me. He suggested I leave through a smuggler's tunnel that left from his basement. It came out several blocks away. Tom called a taxi to meet me at the tunnel's exit door. I went downstairs to the basement, out of the tunnel, and the taxi was waiting. It took me home, and I left my car at the docks until my husband arranged for it to be towed to our house. I stayed home until I heard about the kidnap and rescue."

"Is Detective Morse going to have Tom work with the police artist?" Harriet asked her.

"She is going to interview him and mentioned having him do a sketch."

Robin pulled a yellow legal pad from her shoulder bag. DeAnn handed her a pen. "What do we know?" Robin asked.

"First of all, we know Foggy Point has a drug problem," Beth said.

Robin wrote that down. "Who has died as a result of the drug problem—not from overdosing but murdered by the dealers."

"Maylene, for one," Mavis said.

"Greg Lewis," Harriet added.

"My unknown drug dealer victim," Sarah said.

Bob joined the group at the table, a cup of coffee in one hand and a chocolate chip cookie in the other. "Sorry, I'm late. My mother is doing better, so they are moving her to a step-down unit. I had to stay until she was settled. Her brain is doing a lot better; the swelling is gone. They expect to move her to a rehabilitation facility if she does well in the step-down."

"That's excellent news," said Lauren.

"I see you listing victims," Bob said. "We need a column for the injured but not dead."

Robin wrote "Injured" in large letters. She put Avelot at the top as the most injured. She added Carrie, the girl who had overdosed at the bird festival. Harriet was next with her multiple injuries and surgeries on her hand. Lauren went on the list with her infected wrist and ankle, followed by Connie, Mavis, and Beth with their injured ribs.

"I hope no one asks us to do a quilting project in the next month or so," Lauren said. "Sarah, Carla, and Jenny would have to carry the load."

"Bob should go on the injured list from when we got attacked at his trailer," Harriet told Robin.

"So far, we know a lot about who has been killed or injured, but not much about who has done the killing or injuring," Mavis said.

"We've got the artist's rendition of the people who kidnapped Lauren and me," Harriet said.

Connie picked up a newspaper section from the table next to their big one. It was folded open to reveal the Crime Stoppers page, on which the two sketches had been printed.

"Let's pass this around the table so everyone can take a good look and see if they've seen these two anywhere or know who they are," Connie said, passing the paper to Carla.

Each person studied the pictures and shook their head before passing the paper on. When it reached Harriet, she looked at the pictures again to see if she remembered any more details.

Ta'sean came to the table to ask Harriet if he could get a refill on his strawberry lemonade. He looked over Harriet's shoulder at the pictures. "I know who that guy is," he said, stabbing his finger onto the picture on the left.

"Who is he?" Harriet asked him.

"That's Robbie," he said. "He used to live with us. He was my mom's boyfriend, and he gave her drugs," he added darkly.

"What was his last name?" Lauren asked him.

"I don't know. I was little when Robbie lived with us. Ask my mom."

"Have you ever seen the other guy?" Harriet asked him.

"Nope," said Ta'sean. "Can I go get another lemonade now?"

"Sure, sweetie," Harriet said, handing him a couple of dollars from her pocket.

Mavis picked up her latte and took a sip. "I think we should call Detective Morse and tell her what Ta'sean said."

"I'll call her," said Harriet, but I will ask her to come here. I don't want Ta'sean to go to the police station. Both the boys are traumatized enough by the kidnapping. I'd like to keep them here, where they can be relaxed and within sight of me and Aunt Beth."

Harriet slid her phone to Lauren. "Will you put the Foggy Point Police Department into my new phone and then dial it for me?"

Lauren smiled. "I think I like this dependent, Harriet," she said and used her phone to send the FPPD contact info. Harriet called Detective Morse.

"Could you please meet me and the Threads at the Steaming Cup? My foster son Ta'sean recognizes one of the drawings in the Crime Stoppers article. No, I can't bring him to the station. My boys are traumatized enough since my kidnapping."

"Okay, we'll be here," Harriet said after listening to whatever Morse had replied. She set her phone down and turned to the group.

"She says she'll be here within thirty minutes."

CHAPTER FIFTY

"None of us think this Robbie character is the 'Mr. Big' of Foggy Point's drug ring, do we?" asked Bob.

Harriet and Lauren looked at each other. "I'd be shocked if either of our two kidnappers were 'Mr. Big,'" Lauren said.

"I agree," said Harriet.

"By the way," Bob said. "I finally got the bag of pills away from Red. He pulled a bag from his pocket. He'd put the pill bag into a green compostable zipper bag. "I planned to take them to Detective Morse on my way home. This will save me some time. I've got the birds in the back of my truck. They're overdue to go out hunting."

"Does anyone have any idea who the rest of our kidnappers are?" Robin asked. "Anything that would help us identify them?"

"Just the names Sketch and G-dog," Harriet said.

Robin wrote the names on the tablet. Ta'sean was writing on a worksheet. "Sketch and G-dog are friends of Robbie's," he said without looking up.

"I wonder what the G stands for," Lauren said.

"Grayson," Ta'sean told the group. "I heard Robbie making fun of him. I think his parents are rich." Robin wrote that on their paper.

"That should be easy enough to track down," DeAnn noted. Grayson isn't that common of a name."

They all looked up as Detective Morse came into the coffee shop. She stopped by the front counter and ordered coffee before joining the Threads.

"Do you have anything to tell us before I call Ta'sean over?" Harriet asked.

Morse sipped her coffee. "Not really. I suspect you all are where we are. We're starting to fill in some of the minor players, but so far, no idea who the top person is."

"I wish I could tell you Ta'sean knows that name, but he doesn't," Harriet said. "None of us believe the guys that put us on the fishing boat are the top guys."

"Be gentle with him," Aunt Beth cautioned Morse in a quiet tone. "He's had a tough life."

"I can help if you'd like," Connie said. "I've been tutoring him since he's lived with Harriet and James."

"Okay," Morse said. "You can ask him the questions. I want to know who the guy he recognized is and if he knows other people associated with him."

Harriet walked over to the table where Luke and Ta'sean were sitting. "Ta'sean, this is Detective Morse. She'd like to ask you a few questions about the guy you recognized. Connie will help her ask questions, so it won't be so scary. Luke and I will be right over there at the big table. If you want to stop anytime, just tell Connie you're done. Understand?"

Ta'sean nodded. "I'm not a baby, you know," he muttered.

"Luke, come sit with us," she said.

The group at the table sat quietly, hoping to hear what was being said. Harriet heard Ta'sean tell Morse Robbie's name. Then she heard Connie ask him about G-dog, and Ta'sean told Morse his name was Grayson. He knew that because Robbie teased him about what he called G-dog's "high-brow name."

"Was Robbie a drug dealer?" Connie asked.

Ta'sean nodded. "That's how my mom met him."

"Do you know who he got the drugs from?" Connie asked.

Ta'sean took a deep breath and let it out. "I'm not supposed to talk about him. My mom said he was dangerous. She got real mad when Robbie took me with him to pick up drugs one time."

"Do you know the guy's name?" Connie asked. "You can tell Detective Morse. She's with the police, and she can keep you safe."

"I don't know his name. For reals," he added.

"Do you know what he looks like?" Connie asked.

"It was dark, but I could see he had blond hair, and he dressed nice, not like G-dog and Robbie."

Connie patted his hand. "Is that all you can tell us?" Connie asked.

Ta'sean nodded. "Can I be done now?"

"Yes, Ta'sean, you did very well. Detective Morse appreciates all your help."

Harriet could see that Morse had more questions, but Connie gave her her best schoolteacher look. Morse thanked Ta'sean and went to join Harriet and the Threads at the big table. Luke went back to sit with Ta'sean. "Do you want another cookie?" he asked.

Ta'sean shook his head. "I just want to go home."

"I don't think Harriet's done yet," Luke said, reaching into his school bag. "Here, you can play a game on my phone," he said. Ta'sean smiled and took Luke's phone.

"I doubt if the top guy is the one who killed Maylene," Morse said. "It was probably someone who works for him."

"What about Greg Lewis?" Harriet asked.

Morse sat back in her chair. "That would make sense. Maylene would trust him. I doubt she'd let one of the others get that close to her unless there was more than one."

"I'm sure whoever Mr. Big is will probably try to blame Greg now that he's dead and can't defend himself," Harriet said.

Morse and the Threads sipped their drinks in silence for a few moments.

The bell on the coffee shop door jingled, and Mason Sanders walked in. He went to the coffee counter, his back to the table the Threads were sitting at. He carried a leather backpack. Harriet watched as Mason spoke to the barista. He appeared to be asking for the manager. A man in black pants, a white shirt, and a tie came out from the back area of the shop. He and Mason spoke for a few minutes. The manager set a bag of coffee beans on the counter in front of Mason. Harriet watched closely. She nudged Lauren's arm and nodded toward the interaction.

Lauren got up and went to the counter, asking for the restroom key. The barista gave Lauren the key, and Lauren went to the restroom area, entering one of the two rooms but not shutting the door completely. From her vantage point, she could see what was going on with the manager and Mason.

Whatever the transaction was, the manager returned to the back office, and Mason turned around. "Whoa," Harriet said when she saw Mason's face. Three long scratches angled from his left temple to the right side of his mouth.

Bob set his coffee cup down. "He must be the person my bird attacked in the woods."

Lauren returned the restroom key to the bar and returned to the table. She leaned across the table toward Morse. "Mason and the manager just did the classic spy move. Mason had an identical coffee bag in his backpack. When he put the bag the manager had set on the counter into his pack, he took it out and set it on the counter. The manager took it into the back room, shielding it from view with his body."

"Unfortunately, I can't demand to look in his backpack based on what Lauren told me," Morse said.

Mason got a cup of coffee to go. "We can't just let him walk out of here," Harriet said, watching him head for the door.

Bob stood up. "I can slow him down," Bob said, crossing the room to the door and cutting Mason off.

Harriet went over to Mason. "What happened to your face?" she asked him. "It looks painful."

"I must have gotten too close to a bird nest. I got attacked. It will be okay. I may need a little plastic surgery, but hey, maybe the doctors can take a few wrinkles out in the process," he said with a laugh.

While Harriet was distracting Mason, Bob had gotten Helen from the back of his truck. She still had her hood on. Harriet followed Mason out the door.

"Mason," Bob called out when Mason came out. "Are you the guy who sent people to beat up my mother?" Helen was perched on his leather glove-covered arm.

"Why would I do that?" Mason kept glancing between Helen and Bob. "You aren't going to let that thing loose, are you?"

"I will take her hood off and let her go hunt. Whether I do it here or in the woods is up to you."

Detective Morse came outside. "Is everything okay out here?"

"We're just having a friendly chat," Bob said.

"Is that true?" Morse asked Mason.

Mason glanced over at Helen again. "We're fine," Mason muttered.

Morse went back inside. "Were those drugs you handed the manager in there?" Harriet asked Mason. "We saw you pull the switcheroo in there with the coffee bags."

"I did not switch anything in there. I just picked up a special bag of beans the manager ordered for me."

"Would you mind showing us your special coffee?" Harriet asked.

"Yes, I would mind, very much."

"I'll just have a look," Bob said.

"Bob, maybe we should go back inside," Harriet said.

"I need to let Helen fly," he said, pulling her hood off. She screeched when she saw Mason and then launched into the air.

As soon as she was off his arm, he grabbed Mason's backpack. Mason grabbed at it, but Bob held it aloft. Mason punched at Bob, but his punches rolled off without affecting Bob.

Bob reached into the pack, grabbed the coffee bag, pulled it out, and dropped it. Mason grabbed the coffee bag, and it tore open, spilling lots of cash.

"Whoa, are those one-hundred dollar bills?" Harriet asked.

"They aren't coffee beans," Bob said and turned away, leaving Mason to scramble around picking up bills.

Bob went to the back of the truck and waited for Helen to circle around. Eventually, she returned to land on his arm, a mouse clutched in her talons. Harriet returned to the coffee shop.

"Well, that was interesting," she told the group.

"What was in the bag?" Morse asked her.

"A whole lot of one-hundred-dollar bills."

Morse straightened in her chair. "I guess I'd better chat with the manager here."

Morse went to the counter and asked the barista to summon the manager. The Threads couldn't hear what was being said. Still, they watched Morse pull her badge wallet from her pocket and show it to the barista before being escorted into the back office.

When the barista returned, Harriet went to the counter and ordered a cup of tea. "I'm assuming we're staying until Morse comes back out."

"I'm not moving," Mavis said.

The rest of the Threads went to the counter and ordered second drinks. Before they were all seated again, two police cars pulled into the parking lot, and four patrolmen got out. They bypassed the counter when they came in and went straight to the back office.

"I can't wait to hear what Morse found in the other coffee bag," Lauren said as she sipped her latte.

CHAPTER FIFTY-ONE

"Harriet," Luke called from his table. "Can you come over here?"

Harriet came over and sat beside Luke. "What's up?"

"Ta'sean wants to tell you something, but he didn't want to say it in front of the whole group."

Harriet reached across Luke and took Ta'sean's hand. "What is it, honey?"

"That guy that came in with the scratches on his face?"

"Yes, what about him."

"He's the guy Robbie got his drugs from."

"Are you sure?"

Ta'sean's face was serious. "Positive. There aren't that many blond guys around here."

"Thanks for telling me, sweetie. I will have to tell Detective Morse, is that okay?"

"That's why I told you. His drugs are what my mom is hooked on."

"You did the right thing."

Harriet went back to the big table. "Okay, everyone, don't look at Ta'sean, but listen up. He says Mason is Mr. Big. I'm going to go tell Morse."

She got up and went to the counter, explaining to the barista that she needed to talk to the detective. The barista went to the back room and came out momentarily, signaling Harriet to go into the office. Harriet repeated to Morse what Ta'sean had told her.

"That confirms what we were putting together here. The coffee bag was full of fentanyl. The manager is waiting for his attorney, and I'm waiting for the DA, but I think he will go for a deal. I'm guessing he's been using his baristas to distribute drugs."

"Hopefully, not all of them," Harriet said. "I like the coffee here; It would be a shame if they had to close."

Morse laughed. "I hadn't even thought about that."

More people in suits arrived. "I think our work here is done," Harriet said.

Beth sipped her latte and set her cup on the table. "I suggest we finish our drinks," Beth said. "And leave. We probably don't need to get together again for a few days. After we've all had some time to rest up, we need to plan a memorial for Maylene. I don't know if they've found a family to plan a service, but whether she does or not, we need to have a service in our group. We should invite Bill Park and find out from him who should be invited from her complex. Bob should come, too."

"Should I check at the church to see when their spaces might be available?" Connie asked. "I know she attended our church. I used to see her at the early service."

"Good idea," Beth said.

"What quilting projects are we all going back to?" Harriet asked.

The rest of their time at the coffee shop was spent discussing what people were working on.

It was a week before everyone was ready to get together again. Harriet invited the group to meet at her studio, and everyone agreed.

Mavis was the first to arrive. "I brought lemon bars. I hope that's okay."

Harriet smiled. "You know it is. I love your lemon bars."

"Connie said she's bringing something chocolate, so I figured lemon would be a good contrast."

Beth was the next to arrive. "Jorge made churros for us," she said, carrying a platter stacked high with the Mexican treat.

Robin and DeAnn came in together, carrying a jug of iced tea and one of lemonade. The rest of the group trickled in over the next ten minutes.

"I invited Detective Morse, and told her we were all very curious about what the police learned from Mason. She said she'd think about it."

Harriet got out her schedule book. "While we're waiting for Detective Morse to come or not, would anyone like to guess when their next quilt project will be ready for me to long arm? As usual, this is just your best guess. I have a separate column to keep guesses in. Let's start with anything that needs to be done quickly."

"Can you run your long arm machine with your hand wrapped up like that?" Mavis asked.

Harriet smiled. "I tried yesterday to see if I could, and it went fine. I just took it slow."

"Well, if you're sure, I have a baby quilt I need to finish for a shower next week," Mavis said.

Harriet made a note in her notebook. "No problem," she said. "Anyone else?"

Lauren expected to have a quilt ready in two weeks. Jenny planned on having her next quilt ready the week after that. By the time Detective Morse knocked on the studio door, Harriet had an idea of her next two months.

She stood up. "Welcome," she said. "Would you like lemonade or iced tea?" she asked.

"Could I get a cup of coffee? Morse asked. "I can go make it myself in your machine."

"You sit down," Sarah said. I'll get it for you." She got up and went into Harriet's kitchen, choosing an Italian roast pod from her drawer of selections.

Mavis slid the plates of treats to Morse, who made several selections and put them on a napkin. Sarah returned several minutes later, which gave Morse time to eat some of her treats.

Morse sipped her coffee and then set her mug down. "My boss and I had a pretty strong debate about sharing the investigation results with you. On the one hand, we don't want to encourage you all to continue investigating crimes in our community on your own; on the other hand, you all were instrumental in figuring out who was bringing drugs into our community at some cost to your physical well-being.

"As you saw at the coffee shop, and thanks to Harriet's foster son, we arrested Mason Sanders for distribution of drugs. Seems the bird festival disrupted his drug operation and he may be implicated in Maylene's murder and Avelot's attack as well. We think he personally killed Greg Lewis. It appears he was blackmailing Greg over his relationship with Betty Ruiz. Greg apparently said he was done. He had no more money, and he wasn't going to deliver drugs to area users for him anymore.

"Mason's underling, Robbie, has cut a deal with the DA and is providing a lot of information on the drug dealing operation—how they were using fishing boats to smuggle the drugs in, and then using drones to deliver the drugs to their dealers for distribution. He will be going into witness protection when the trials are over. Sanders and his people will be prosecuted for kidnapping you all and possibly attempted murder for setting your boat loose in the strait.

"We confiscated the drones. They will be repurposed for use by the Foggy Point Police Department."

When she was finished speaking, Detective Morse picked up a lemon bar and took a bite. "These are delicious."

"Thank you," Mavis said.

"This should help the drug problem at the school," Connie said.

"We're going to have some officers go to the high school weekly for a while. As we question the other involved in Mason's empire, we might pick up a few names of high schoolers," Morse said.

"I'm glad all our trauma was worth it," Harriet said, looking at her hand.

Morse took another bite of lemon bar and said, "Was that your schedule I saw you writing in when I came in?" Harriet nodded.

"I have a quilt that will be ready to be long armed in a few weeks," Morse said.

Harriet pulled her schedule back in front of her and opened the appropriate page, glad things were back to business as usual.

ABOUT THE AUTHOR

 Arlene Sachitano read her first Agatha Christie mystery at age eleven, and she was hooked. Already a knitter and sewer at that tender age it made sense she'd grow up and combine her favorite pastimes to write cozy crafting mysteries. A thirty-year side trip into the world of high tech along with raising multiple children, dogs, and cats derailed her writing ambitions for a while, but eventually the writing compulsion won out.

Arlene is the author of the Harriet Truman/Loose Threads Mysteries and the Permelia O'Brien and Harley Spring Mysteries series. Along with her husband, Jack and their dog, Navarre, she divides her time between Tillamook and Portland, Oregon.

ACKNOWLEDGMENTS

Thank you to the many people who contributed to this book in ways both large and small. A special thank you to Kate Poirier for her beautiful cover drawing. Also, thanks to her mum Bette Forester for her promotional materials. Additional thanks to my son David for redoing my web page and for other technical support. My on-the-road marketing team, Jack and Beth, deserve thanks for helping me bring my books to quilt shows across the country.

Finally, thanks to Jeff and Sharleen for taking the Loose Threads (and me) on, so I can bring them to my readers.

Other Books by Arlene Sachitano

The Harriet Truman/Loose Threads Mysteries
Quilt As Desired
Quilter's Knot
Quilt As You Go
Quilt by Association
The Quilt Before the Storm
Make Quilts Not War
A Quilt in Time
Crazy As a Quilt
Disappearing Nine Patch
Double Wedding Death
Quilts Make a Family
The Twelve Quilts of Christmas
A Quilt of a Different Color
*Quilts of a Feather

The Permelia O'Brien Mysteries
Double Knit
Louies Knit Shop

The Harley Spring Mysteries
Chip and Die
Widowmaker

*Published by GladEye Press

More books from GladEye Press

Follow the adventures and missteps of time-traveling PI Imogen Oliver as she recovers lost items and unearths long-buried stories and secrets from the past in this exciting series! (*The Time Tourists is available on Kindle Unlimited.)

The Time Tourists Trilogy
Sharleen Nelson

*The Fragile Blue Dot
Ross West
Veteran science-writer and journalist Ross West's collection of award-winning short fiction touches on the human aspect of living in a world on the brink of ecological disaster.

Teaching in Alaska
Julie Bolkan
In this candid and often funny account, the author describes how she dealt with culture clashes, isolation, weather, and honey buckets as one of the first outsiders to live and work with the Yup'ik in their small villages.

  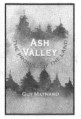

Join 19-year-old Ben Tucker for a passionate and revolutionary tale of protests, parties, trials, and a band of idealists who set out to build a countercultural utopia in the southern mountains of Oregon.

The Risk of Being Ridiculous Trilogy
Guy Maynard

*Available as an ebook on Kindle Unlimited.

All GladEye titles are available for purchase at
www.gladeyepress.com and your local bookstore.

*Federation of the Dragon
*Footman of the Ether
Jason A. Kilgore
Enter the ancient world of Irikara for
high-stakes epic fantasy adventure
in a mythical land filled with dragons
and demons, dwarves and elves,
magic and mages and gods.

*The Midnight Show: bohemians, byways, and
bonfires*
Camille Cole
During the early days of Oregon's famous Country
Fair, the Midnight Show was a stage shared by icons
of the counterculture, lovers, children and family,
and those of us finding our way through.

Coastal Coffee Club Mysteries
Patricia Brown

Five cozy mysteries follow retired poet Eleanor Penrose and her band of quirky friends as
they solve mysteries along the Oregon coast.

Dying for Recipies
Patricia Brown
Follow the clues while enjoying twenty-two of Eleanor's
scrumptious, mouth-watering recipes drawn from the
pages of Patricia Brown's charming Coastal Coffee Club
Mysteries series.

COMING in 2025 *from*

GladEye
Press

Far Side of Revenge
Anne Dean
A fictionalized account of the life of Brian Boroimhe and his rise to King of Ireland.

Black and Tan Fantasy
Randall Luce
In the turbulent and often violent nascent civil rights movement of the Mississippi delta, racial identities, culture, and attitudes collide and shift in this taut drama.

The Extraordinary Voyage of a Tall Ship in a Tiny Pool Far from the Sea
Donovan M. Reves
With gentle absurdity and copious humor, Donovan Reves weaves an exciting adventure yarn with a tender love story all set in a ridiculous landlocked tallship built in a tiny pond. As hard to describe as it is to put down, this tender fable evokes the magic of *The Princess Bride*.

RERELEASES FROM JASON A. KILGORE

The First Nova I See Tonight
Star pirates, alien lovers, tentacled mafiosos, this space opera offers a return to the beloved "zap gun" stories of the past!

Around the Corner from Sanity: Tales of the Paranormal
Fourteen short stories of spine-tingling horror will scare you AND tickle your funny bone!

Guide Me, O River and other poems